DESTINATION
UNKNOWN

BILL KONIGSBERG

DESTINATION
UNKNOWN

SCHOLASTIC PRESS • NEW YORK

All rights reserved. Published by Scholastic Press, an imprint of Scholastic Inc., *Publishers since 1920*. SCHOLASTIC, SCHOLASTIC PRESS, and associated logos are trademarks and/or registered trademarks of Scholastic Inc.

Lyrics from "Love Don't Need a Reason (What We Don't Have Is Time)" by Peter Allen, Marsha Malamet, and Michael Callen © 1987 Woolnough Music, Malamution Music, and Tops and Bottoms Music. All rights on behalf of Woolnough Music administered by Warner-Tamerlane Publishing Corp. Reprinted by permission.

While inspired by real events and historical characters, this is a work of fiction and does not claim to be historically accurate or portray factual events or relationships. Please keep in mind that references to actual persons, living or dead, business establishments, events, or locales may not be factually accurate, but rather fictionalized by the author.

Library of Congress Cataloging-in-Publication Data available

ISBN 978-1-338-61805-1

10 9 8 7 6 5 4 3 2 1   22 23 24 25 26

Printed in Italy   183

First edition, August 2022
Book design by Christopher Stengel

To my friends who didn't make it to the 21st Century.
I miss you.

What are words for when no one listens anymore?
    —*"Words" by Missing Persons*

CHAPTER ONE

NOTICEABLE ONE

September 1987

The first thing I noticed about CJ Gorman was his plexiglass bra.

Alone he skulked in a dark corner of the Tunnel. I say *skulked* because his head bent down and his posture curled in, which I thought was interesting because he was dressed to be seen, obviously. His short hair was dyed platinum blond with shocking pink highlights in front. His tall, thinner-than-rail frame would have cut an imposing figure without the clincher: He was shirtless, with an open black sequined jacket over a plexiglass bra that was only half covered in tin foil, allowing his obvious lack of mammary glands to be seen.

"Brand New Lover" by Dead or Alive blared over the speakers and rumbled the floor. The air was hazy with cigarette and who-knows-what-else smoke. The haze smelled faintly of paint thinner. My friend Deena had dragged me out with a group of school friends on a Friday night when I could just as easily have been comfortable at home, watching the replay of the MTV Music Video Awards, hosted by Downtown Julie Brown. My friends were all out on the floor dancing, while I stood alone near the bar.

Story of my life.

I'd barely made it in. This guy with an eye patch stood out front, pointing at various groups and people from the mob wanting to get into this former-railroad-terminal-turned-chic-nightclub. I was praying I'd be disallowed so I could go back home, but Deena was hanging on my arm and Deena is hot. So yeah, I made it. Yay.

The lights and movement on the dance floor dizzied my already heavy brain. A girl with Goldilocks braids in a peppermint-striped skirt swirled, her dilated pupils at the tops of their sockets. A white guy with dreadlocks, wearing what appeared to be a plastic bag, ground against her.

I looked away, and found myself drawn again to CJ, his arms folded across his plexiglass bra, surveying the crowd. He looked to me like everything I never would be. He postured like he owned the place and was a little over the whole scene.

I was transfixed. I wasn't sure if it was the height, the unapologetic attitude, the thinness, or all of the above.

Maybe I gawked. Maybe I stopped myself. I had to be careful who saw me taking this boy in.

Yes, we were at a club with plenty of gay people around.

But no, none of my friends besides Deena knew I was one of them.

CJ turned and caught me checking him out. He uncrossed his arms and put his hands through his wild platinum-and-pink hair, entirely unselfconsciously. I spun away and almost crashed into Deena, who appeared amused by my embarrassment.

"Take a picture, it'll last longer!" she screamed over the

thumping beat. Strobe lights illuminated the floors and walls. Next to us, a bald, brown-skinned woman in a neon-pink tank top was spinning for some reason, even though we weren't close to the dance floor.

"I'm not—"

"So now you're into drag queens?"

I crossed my arms over my chest. "Yeah, no. Not my scene."

She laughed and ordered a vodka tonic from the (extremely cute) bartender. "Your scene is closet cases. How's that working out for you?"

True, the only gay experiences I'd had were with two closeted jocks at Trinity, where we were juniors. I wondered what parallel universe I'd have to live in to have a friend like the boy in the corner. Or, better yet, a boyfriend. He was taking everything in; I was busy keeping it all out. He was so beautiful and thin. I was like a sixth grader who'd expanded sideways without growing up. He probably had plenty of other gay guys to talk to. I didn't have a single one.

I dropped my head onto her shoulder. "Can we just go? I hate this."

She looked at her pink-and-aqua Swatch, then pulled my hair lightly until I was upright again. "It's literally ten thirty. No, you cannot go home. I'm trying to expand your horizons beyond the closet."

"MTV is not going to watch itself. Come on. Please?"

She pulled on my arm. "Come out here and dance. That's like the one perk of being a fag hag, and you're ruining it."

I lowered my voice. "I'm not a fag, and you're not a hag."

She rolled her eyes. "Fine. That's the one perk of being a

needlessly closeted gay boy's, um, what's another word for *hag*? Witch? Whatever the case, you're standing here like some demented straight guy in your awful Members Only jacket."

"I like it," I said, caressing the beige collar strap.

"Yes, that's been abundantly clear for some time. Come on. Dance!" She grabbed my arm and pulled.

"I'll be right there," I said, jerking away. "Gotta piddle."

Deena couldn't argue with that one, even though I could tell she wanted to.

"Fine," she said. "Be that way."

I felt like I'd won the skirmish when she rejoined our friends on the dance floor. Then I realized the weakness of my plan: Now I had to face the bathroom.

The Tunnel didn't believe in men's rooms or women's rooms—all the bathrooms were unisex, first come, first serve. When I walked in, Club Kids filled the space, hogging the mirrors. Company B was busy screeching about how fascinated they were by my love toy.

I sincerely doubted they would be.

My head pounded, I didn't have to pee *that* badly, and I wished there were a black hole I could climb into, perhaps hidden in one of the stalls. Or some sort of fast-forward button I could press to jump past junior and senior year and be at college somewhere calm. Earlham in Indiana was calling me. Maybe I'd become a Quaker.

"Hey, fatty, are you actually going to use that stall, or are you just going to stand there?" this bald kid with a glittered forehead and painted-on eyebrows asked.

"Sorry." I covered my belly with my hands and moved

toward the sinks, inadvertently bumping into someone, which made me say "Sorry" again.

The person into whom I'd bumped had a blond pompadour and wore too much blush on his powder-white face.

"Excuse you!" he said, pushing me lightly with the backs of his fingers. Then he looked me up and down with his hands on his hips. "Pure bridge and tunnel. Go back to Long Island, honey. Leave us one place that's just ours."

I froze. *Long Island?* I was Upper West Side, born and bred. I opened my mouth to defend myself, but no words came out.

"Great comeback," he said, sneering.

"Kindness. Give it a try," a low, booming voice said behind me.

It was CJ, standing in the doorway. His voice was very *Top Gun*, even if the bra and hair pointed in a different direction.

"Oh my God! It's Dale Bozzio!" Pompadour Guy said, all nasal and deadpan. "If she had AIDS."

I felt like I'd been dropped into the middle of a parallel universe.

Dale Bozzio put his hands on his hips, which only emphasized his bare midriff. "Be gone, before someone drops a house on you," he said, expressionless.

The bald guy laughed. So did the guy with the pompadour. He leaned in, and he and Dale Bozzio did this air kiss thing, one on each side, like they hadn't just been insulting each other. Baldy and Pompadour went over to the mirror, leaving me and Dale in front of an empty stall.

I must have been staring, because Dale sized me up. "Why

are you dressed like this? Who hurt you?" Total unsmiling delivery.

I looked down. I was wearing an aqua-blue Lacoste polo shirt with the collar up, a pair of ill-fitting Lee jeans, green Keds, and my beige Members Only jacket.

"What?"

"Are you a plant? Are you a narc? Did the Russians send you? Only the Russians dress this way."

I shrugged, utterly unprepared for whatever kind of joking this was.

He pursed his lips. "You're cute. But that jacket. It must be burned."

"Everyone keeps saying that."

"Everyone is right."

I laughed, frustrated and surprisingly disarmed by this person who was obviously way cooler than I would ever be. I glanced around to make sure no one from school had decided that they, too, needed to pee.

"Thank you, by the way," I said.

"No sweat. I'm so over mean people right now."

"Well, I'm not mean."

He smirked again. "I wouldn't imagine you are, or could be."

"So your name is Dale Bozzio?"

The slap stung my cheek.

"Ow!"

"How do you not know Dale Bozzio?"

"Is she a drag queen?"

The second slap stung my chin less, but my pride a little more. I felt like slapping him back, but some weird chauvinist thought came to me that maybe you don't slap a person dressed as a woman. I took a calming breath and tried a different tack.

"'Don't slap me, I'm not in the mood,'" I said, quoting a line from one of my favorite songs.

That got a laugh of recognition. "And we are, in fact, 'meeting in the ladies room.'"

That made me grin and blush.

"So you know Klymaxx but not Missing Persons?"

"If I knew them, would they be missing?" I said, realizing too late this made no actual sense.

He rolled his eyes. "What are words for?"

"To . . . speak?"

He sighed in exasperation. "Famous lyrics. 'Destination Unknown'? 'Life Is So Strange'?"

I squinted. "That one sounds vaguely familiar."

He lifted his left hand, but this time I made a time-out sign with my hands and he abstained from slapping me.

"You need education," he said, moving in closer. "Such exceeding cuteness cannot be left to carry on with only what it knows."

I blushed and popped a boner in the restroom of the Tunnel.

"I'm Miles," I said, lying. (My strange logic being: *What if he calls my name and one of my friends hears?*)

"CJ," he replied, and I wondered if he was lying, too. Probably not. He smiled for the first time. His teeth crowded together like he had a few too many molars. I liked this surprise. It made him seem human.

We stared at each other, and it was so weird, because I

wasn't really into drag or whatever, but he thought I was cute, he was obviously stunning, and even more than that, it was like I'd just met someone important, like my body knew it, like the universe was whispering to me, *Pay attention.*

I shivered.

And then I realized I wasn't sure how to keep him focused on me. That he was standing in front of me, ostensibly waiting for me to say something, and here I was, lacking a certain luster while the restroom was bursting with color and people whose whole presence screamed, *Look at me!* I recognized that if I wished for this dialogue to continue, I needed to say something interesting, and though this moment was perhaps the most interesting in my life so far, I couldn't think of anything stimulating to say about it.

The best I could do was lower my voice a few decibels and ask, "Are you openly gay?"

He snorted. "Oh, sweetie. You're green, aren't you, Miles?"

"I'm emerald green. I'm the greenest possible green."

CJ adjusted his plexiglass bra. "High school?"

Somehow, the right banter tone appeared in my mouth, and I said, "As is required by law."

"I'm a senior at Bronx Tech," he said. "Turned eighteen in April. One more year to freedom."

"I've got two," I said, pouting my lip.

"Poor baby."

"I've never met a gay person before," I said. He raised an eyebrow and I corrected myself. "I've never met an openly gay person and talked to them. As a gay person. Which I am. Obviously."

"Obviously," he repeated. "Well, you're in luck, because I have actually been looking for a sidekick, and green is my favorite . . ."

He glanced past me toward the door and must have seen something, because all of a sudden he grabbed my arm, yanked me into an unoccupied stall, and slammed the metal door shut behind us.

CHAPTER TWO

CAUSING A COMMOTION

Still September 1987 (really, just seconds later)

"Shit," he whispered as we stood mere inches from each other in the tiny stall.

"What is happening? What—"

"Shh." New Order's "True Faith" was sounding through the club now, and CJ closed the toilet lid, sat down, crossed his leather-panted legs, and exhaled dramatically.

"Sorry," I whispered . . . but in reality, I was anything but. There was something shockingly exciting about being locked in a tiny bathroom stall with a scantily dressed near-stranger who thought I was (exceedingly) cute. I could feel myself getting further stirred.

"Ugh," he mumbled. "Long story. I promise I'll tell you. But right now? No sound, okay?"

As I pantomimed zipping my lips, he reached into his jacket pocket and took out this plastic yellow banana. It was the kind I used to love as a kid, the kind that came in packages alongside plastic strawberries and grapes. You found them in the candy section next to circus peanuts and gumballs, and they usually cost about fifty cents for a pack. The banana ones were typically filled with banana-flavored sugar. But I wasn't a total idiot—I knew that other substances could be kept inside as well, especially at a club like this one.

The balloon of excitement deflated. I swallowed, utterly disappointed.

"Oh, um. I don't . . ."

He put his finger to his mouth again, and I turned, figuring it was time to extricate myself from this.

As I reached for the door handle, CJ grabbed hold of my arm, and I turned to look at him. His face was pleading. I sighed and leaned against the door, crossing my arms over my chest.

He nonchalantly turned his attention back to his banana, pouring powder into his palm. The powder appeared yellow, like the candy. But I remembered from an episode of *Miami Vice* that cocaine could be mixed in with other substances. Was that what was happening here?

CJ licked the powder from his palm and smiled.

I must have looked alarmed, because he finally rolled his eyes and whispered, "I'm a sugar fiend. I needed a hit. Bad."

At first I thought *sugar* was a code word, but the way he smacked his lips said otherwise.

"It's candy. Honest."

I was dubious, and I guess he could tell from my expression. He poured out a little more into his palm, the same one he'd just licked. "Pure as the driven snow, I am," he said. "In terms of drugs, anyway. God no."

He offered his palm to me.

"Um . . ." Again with the arousal. My eyes sought something else to focus on. Just bathroom walls, covered in lewd drawings of cocks and boobs. That didn't help.

"You still think it's cocaine, don't you?"

I shrugged and willed my dick to deflate. I shuffled my feet and glanced back at his face. His expression was so sober that I almost broke out laughing, because it totally didn't match the outfit.

"I promise. It really isn't. It's banana-flavored and one-hundred-percent sugar. Honest."

There are moments your existence flashes before your eyes and you hear the voice narrating your life saying something like, *And that was the moment it all went downhill for Micah* . . . But I closed my eyes and tentatively licked his frosty palm, waiting to see what licking potentially unidentified drugs felt like.

Two things: One, licking his skin made my heart pulse like crazy. And two, sugar. Delicious.

I smiled, relieved.

"Would you do me a favor and peer over the door and let me know if a tall douchebag in a brown bomber jacket, with a mustache, maybe about thirty, is still here?"

I stood on my tiptoes and peered out. Club Kids, mostly. A couple of adults at the urinals. No one close to matching that description.

"Nope," I reported. "He must have left."

"Thank God," CJ said, speaking at a normal volume again.

"So what was that all about?"

He grunted. "I'm ditching his sorry ass."

"What did he do?"

He swigged more sugar and sucked it into his cheek. "It isn't what he did. It's who he is. It's his essence. Sometimes you have to ask yourself: What would Sally Jessy Raphael do? And in this case, she'd tell me to give him the boot because I'm a beautiful flower and he's a weed. Like the worst kind of weed, the kind that has bad breath."

"I hate weeds with bad breath," I said.

"His is like pickled dog shit."

I blanched. "That's pretty bad."

CJ sighed and chugged the final bits of sugar from the banana, tapping the bottom and then tossing it on the floor.

"You're littering?"

He gestured dramatically with his hands. "By four a.m., that piece of plastic will be easily the least offensive thing found on this bathroom floor. Anyway, the thing is, shit breath was my cab ride home. And he has all our money."

I studied CJ. Was this a con? He certainly had the pizzazz of a con man. But there was something else there, too. When he'd stood up for me against the other Club Kids, it had been sincere. I was sure of it.

Well, pretty sure.

"So you need cab fare?" I said. His story didn't quite add up. Who leaves their money with a guy and then ditches him?

"No, no. Well, yeah. I mean, I need to get home. I have a token in my pocket—"

"I thought you were just happy to see me!" I said, channeling my best Mae West.

"Ha! But yeah. I have a token, but this may not be the best

outfit for the subway. I'm not sure I want to be pushed onto the train tracks by the brawling boys of Bensonhurst."

He said this with such a gleam that I couldn't help but feel myself gleaming back at him. I realized that in some ways I didn't care if he was a con man. This conversation, in this place, was by far the most interesting thing that had ever happened to me. Even if it seemed to barely register for him. Or maybe especially because of that. This was natural to him, but for me this was a leap into the great queer unknown. He was a gay guy just about my age who was actually talking to me. That was new, and needed. Even if he was conning me, I was a willing target, if that was what it took for me to see what happened next.

"Okay," I said.

"Okay?"

"Okay, I'll help you get home. I'll put you in a cab and give you the money for it."

"Oh my God, would you? That's so nice of you. Thank you. You're literally the nicest person in the history of the world. Like, if Mother Teresa, Florence Nightingale, and Oprah Winfrey got together, they'd say, *Why can't we be more like Miles?*"

Feeling myself blush, I told him to meet me at the front of the club because I had to say goodbye to my friends. Unsaid was that there was no way I was going to walk out of the bathroom with this guy. I wasn't sure what the reaction would be at school, but I knew I didn't want to find out.

Deena was dancing on the sunken dance floor with Rolando and Cherise, who were doing a faster, more manic version of the shuffle from *The Breakfast Club*, arms akimbo and flailing. Deena was cackling, having the time of her life, doing that Tiffany heel-shuffle thing. Too bad I'd never be able to move that fast. I tapped her on the shoulder.

"Sooo . . . I'm gonna go," I said.

I must have looked different, because her eyes got wide, she stopped dancing, and she pulled me off the floor, up the stairs, and into this rafters area where we leaned on a black metal railing.

"Tell me you met someone. Tell me!"

I mugged for the camera.

She punched my chest with her fists. "Oh my God! My baby boy—he's all grown up! Where is he? Let me meet him! Is he our age? Please let him be our age and not some grody pedophile."

"He's definitely the right age, and you're definitely not meeting him yet."

"Ooh. No. You have to introduce him to your friends. That way if you're hacked to death and dumped into the Hudson River, we'll at least know what to tell the police sketch artist."

"I'll be fine. I'm not going home with him. Just living a little, for once."

"I'm going with you!"

"But you so aren't." I leaned in. "It's the boy in the bra."

She shrieked. "Omigod! Omigod omigod omigod!"

"Like, gag you with a spoon?"

"No! Not at all. I'm just impressed, that's all. He was a babe."

"Call you tomorrow?"

She hugged me tight. "Remember everything. Everything. And be safe, please. Use a condom for everything, and be the boy, not the girl. That's safer."

I pulled back and looked at her. "Did you really just say that?"

"I'm just saying."

I didn't have the energy to tell her how not cool the whole *be the boy* thing was, so I dropped it. With Napoleon from the basketball team, I was always *the boy*. Did that make Napoleon a girl? I didn't think he'd like that too much.

"Can you believe—" I started, but she was running down the stairs back to the dance floor and I felt this sudden twinge of abandonment, which was weird because I was actually the one leaving. I knew I could do things without Deena, but I almost never did. Which made this a very big deal.

CJ seemed to go way back with everybody at the door of the club, or maybe he'd just made fast friends with everyone and become the center of it all. A guy pulled a Polaroid camera out from his knapsack and snapped a picture, and CJ's face came alive as it emerged from the cloudy gray square. In the photo, he looked completely at home in the glare of fame's flashbulb, as if he were Dale Bozzio herself and hadn't just needed to ask a stranger for cab money in a bathroom stall. When he saw me watching, he started saying goodbye to the crowd, and a bunch of people hugged him like they were old friends. I was left wondering why, with all these people to choose from, he'd picked plain old me to leave with.

Was I just an easy mark?

We crossed Twelfth Avenue and walked east on Twenty-Eighth Street under some scaffolding. There was nothing there but industrial space and darkness. This wasn't a neighborhood for walking. For anything, really. If CJ turned out to be some sort of dangerous killer, like Deena had said, he wouldn't have to carry my dead, chubby body far. It would blend in fine in this West Side wasteland.

He clutched his thin, sequined jacket over as much of his exposed skin as possible. "Brr," he said.

"You look cold. You want my jacket?"

He looked over at me and laughed. "I'm good. Put me naked on an ice floe in the middle of the Arctic Ocean and I still wouldn't want to be seen in that thing. No offense."

"You'd die for fashion," I said as we approached Eleventh Avenue.

"Yup. And eventually, I intend to make fashion die for me. What about you? Would you rather die than be seen with me?"

"No!"

"Then what was that all about? Meeting me at the door?"

"Oh."

"Nothing? Okay, then."

I couldn't come up with a single lie to tell him, so I said, "Well . . . I guess it's because I'm not exactly out to all the people I was there with."

He laughed. "Are they terminally oblivious? You basically scream gay. *Gay!*" he shouted into the night sky, and I instinctively shrank into myself.

"Do I?"

"Well, not your outfit. But you? Yeah. You're very . . . gentle. What is it with your outfit, by the way?"

"It's kind of my thing. The absence of fashion."

He pursed his lips. "Okay. Not fully getting it, but it's your thing, so."

"I just wear what I like, I guess."

"There's something to be said for that. This," he said, pointing to his bra and sequined jacket, and then up to his hair and makeup, "is what happens when you put your faith in an older guy who turns out to be an asshole."

"Yeah?"

"The guy we were hiding from. This dipshit from Union Theological Seminary I met at this Columbia dance last month. We've been kind of dating. Or I thought we were. He insisted I dress as Dale Bozzio, because he knows I worship her. He suggested it and bankrolled it. I never dressed as a woman before in my life, but what do you know? A humpy older guy asks me to do something and I spend all day working on it. We get here and, I don't know, maybe he didn't like the way it turned out. He pretty much abandoned me for a walking cliché in a gold Speedo and angel wings, *as older men do*." This last part he shouted, and then went back to his normal tone. "And now here I am, cashless and cabless, leaving the Tunnel. I guess sometimes I'm too trusting? Sigh. 'Women who love too much,' next time on Lifetime. Television for Gay Men with Too Many Emotions."

I stopped walking. "Wait. I thought *you* were the one ditching *him*."

He looked away. "Oh yeah. That. Well. I meant ditching

him as a metaphor, more than as the absolute, actual truth."

"Huh."

"In that way, it's true in a larger sense. Which makes me brave. Yes. Very brave."

I laughed and rolled my eyes. "I have a feeling that you can be a little fast and loose with the truth?"

He shuffled his high heels. "I have been known to tell a tale or two. To embellish, maybe a smidge. But it's all in the name of benevolence." He looked into my eyes. His were this incredible cool gray color I'd never seen, and suddenly he was looking at me in a very serious way. "I can stop, though. I only lie to them, not us."

Them? Us? "Okay . . ."

"Seriously. I am ditching him, but I don't have money. And I like you. You're smart and funny and age appropriate. You can carry on an intelligent conversation, which is rare, believe me. And as I said, you're cute as a button, which is weird because I don't usually go for guys our age. Or buttons."

I looked away, unsure I could believe him, but he softly said, "No, really. You are, Miles."

I grimaced. "Micah."

"Oh, I misheard."

"Nope," I said. "Not exactly."

He cracked up. "Well well well! I'm starting to think that you have your own special relationship to the truth, too. I'm all for that. I actually think we're going to be great friends. Partners in crime. And who knows? Maybe it's time I give up the older guys, who totally suck, by the way. In case that wasn't clear."

He took my hand, gently, and we walked toward Tenth Avenue along abandoned Twenty-Eighth Street, hand in hand. My body was absolutely buzzing. His hand was tepid, bony, tentative. Part of me wanted to pull away, so no one would see. Part of me wanted to feel my hand in his forever.

"So you're in the closet," he said.

"Yup. I just don't think it would be a good idea for most people to know I'm, you know . . ."

"Gay. And would it be that bad?"

"It would."

"Your parents are homophobes?"

I nodded. It felt like too much trouble to explain that no, not really—what they were, other than liberal New York Jews, was entirely blind to the possibility. My dad's best friend, Rick, was gay, but any time I got ready to bring up my sexuality, they'd ruin it by saying something that made it clear that I had to be straight. For them.

CJ and I walked on in a semi-comfortable silence, our arms swinging together like we were schoolchildren holding hands. The night stretched thin before us, and I was glad we were alone together. I wondered what he was thinking. I was thinking about maybe trying again with my parents. Because maybe they'd be okay with it. I was just scared. I was just—

My thoughts were interrupted by CJ muttering something I couldn't quite hear, and then I saw these two white guys, maybe in their twenties, walking toward us. One wore a Yankees cap and had a sloppy mustache. The other, wearing a white down jacket, looked greasy to me. The thin night thickened. The energy changed around us in an instant.

"Fags," Yankees Cap called out, loud, menacing.

CJ grabbed my hand harder in defiance. "Brothers," he said.

"Fuckin' fags, you're gonna give us all AIDS," Down Jacket said. They were near us now, and CJ stopped walking. I wanted the world to stop. I wanted to disappear. I wanted the safety of my bed.

"And what if we were fags?" CJ asked calmly. "You think you're gonna do something about it?"

The guy cracked up. "Yeah, some dude dressed like a slut really scares me. I'll do something about it. I'll kick your fuckin' ass and—"

CJ reached into his pocket and pulled out a Swiss Army knife. He pulled out the gleaming blade and showed it to the guys.

"Your pansy ass wouldn't—"

CJ picked up his other hand and, emotionless, sliced a small cut on his index finger with the blade. A crimson line emerged from the gash. He looked at the guys.

"That's exactly it," he said, still calm. "We're all here to give you AIDS. Which one of you is first?" He moved toward the guys, and they jumped back.

Down Jacket backed off. "Crazy faggot," he muttered.

"You have no idea," CJ said. "Please test me. Please."

The guys turned and walked away, and CJ closed the knife, put it back in his pocket. We started back walking toward Tenth Avenue.

I was trying not to hyperventilate. Telling myself it was okay, we were okay, and that, dangerous or not, CJ's tactic had worked. No way were those guys coming at us again.

"I don't have AIDS, don't worry," CJ assured me. "I was just playing off their fear."

I may have nodded. Or my head may have been frozen.

"You learn to take care of yourself," CJ said after putting his bloody finger in his mouth and sucking it. "You learn to take care of yourself when no one else does."

My thoughts ran in so many directions, and the nausea I felt from nearly getting gay bashed threatened to empty my stomach.

CJ stopped and turned toward me, wiping his wet-but-not-as-bloody finger on his leather pants. "I'm sorry you had to see that. You're new. You don't know yet what it can be like."

I looked away. I wanted to say, *I'm not like you. I don't wear women's clothing on the street.* But I also knew that was bullshit. The guys stopped two fags. Not one fag and one random innocent person. If he was a fag, so was I.

"I promise that most of it is really fun. It's just the assholes that aren't. That and AIDS. AIDS. Is really not fun."

"Understatement of the century," I said. I knew about AIDS from the news and everything, but I felt its presence the most when I was working at the Lortel Theatre on Christopher Street. Walter, the concessions guy, had it. My boss, Felicia, talked about it all the time.

But even with that, the disease wasn't *real* to me.

Not yet.

CJ and I started to walk again.

"Damn, I'm cold," he said, shivering.

I began to shimmy out of my Members Only jacket.

"No means no, Micah."

"Take it. You're cold. I have more on than you." We stopped walking again and I handed him my jacket.

He sighed and took it, holding it like it had kryptonite lining. "I guess it's better than nothing."

Watching CJ Gorman put my beige Members Only jacket over his plexiglass bra is something I will never, ever forget.

"Thanks," he said.

"Don't mention it."

"I'll give it back to you. I'll give you my number. Is there a pen in one of these many, many Members Only pockets?"

I shook my head. "Members only. Pens are not members."

He fished around. "Is this a typewriter in here? No. Just tissues. Lots and lots of tissues. Are you a crier, Micah? Do you masturbate in public? Which is it?"

"No and no. Are those seriously the only options you can come up with? And why are you going through my pockets?"

"Well, without any writing or typing implement handy, can you memorize?"

I nodded, knowing that as much as I was drawn to CJ, as much as I wanted to get to know this person, I was still Micah Strauss, son of Ira and Dalia Strauss, and that person just wasn't going to be able to keep up with CJ, who carried a knife, wore women's clothing, and lied a lot. So I nodded, he recited it, I pretended to memorize it, and we walked on.

We hailed a cab, and I handed him a twenty.

As he got in, he said, "I'll pay this back, too. I promise."

"Sure, CJ."

"You have my number memorized?"

I nodded again.

"Repeat it back to me."

I paused and looked down, and when I looked back up, the life had left his eyes, like the gray had dimmed. I could see, in that moment, that this was a thing for CJ, people not calling him back. I suddenly hated myself.

"I'll definitely call you," I said, feeling like the worst person.

"I'm certain that you will," he replied, monotone.

The cab drove off.

I never even got to say goodbye.

CHAPTER THREE

BRILLIANT DISGUISE

October 1987

The second time I met CJ Gorman, he was wearing aviator glasses and a brown leather bomber jacket.

It was a Saturday night about three weeks later, and I was tearing tickets at the Lortel, on Christopher Street. The play was *Steel Magnolias*, about a close-knit group of Southern women who hang out in a beauty parlor. I'd started ushering over the summer. The ten dollars I made per show wasn't much, but I did get to meet all the actors and see the show every night.

I had the entire play memorized.

"Laughter through tears is my favorite emotion."

"Shelby? You need some juice . . . drink the juice, honey."

Felicia, the feisty, birdlike lesbian theater manager, was supervising, which is to say she was standing around talking to me while I tore tickets. She'd just whispered a stupid joke about a penguin with a lisp to me when the person to whom I'd just handed a ticket back didn't enter the theater.

I looked up and saw a tall, skinny, cute guy with wavy brown hair who otherwise looked like he had taken a wrong turn on his way to pilot school.

"It's you!" he said.

I had no idea who this person was, though I admit I was intrigued that someone so handsome was excited to see me. I wondered who he'd mistaken me for. The redheaded kid with the glasses from *Revenge of the Nerds*? A chubby Anthony Michael Hall? ALF?

"It is me. And it is you. It is us!" I said.

"I still have your jacket, by the way."

"Oh shit!" I said, and even though Felicia was generally cool, I glanced back because ushers and ticket takers really aren't supposed to curse. It frightens the old ladies. But Felicia didn't seem to care, because she did the thing where she made one of her eyes go cross while the other stayed still. She stuck out her tongue and walked away.

CJ went on. "I've been hoping against hope I'd see you again one of these days so I could return the jacket, which you clearly covet. I've made a shrine to you. Our Lady of Questionable Fashion Taste."

I reddened, aware our conversation was in public. He stood off to the side and allowed the line of old people to approach with their tickets. The lobby was chaotic, loud with conversation on our side and will-call tickets being picked up on the other. An old woman with a cane handed me her ticket with a shaking hand, and I tore it, trying to split my attention between the line waiting to get in and the guy I'd blown off.

"CJ, right? Thank you, enjoy the show."

"Right! And you were Micah?"

"Still am! To your left, up the stairs."

"Carlo, are you coming?" The decrepit, gravelly voice came

from inside the theater. I turned to see a man with gray hair, small, round eyes, and a perfectly trimmed mustache. He was talking to CJ. "We should take our seats."

"Of course," CJ replied. "I'll be right there. I ran into a friend from AMDA. Would you be a doll and get me a gin and tonic?" The man winked, nodded, and walked away.

"Carlo?" I asked. There was a lull in the line, thankfully.

CJ shrugged.

"AMDA?"

"Academy of Musical and Dramatic Arts. I'm a student there."

"I know what it is. But you aren't really a student there, are you?"

He screwed up his face at me like I was asking a crazy question.

A line was beginning to form again, so I gestured him inside. I thought of the weird, scary night we'd had, and I told myself, *Just say goodbye, Micah.*

My mouth disagreed. "Maybe I'll see you at the break?" I asked.

He gave me this adorable full-toothed, exaggerated smile, which, combined with the pilot gear, looked utterly ridiculous.

Suddenly, I couldn't wait for intermission.

When the curtain went up, I headed down to the office.

"Cursing while tearing tickets," Felicia said. She had a wry half grin on her face, though, so I knew it was basically okay.

"Blue-haired ladies running for cover," I said, hanging my head. "Sorry."

"The guy seemed pretty smitten!"

I blushed. "What? Naw."

"I don't know. That could be your future lover."

Felicia wasn't just my boss; she was the closest thing I had to a mentor. I think part of it was the fact that the typical usher was an aspiring actor, a headshot come to life. The thought of being on a stage terrified me. But there was still something about the theater that I loved. I was there to figure out what it was. Even though I was just a lowly usher, Felicia had made sure I'd met everyone associated with the production, all the actors, including Rosemary Prinz and Margo Martindale; the director, Pamela Berlin; and even Kyle Renick, the producer. "Can't hurt to know people," she said.

She was also a mama bear, small as she was; when this creepy college-aged usher was with us for a week in July, she carved a wedge between us, making it clear to him that I was not available.

"You're better than him," she'd told me flatly as she did her daily paperwork. "We'll find you a boyfriend who will get how special you are."

So yeah, I kinda loved Felicia. Had a little crush on her, maybe, if a gay boy can have a crush on a lesbian. (He can.)

My coworker Walter stuck his head into the room. "Concessions set up for intermission," he said in his raspy voice. "Okay if you take it today? I think I need to get home."

Felicia nodded, then asked, "You okay?"

He stepped fully into the room. His face was shrinking in, like a deflating balloon. He looked noticeably worse than he had when I'd first met him in June. You could kind of tell he had AIDS then; now he was cheekbones and hollow eye sockets, basically a skeleton with raggedy brown hair that was rapidly falling out. I made sure not to look away, though that was always my impulse.

He was twenty-eight.

He rubbed his belly. "Yeah. I think probably," he said.

"Go go go," Felicia said, and Walter nodded and hurried out. He lived around the corner in a brownstone, so it wasn't too far he had to go. Thankfully.

Felicia gave me a meaningful look. We'd talked about AIDS, a lot. She and Raina, her girlfriend, pretty much harangued me with information. I told them it didn't matter, that my only experience was with a straight guy. What I didn't tell them was that we weren't using condoms, because neither Napoleon nor Lucas nor I had ever been with any other guy. I knew they'd kill me themselves if they found out. Felicia had said, "A condom every time, hear? You think you're the only one. You never are. Even some so-called straight jock."

I had promised myself: When I got my first gay boyfriend, things would be different and condoms would be used, every time, for sure.

"So, this boy. Worthy of you?" Felicia asked. "How old is he?"

I thought of the different versions of CJ that I'd met, weird as they were. I thought of his gray eyes and electric presence.

"Eighteen," I said. "And definitely."

I could see in her smirk that she knew I was hardly sure.

"Just be careful. You boys go too fast."

I nodded, thinking about what Walter would say to that.

Over the summer he used to joke about how lesbians just about got married as soon as they met. Then my mind got lost in what "too fast" might mean in actuality, with CJ.

If he was actually interested, I was probably, against my better judgment, all in.

Whatever that meant.

At intermission, he did indeed come to see me, and after introducing me to Irving, his . . . date?—who was my grandfather's age, probably older—CJ sent him off to get him another G&T.

"So . . . explain? Every time I see you, you're a different person."

He ran his long, thin fingers through his wavy hair. "One personality cannot contain all of this."

"And you're here with a septuagenarian because . . ."

"A guy's gotta eat."

"Okay . . ."

He smiled and took his glasses off. "Over at Ty's, this guy was asking a friend if he wanted his extra ticket for tonight. He didn't. I did. So I turned on the charm."

"But . . . *Carlo*? Why?"

"To get to the other side. Duh."

I laughed, remembering how that night, before things got out of control, my every nerve had been on overdrive with each unpredictable thing he'd said. (It had all gotten lost in the translation when I'd told Deena about him; she decided he was "dicey as hell.")

"I feel like maybe you're avoiding the question?" I said. He shrugged. "And anyway, you don't even look like a Carlo. I look more like a Carlo than you, and that's not saying much."

"Well, what you don't know is that Carlo's mother is Portuguese. And a former Olympic figure skater, to boot."

"Is she?"

CJ rolled his eyes. "You wanna do a scene study after the show?"

"What does that mean?"

"It means I ditch the old guy, who is pretty sure he's getting at least to gay second base with Carlo, and we go to David's Pot Belly Stove and eat mozzarella sticks?"

I was struck silent. The level of unnecessary deceit both repelled and compelled me. I found myself pulled in, as if this were a mystery I might solve.

"Yes," I said. "On one condition."

"Name it."

"I'd like to go with CJ."

He seemed to consider this. "I'll check and see if he's available."

Cigarette smoke, sweet wine, and fried potatoes merged into a singular scent as we walked into David's Pot Belly Stove. I'd walked by the restaurant many times, but I'd never gone in. All I knew was it felt vaguely descriptive of my midsection, and that made me feel annoyed every time I walked by.

Kenny G played softly in the background, and the place was filled with adults, not another teen in sight. It was packed though it was nearly eleven. Same-sex couples sat in brown leather booths, eating omelets and drinking martinis. I excused myself and called my mom from the pay phone on the corner of Bleecker and Christopher. I was nervous that she'd ask a lot of questions, but frankly she was just glad I wanted to stay out late like a normal kid and gave me carte blanche to do as I pleased.

"Just don't get anyone pregnant, please," she pleaded.

I promised to do my best.

CJ had secured us a table. When I sat down, he was gazing at the menu, perplexed.

"I'm a picky eater. Are you?" he asked.

I pointed at my belly and he frowned. He shook his head and said, "I'm not sure there's an absolute correlation between girth and willingness to eat a wide array of foods. You wear it well, by the way. What I wouldn't give to put on some weight, actually."

It was hard not to feel a little defensive, as I'd spent a lifetime dodging nicknames like Fudgie the Whale and Stay Puft Marshmallow Man from people who were blessed with CJ's build.

CJ ordered for us. Two plates of mozzarella sticks, which he claimed were the best in the world, and two pot belly burgers, which inexplicably had a pineapple ring and teriyaki sauce on them. Cokes, which surprised me, because he'd been drinking gin and tonics, apparently, at the theater. And a salad to share, so that we would, as he put it, "appear health conscious."

"How are we paying for this?" I asked. "That's gonna cost like a week's worth of ushering."

"Don't worry about it. You took care of me when I needed it. I got you this time. And get a raise or something. They're ripping you off."

While CJ arranged the salt and pepper shakers to be in perfect alignment, I drank him in. His face was long and thin, his jaw square, his mouth full. Not full of food, but full like substantial, like the mouth of a person who is worthy of existence.

I wondered what that felt like.

"Sorry I didn't call," I said, and he waved me off like he hadn't even noticed.

Then he went back to arranging the items on the table and not speaking, so I said, "Dale, Carlo, CJ, tell me all about you." I sipped ice water from a mason jar.

"Oh, you know. Long walks on the beach. Piña coladas and getting caught in the rain. I won't cum in your mouth. The usual."

I spat water all over the table. He seemed pleased.

"Sorry," I said. "Drinking problem."

"One day at a time, my friend," he said.

"Right. But actually. Who are you, actually? I'm curious."

He reclined and sighed dramatically. "It's so *not* interesting, you know? And really, this is about you, rookie boy. This is brand-new to you, isn't it?"

"Kinda," I said. Truthfully, my body was almost too tingly. There was a gay couple, middle-aged and mustached, sitting next to us. Across the table from me was a completely crush-worthy—if somewhat unpredictable—guy who had actually befriended me, sought me, held my hand on the street.

"So let me be your tour guide, okay? I feel like I should do for you what no one did for me."

When he said that last part, he averted his eyes, and for a nanosecond it was like I almost saw something real there. I wanted to know more.

And somehow, I knew not to ask.

Instead I said, "So you were in a gay bar before the show? Ty's?"

"Oh, puleeze," he said. "I go to all of 'em. Boots and Saddle, which we call Bras and Girdles, or Beer and Sympathy. Julius', Ninth Circle. Total chicken bars, which is good because we're chicken. Uncle Charlie's, which is total S and M."

I wondered if there might be a CJ-to-newbie dictionary I could ask for. I was doing my best to use contextual clues. But the last one stunned me because I *did* know what sadism and masochism meant.

"An S and M bar? And you go there?"

"Stand and model."

I smirked.

CJ kept going. "Actual S and M places . . . I wouldn't rule them out. I wouldn't rule anything out. Try anything once, I always say. One time I went into Badlands on the corner of West and Christopher."

I remembered that one from driving home along the West Side Highway from my grandmother's place in Brooklyn. I must have been thirteen, and on our right in the distance was a dark and dingy brick building with smoky (or possibly dirty) windows and a white placard that read BADLANDS. I somehow knew it was a gay bar. There was a sign in the window that read TUESDAY NIGHT IS DYNASTY NIGHT. A few men in leather pants milled outside. It took everything I had not to turn my head as we drove by, but somehow it was like my mother was seeing through my eyes.

"That's a *gay bar*," she said. "Such a shame what's happening to gay men."

My heart pulsed, and even though I didn't know what was such a shame, I felt as though there was a life out there that I wasn't living, and it was alive at that bar, where they might be watching *Dynasty* and drinking and laughing and talking, and I wanted to be there, too, I wanted her to stop the car so that for one moment I could step out of my little Micah Strauss bubble. I needed to understand how it all worked. How men met other men. How they decided to have sex. How that worked.

"What was it like?" I asked CJ.

"By the end of the night, I was doing a striptease on the bar. Guys were throwing hundreds at me. They have a signed poster of me in the corner of the bar."

I was disappointed that he was still joking with me. "How come I feel like this may not be entirely all true?"

He raised his right eyebrow. "A boy likes to be mysterious."

"Is any of that true?"

He shrugged. "It's all metaphorically true. Some of it is literal truth."

"And you're not going to tell me any more than that?"

"Someday, maybe."

Over mozzarella sticks that were indeed amazing—the cheese beautifully melted and not chewy, the breaded vessel not greasy and with just a hint of salt—CJ told me he had the night off, and then, when I asked him from what, he changed the subject. Big shocker.

"So really. What can you tell me about CJ?" I asked.

"My dad was abducted by aliens. My mom died on an oil rig off the coast of Bora Bora last year. You know, the usual."

"Ah."

"I live with Tom Selleck in Tribeca."

"Ah. And how is that going?"

"Ugh. All he wants is sex, sex, sex."

I cracked up. "Who do you actually live with?"

"My mom had this boyfriend for a couple years before the oil rig mishap, so I live with him. His name is Jack. Jack is a part-time carnival barker and full-time asshole."

"Sounds fun!"

"Oh, it is!"

"What's it like to live with a carnival barker?" I asked.

He took a deep breath. "Do you have several hours?" he asked.

"I kinda do," I said.

"Another time."

CJ toned it down over dinner and he got a bit more real, and we talked about our school lives. (Neither one of us was particularly popular, but we weren't alone, either.) A little about how his coming out had gone at home (not well), and why I hadn't yet. Favorite albums. His was *Spring Session M* by Missing Persons. I'd never heard of it, and that led him to nearly slap me again.

"It's about five years old and already it's a classic," he told me.

"I didn't get into music until freshman year," I explained bashfully.

This was an acceptable answer to him, apparently.

"No shame in being a late bloomer, as long as you make the most of your bloom when it arrives," he said. "So what's your post-freshman-year favorite album?"

I tensed up. Deena already gave me enough shit about my musical tastes, and I didn't want more of that from CJ. So I didn't tell the total truth. I picked something I thought would be less ridiculous.

I was wrong.

"Tina Turner?" CJ almost shrieked. "How old are you, Micah? Are you my long-lost mother?"

"She has an amazing voice," I said, defensive and wishing I'd just said my real favorite. "I like her. I guess I'm not as cool as you."

He cracked up. "Oh, please. I'm not cool. Liking Missing Persons gets me all sorts of shit, too. I'm just . . . of my generation, I guess. It's cool that you're different. You don't know how to dress. You like yuppie music. You're—oh, never mind. The point is that I like these things about you."

I wondered what the left-out part was.

Again, I didn't ask.

As we finished our dinners, we fell into a comfortable rhythm of give and take as we talked about *Steel Magnolias* and which MTV VJ was the sexiest and the strange way straight people had become obsessed with the musical *Cats*. I explained Deena and he explained how 'Til Tuesday was not a one-hit wonder. There were plenty of delicious silences and just a hint of lingering eye contact. I couldn't believe this was happening, finally: I was out with a guy. Of course, I was out with a guy who was out of my league, and who may have only flirted with me when he wanted something from me at the club. But still. Progress.

I watched as he put his fork down, ran his hands through his wavy hair, cocked his head, smirked, and said, "You're cute. I like you. You wanna go down to the piers after this and do perverted things to each other?"

I put my hands on the table to steady myself; suddenly it felt like the restaurant was a Tilt-A-Whirl.

"Oh!" I said. "Okay, um."

"God, you're adorable. You're so flustered."

I whispered, "I'm a virgin."

This wasn't entirely true, but it felt—as CJ might say—*emotionally* true, since the two guys I'd been with were both straight, and therefore both not particularly interested in me as a human being. No kissing, which was actually the thing I most longed to try.

"Yes, yes," CJ said, grinning. "Me too." And then he ducked under the table and cloaked his head with his hands as if to avoid a lightning strike.

"No. Really. I am," I said.

"How is that even possible? There's so much temptation!" He gestured around the restaurant. "So many men, so little time," he sang.

"You don't get it. I wouldn't even know how to begin to find a willing partner."

He gestured around the restaurant again. "Any. Man. Here. Any. Even the straight ones after a few drinks, in my experience. Check this out." He turned to the two middle-aged men at the next table. Besides the mustaches, they both had thinning brown hair and drawn faces.

"Hey!" he said, and the two men turned toward him. He smiled at them. "You wanna take us home? We're down for literally anything."

"What?" I said, but he put his hand up.

One of the men turned to look me up and down. He raised an eyebrow. "Honey? You're chicken. Are your fathers available?"

CJ cackled. "I think if you catch my stepdad after his fourth G and T, probably."

The guys laughed and went back to their meal. CJ turned back toward me, openmouthed and enchanted. And I was like, *What is this? Who is this person? What is happening?*

"Do you want dessert?" he asked, and I paused because I didn't know if this, too, was code for something he planned to do to me at the piers, where I was clearly *not* going to go with him, as I had no idea what I was doing, and this was like a real gay guy, and I didn't even have condoms, and who has sex outside anyway?

Noticing my pause, he said, "I mean, like, actual dessert. Häagen-Dazs, next door."

I didn't want him to see how relieved I was. "Sure."

"Good. I'll take care of dinner if you buy me a small rocky road cone. *Rocky Road*: the name of my future autobiography."

My shoulders sagged. He didn't actually like me; he wanted a free ice cream cone and he didn't want me to see him dine-and-dash. Shit. I was part of his free night out.

"How are you going to pay for all this?"

"Don't worry about it," he said. "If you're ready, why don't you go get us ice cream and I'll meet you outside in five."

I paused.

"Go," he said. "Git."

My stomach crashed. I hadn't ever broken a law before, and I didn't want to start doing it now. I also didn't have nearly enough money to pay for whatever this meal was going to cost. I did, however, have a credit card *just in case of emergencies*, as my mom always said. I had never used it before.

Was this an emergency?

No, I decided.

Or maybe I was just afraid of what CJ would think if I tried to pay.

I got up, put on my jacket, and went outside, sure that the waitstaff was onto us and that at any moment they would call the cops on me. It was a relief when I got outside into the chilly night air.

Next door, Häagen-Dazs was apparently now a gay bar.

The line appeared to be all gay and lesbian couples, mostly drunk. A dark-haired couple wearing matching gray overcoats was making out, which fascinated me and made me want to stare. The white guy with thinning brown hair in front of me was wearing what I'd come to understand was the gay uniform: tight black jeans and a black bomber jacket with silver zippers on the sleeves. He turned so I could see his profile, and I saw several purple splotches on his neck and cheek.

I caught my breath. Walter didn't have any, but I certainly knew Kaposi's sarcoma lesions when I saw them. I'd see guys like this sometimes coming in to see *Steel Magnolias*, and

I knew what it meant: AIDS had gotten its hold on these men and wouldn't let go. Although I tried to rip their tickets like everyone else's, those lesions looked like death to me.

The man in front of me must have sensed me looking at him, because he turned. I stared across the street, straining my neck as much as I could so I could ignore what was right in front of me.

When I got to the counter, I ordered CJ's rocky road and my plain chocolate. Just as the poor overworked sap on the midnight shift gave me my change, CJ came in, grabbed his cone from my hands, and said, "Thanks! C'mon."

I hated how casually he said it, and how complicit I was in what he'd just done. I kept my feet planted where they were. CJ was lots of fun, but I wasn't a thief, and no way was I going to walk by Dave's Pot Belly Stove every night and worry that they'd recognize me.

"What are you—?" CJ asked, but I was already walking back into the restaurant.

CHAPTER FOUR

DIGGING YOUR SCENE

October 1987

I hurried over to our table and was about to pull out my wallet and the emergency card when I saw something shocking.

A fifty-dollar bill on the table.

I looked at the check and it was for thirty-nine and change, so that meant CJ had given the waiter a generous tip. Stunned, I turned around and walked out of the restaurant.

Who was this guy, who was so full of surprises?

I prepared to apologize, but when I walked out, CJ had this impish smile that drooped his lip slightly on the left side of his face.

"I can see why you'd think that," he said.

He started walking west on Christopher, so I followed. "Sorry."

"No sweat. I get it. I have perhaps not seemed like the most honest and credible person on earth so far." He turned his head sideways and licked his cone. "But the truth is that I am honest. In the important ways. I don't lie to friends. And I like you, Micah."

We walked west in silence along the crowded sidewalk. I

was thinking about how he'd said we were friends. But he'd also said I was cute. Was this a date? Could there be a date in the future if this wasn't one?

This was the latest I'd ever been out. *Saturday Night Live* was already over, and Christopher Street was filled with people who had better things to do than watch it. A bevy of chattering gays gallivanted up the other side of Christopher Street. A drunk woman sat against the wall of the army/navy store, muttering to passersby that she had crack for sale. A bunch of men in leather vests stood smoking in front of Ty's, the gay bar where CJ had scored his theater ticket earlier that night. Two balding white guys sucked face in front of Li-Lac Chocolates, across from the shuttered-for-the-night Lortel Theatre.

As we wandered farther west, I felt this sense of elation pushing out against my chest, as if I were discovering a hidden wonderland. Because I was. Not only was it late, but I had never walked west of Hudson Street, where the streets seemed to widen and the crowds thinned out.

A Latino kid maybe our age, wearing impossibly tight stretch pants, walked past. Then we passed a frail white man with a cane who looked to be about eighty but was probably thirty, like Walter. His head was down, like each step took concentration.

"Jesus," I muttered, once we were well past him.

"Tell me about it."

"How do you even deal?"

He didn't answer. We walked on, and an older-looking Black woman wearing a fur coat and flowers in her hair was walking toward us, swinging a paisley pocketbook, and

CJ elbowed me in the ribs and said, "Yay, it's Marsha."

Her face was lined like she'd seen some stuff, but what was most memorable was her wide, perfect smile, framed by ruby-red lips.

"Hey, babies," she said. "Be safe, okay?"

"Yes, Marsha. Love you," CJ replied.

"Love you, too, baby."

"How do you know her?" I asked as she walked past.

"I don't, personally. She's a Village legend, like Rollerena. I see her all the time. She always says hi and tells me she loves me and to be safe."

There was that word again: *safe*.

"Really—how do you deal with it? This AIDS thing?" I asked again.

He sighed and put his hands in his jacket pockets. "That, my friend, is too long an answer for this late-slash-early on a Saturday-night-slash-Sunday-morning."

"I've never walked this far west on Christopher," I said.

He stopped in his tracks. "Is that right? Well . . . you're in luck."

He cleared his throat and gestured dramatically as if onstage, and he channeled the intro to Robin Leach's *Lifestyles of the Rich and Famous*. "Welcome to television's unchallenged authority on debauchery, excess, and syphilis!" he announced to me and anyone else within fifty feet. "It's another dazzling *Lifestyles of the Gay and Infamous*. I'm your host, CJ Leach."

I looked around to see who was seeing and hearing this, and my reticence just egged him on.

"Tonight, meet the movers and shakers of homosexual New York, from its epicenter, Christopher Street. For all the yuppies from hell and midwestern ladies on this tour, I must tell you that we're about to see things that will shock and appall you and send you running back to Iowa."

Neither group, unsurprisingly, was represented.

"I look forward to this tour," I said as we passed a metal awning and some stairs leading down.

"And this, ladies and gentlemen, is the PATH train station. It's where the queens from New Jersey congregate every weekend night at three a.m., to venture back to their homes after sampling the fine drinking establishments of the West Village." He gestured as we crossed Washington. "Such as Two Potato, catering to a mostly Black and Latino crowd of homosexual men due to rampant racism and segregation in the gay community—great rum and Cokes, by the way."

"How do you even get into all these places?"

"And coming up, the Church of St. Veronica, where pious homosexuals pray to a God who does not exist on Sunday morning . . . and then Golden Woks, the Chinese takeout hole-in-the-wall where men purchase egg rolls after doing unmentionable things to each other on the piers. Across the street, you'll see Bailey House, which is housing for homeless people with AIDS."

Out in front of Bailey House, a man lay in the gutter. Just across the street stood a crowd of men in leather outside a bar, ignoring the body. Many were shirtless, wearing leather vests. Some were also in leather chaps, some wearing jeans under the chaps with handkerchiefs in the pockets, and others with their bare asses hanging out. Bare asses!

I didn't want to stare, but I couldn't stop myself.

"And here is the aforementioned Badlands," CJ announced as we waded through the crowd. Suddenly I was standing in a sea of older male gayness. A cigar-smoking guy with big fat nipples protruding from his vest grinned and went to pinch CJ's nipple. CJ karate chopped his hand away. "And you, sir," he said, not really addressing the guy but still in character, "cannot afford my rent."

"Whoa," I said as we continued to weave through the maze of men. It all made me feel a little dirty and uncomfortable.

"This is the Badlands, where men whose day jobs are spritzing cologne on passersby in Bloomingdale's try to look tough."

I ducked my head, and we hurried on before any of the men could further molest CJ. None of them tried anything with me. Which was good. I guess.

"I feel like I'm in a parallel universe," I said as we hurriedly crossed the West Side Highway, three lanes of traffic in each direction with a median in the middle.

On the other side, he lowered his voice. "And here, it might behoove me to control my volume, as we are allies and visitors, and hence this is NOT a place for a white boy to make a spectacle of himself at one in the morning."

We had approached the waterfront, and here, a very different, very young crowd had assembled. A boombox nearby blared "Don't You Want Me" by Jody Watley, and lots of Black and Latino kids stood in clusters, some cackling, most just talking, but some dancing. One boy danced with his hands, using them to frame his face in different poses. Another bent over backward until his head almost touched the ground behind him, and a third balanced on one hand, his legs akimbo.

We stood and watched, and for just one moment, all was good in the world.

At Trinity, my school, there wasn't a single out kid, and other than Deena, no one there knew about me. Well, two athletes did, but it wasn't like we talked about it. And here, on the Christopher Street pier, was a veritable world of young, apparently gay and lesbian people, and transgender people, too, lots of them. We walked out a bit, past various groups. Some were dressed to be seen. Either in revealing, tight dresses in DayGlo colors, or, in some cases, very straight-looking outfits, like sweatpants, Tommy Hilfiger, and baseball hats.

CJ continued to speak softly. "Banjee boys and banjee girls," he said.

I had no idea what that meant.

"I get along with everyone, but you gotta be aware that we're visitors here. Lots of these kids don't trust white people. With good reason."

We climbed over a barricade and made it to water's edge. Across the river, the eyesore of dank Jersey City warehouses lurked in the shadows. The moon glowed, yellow and full, off the water. A chilly breeze hit me in the face. I looked down. My reflection was a Cheetos wrapper. My heart pulsed. We were so close to the water, with no barrier between it and me. CJ took my hand in his.

We faced each other. "I'm glad I met you," he said. "In all seriousness. With all the guys I meet, I feel like I have to be someone else. But with you, even though, yeah, I like to entertain, I feel like maybe I don't have to."

Shivers. "You don't," I said.

He leaned in and tilted his head slightly, and for the first time in my life, my lips met those of another boy. His were soft and plump and delicious. His breath smelled sweet like ice cream. He just barely opened his mouth, and I copied him. The tip of his tongue tentatively met mine, and I shivered. When he pulled back, he smiled. I did, too.

"Wow," I said, a million warring thoughts going through my brain at once. Sensory overload. My first kiss. With a real gay person. Trading saliva and germs. Walter and his deflated face.

"You ain't seen nothin' yet," CJ said.

He went in for another kiss, and I wanted to, but I couldn't. My mind was spinning with images of Walter, and the guy with the lesions, and the guy with the cane. And Felicia's admonishments.

"Is this safe?" I asked, pulling back. I'd seen the guidelines that it was, but reading something was okay and actually doing it were two different things.

He stroked my hair, which felt incredible. "Yeah," he said. "Believe me, I'm basically the condom queen of Tribeca. Kissing is safe. Oral? Unclear. Anal, gotta use a condom every time."

What does unclear *mean?* I wondered. This disease wasn't unclear in the least. It killed people. And before it killed them, it robbed them of everything. And what risk would I be willing to take, if those were the end results? With Napoleon and Lucas, I didn't really think about these things, because they were straight and had never been with anyone else. But CJ obviously had.

"Have you been tested?" I asked.

"Yes, Mother. Negative. And I don't take risks. I talk a big game, but I'm pretty safe."

My mind went to the word *pretty*, and when he went in for a kiss again, I shrank back.

His face registered hurt in the crease formed by his eyebrows and forehead.

"I want to," I said. "I'm scared, I guess."

He nodded and sighed. "That's cool. I mean, no biggie. I just . . . how are you seventeen, gay, live in New York City, and not know this stuff?"

I opened my mouth to disagree, and then I shut it again. Yeah, Felicia had told me a lot, and I knew Walter. The Lortel had made me far more aware of it than any of my classmates, that was for sure. So many guys with canes walking along Christopher Street and coming to see the show. I read up on it every chance I got, locking myself away in the periodicals closet at the school library and reading every article I could find about AIDS. But there was knowing, and then there was *knowing*. My mom's hairdresser, Lorenzo. He used to save all the red lollipops for me when I went with her to the salon. He died in 1984. My mom had told me. It didn't seem possible that someone who had once been so alive could no longer be, and yet I knew that didn't make logical sense as a feeling. I knew everyone died, but I guessed until you really knew someone who had, it didn't feel real.

"I wonder how you can put yourself out there at all," I said. "I'm not judging. I just . . . It's so scary."

He shrugged and looked out at the water. "Not sure I really have any choice. This is life. I like this life. I like gay life. On any day, anything can happen, you know?"

I nodded, but I definitely didn't know.

"So," I said, trying to figure out what I wanted to have happen. I wanted to experience another kiss, and yet I wanted to not have to worry about him only being *pretty safe*. I wanted to be in a place where I could admit who I was, yet not graduate into this gay world where I'd have to worry about my own health. To have to worry about dying.

"Do guys, like, go on dates?" I asked.

He smiled that toothy smile again. It was truly dazzling and alive to me, like his personality was too big for his facial muscles.

"They do," he said. "How about we do this: Your assignment, should you choose to accept it, is to go out and buy *Spring Session M* by Missing Persons and listen to it. What album should I listen to?"

I took a deep breath and told the delicate truth.

"*Music from the Edge of Heaven*, by Wham!"

"Oh dear. Okay. Accepted. Let's do that, and why don't you do a little research so you can come to the conclusion that, yes, it's safe to kiss me. And then, let's talk by phone, and see where we're at. And if I even want to see you again, after suffering through Wham! Deal?"

His impish grin let me know he was giving me crap about my musical tastes and wasn't serious, and the possibility of a date with CJ made me feel like I could jump out of my skin.

"Deal," I said.

CHAPTER FIVE

CRUSH ON YOU

October 1987

"So this boy, CJ. You met him at the Tunnel, and he took you to the piers. Red flags, honey," said Raina, Felicia's girlfriend. Her voice was deep and wide, sort of like the way she was built. We were sitting in Felicia's office on a Tuesday night after the curtain had gone up.

"He's my age," I said. "He can't possibly—"

"HIV doesn't care how old you are," Felicia said. "Please be careful. Think of Walter. We know so many people who are sick and dying."

I nodded, feeling that buzzing sensation in my head, the one that always came with this discussion.

"Brent lost his job," Raina said to Felicia.

"What? No!"

Raina shrugged. "He made the mistake of telling the guy he was understudying for that he tested positive, and what do you know? Suddenly they decided to go in another direction. Just like that. And the director and producer are gay, of course. People suck."

I wanted to stand. I wanted to walk out of the room. Not because they were wrong, but because I wished this cloud wasn't always everywhere. I was seventeen, and I couldn't seem to go a day at the Lortel without hearing about it. I couldn't go to sleep without dreaming of contracting it and having to tell my parents and then dying a terrible death. And weirder, at school it was just the opposite. I couldn't remember the last time anyone at Trinity had mentioned AIDS outside of a mean joke.

"I know, Mother," I said. "I will put a condom over my entire body the next time I see CJ."

She gave me that half smirk of hers and said, "Kids these days."

"He wants to date me. Let me say that again, and slower. He. Wants. To. Date. Me."

I guzzled my orange soda, and Deena popped a piece of Bananaberry Split Bubble Yum into her mouth. We were heading toward Broadway after school on Monday.

"I honestly don't know why this surprises you," she said, smacking her gum rudely. "I mean, you're not even close to grody. Yes, your clothing is unfortunate, and your taste in music is putrid, and at this moment your breath is not lilacs, but . . ."

I sank my head in mock shame, and Deena, to rub it in, poked me in the shoulder and pointed out a slight red stain on my yellow Lacoste shirt. Probably been there since lunch. Hopeless. I scratched at it, to no avail.

Deena was wearing a skintight pair of Sasson Jeans that shaped her butt like a lovely teardrop, and a black blouse with big shoulder pads from Charivari. Her wrists were covered with rubber bracelets, and the silver rhinestone necklace around her neck sparkled. Red Reebok high-tops finished off the look. She was nothing if not trendy, and it worked for her. It would not work for me, so I never tried.

"What would you do without me?" Deena asked as we crossed Amsterdam at Ninety-First.

"Have self-esteem?"

She laughed. We passed the pristine new Luv's Pharmacy with its bright and shiny exterior. Right next to it, a craggy-looking white guy stood in the doorway of a dilapidated building that looked like its windows had been smashed. That was pretty much the Upper West Side in a nutshell. Growing up, I hadn't been allowed to cross east of Amsterdam Avenue alone until I was fourteen, and now, a few years later, though evidence of its former self remained, it was becoming almost chic.

"I'm going to Crazy Eddie's," I said. "Wanna walk me up to Ninety-Eighth?"

"Their prices are INSANE!" Deena said, imitating the annoying commercial.

"I have to buy this album. Have you heard of Missing Persons? We're doing a music swap."

I gritted my teeth for what was to come.

Deena stopped right in the middle of Broadway. An older Latina woman wearing a paisley headscarf had to do some quick gymnastics to not run into her. "Oh no! Micah! Why would you . . . this is why you have to ask me before you make any decisions in your life. Tell me you lied and said your favorite was Echo and the Bunnymen or R.E.M.?"

I ducked my head in mock shame.

"You have literally the worst taste in music," she said.

Yes, I liked Tiffany. And Debbie Gibson. And Lisa Lisa. Deena didn't get it. No one at school did. The people I hung out with liked U2 and The Smiths and Hüsker Dü, and that was all fine. But really? Give me Lisa Lisa any day. Maybe it was a gay thing?

"Which one? Don't tell me . . . not The Jets." She snapped her gum and started walking again.

"Bubble Yum is made of spider eggs," I said, and she swatted at me from the side.

"The Jets? Really?"

We passed a newsstand where an elderly lady was yelling obscenities at the guy behind the counter because, apparently, her newspaper was creased. "Their music is highly underappreciated, and one day we will all celebrate their greatness," I said.

"Sure. Of course we will. George Michael? You want his sex?"

"I went with Wham!, actually."

"Oh no. Date over before it started. And maybe it's for the best. That boy is dicey."

"He isn't, though. He's different and he's wild, but there's something about him that is as undicey as it gets. You'd have to meet him to understand."

She raised one eyebrow.

"And of course, you never will."

I sat down on my captain's bed and took the album out of its wrapping as soon as I got home. There she was, the famous

Dale Bozzio, with her wild platinum-and-pink hair that CJ had been imitating. She had a blue slash painted over her eyes, a mole on her right cheek, and shapely red lips. Those had not been part of CJ's ensemble.

I had to admit: She was hot.

The music started. Harder rock than I tended to like, with blaring guitars and a driving drumbeat, and then, as soon as she started singing the very first song, "Noticeable One," Dale took over. Her voice was brassy and determined and unlike any voice I'd ever heard, and colors seemed to flood my room—pinks and purples and oranges. I closed my eyes, laid my head back, still in my coat, and let the music take me on a trip. My mind traveled to six places at once, but mostly I thought of CJ, and what his life must be like, and where he lived, what his eyes did when he smiled that toothy smile. The chorus, with its call-and-answer of *notice me*, made me think of CJ standing in the corner of the bar, alone. *Notice me.* Sometimes, not very often, I wanted to be noticed, too. Not as Hot Deena's tagalong, but for me.

CJ had noticed me.

On the second song, Dale squeaked. Actually squeaked. I jumped up and picked up the record needle and put it back some to hear it again. A squeak! Like Betty Boop!

Awesome!

CJ had brought this music to my mundane life. He had flipped a switch, and suddenly I was experiencing higher levels of color, the sound and taste and smell of them. He was taking my monochromatic world and making it neon. Dale Bozzio was neon.

Where had this album been all my life?

"Destination Unknown," with its haunting refrain of *Life is so strange*, utterly hooked me. "Walking in L.A." dizzied me. And then, on side two, I finally got to understand why CJ had said, "What are words for?" That song, "Words," exploded from a single synth note into a blowout of ethereal keyboard, slashing guitar, frantic drumming, and Dale's squeaks. It was like a teenage protest song, like everything I had ever felt but never got to say.

My body shivered with recognition, and suddenly it was like the music I had listened to all my life had been mono and this was stereo for real. I suddenly got it. I suddenly got CJ. This connected us in a way that gave me a full-body rush. It was basically my whole life, summed up in one song.

What are words for
When no one listens anymore

By album's end I was crying. And it wasn't a sad album. It just . . . understood me. It got my pain and it got my quirky weirdness and it celebrated it all. I knew that this was a side of me Deena wouldn't get at all, and that was okay. When the needle automatically went back to its holder and the record stopped spinning, I felt changed.

I also felt incredible shame. Because this was NOT Wham! And I was suddenly a bit afraid CJ might actually give up on me for making him listen to it.

I went into my parents' bedroom, grabbed their phone,

pulled the cord as far as it would go, and went back into my room. I shut the door. My mom and dad weren't home yet, but in case they came home, this was a conversation I wanted to have alone.

"Connell/Gorman residence, kindly start speaking," the voice on the other end said in lieu of a hello.

"Um," I said. "Um. Does CJ live here?"

There was a pause and a shuffle on the other side of the phone, then a familiar voice.

"Hello?"

"CJ?"

"This is me."

"Oh, um. This is Micah?"

He laughed. "Are you asking me, or are you telling me?"

"I'm telling you?"

"Are you sure?"

I froze, unsure of what to say. After a few seconds, CJ laughed.

"Oh, relax," he said. "Just razzin' ya. Hey!"

"Who was that who answered?"

"That would be my riotous stepfather," he mumbled.

"Ah. The famous Jack."

"You remembered!"

"So, um, I'm calling you in tears to repent, because I just finished listening to *Spring Session M*, and, wow. I have officially found life."

"Are you being serious? Do not kid me like this."

"Totally serious."

"Oh my God oh my God!" he yelled, and I could hear his

feet stamping a bit. "It's so rare that someone GETS IT. Jack! Someone else gets Missing Persons!"

"Slick and suave," I heard the voice in the background say. He pronounced it *sway-ve.*

"No, I totally get it," I said, lying on the floor and looking up at the yellow, orange, and peach sunrise my mom had an artist paint on my light blue wall back when I was about eight. "It spoke to me. What are words for? Yes."

"You have no idea," CJ said.

"I have a clue."

"Anyway, I'm so glad you get it."

"She's amazing!"

"You have to see their videos. The visual is important."

"Cool," I said.

"Way cool."

I smiled, and then I remembered the bad news. "So, um. Maybe don't listen to that Wham! album?"

He snorted. "Too late."

I buried my face in my hands. "Oh no."

"Yeah. It was nice knowing you."

"But . . ."

"Kidding, God. It's poppy, but. You know what? It was really fun. And there's this one song that totally doesn't suck. Not even a little."

"Oh?" I had no idea which one he was talking about.

"The quiet one. 'Turn a different corner and we never would have met'?"

"Oh! Yeah! That was a single. Went to number one."

"I don't pay attention to that shit, but that song has depth.

Seriously. I thought he was just this bubblegum guy, but that song, you can't fake that kind of emotion. He's also completely hot, and obviously gay."

"Do you think so?"

He snorted. "Gayer than the French army."

I laughed. "Is that a saying?"

"It is now. And . . . he's gone. It's interesting. I mention something gay and suddenly my stepfather needs something in the other room."

We talked and talked and talked, and it was amazing how it never got weird. It was almost like I was talking to Deena, which was crazy, because first of all it took a long time to get that comfortable with her on the phone, and second, I didn't want to sleep with Deena. That thought made me shiver, and I jumped up on my bed, throwing my coat to the floor. I scanned my room and wondered what CJ would think of it. Would he get my huge collection of albums and 45s? Would he think it was weird that I had a Nerf basketball hoop over my closet door?

Maybe one day I might find out. And that thought made my entire body blush.

We talked some more about MTV, and his homophobic high school, where he had altercations basically every day, and my liberal-but-blinded parents. As the conversation wound down, about an hour later, I felt so confident that I did the unthinkable. Or at least the unthinkable before Saturday night at the piers and hearing *Spring Session M*. Life was so strange, indeed.

"So," I said, "could you be coaxed out on a date? Friday night?"

There was a pause on the other end of the line, and my heart sped.

"Let me ask my girl," he replied. I could hear him put the phone down and move away from the mouthpiece. "Holly, dear? Do you have my book? No, not *that* book—who keeps their calendar in a Bible?" he muttered. "Yes. This Friday night. Can we work around that? Should I have you call him back? Uh-huh. Uh-huh. Okay, okay. Thanks, dear. Love your hair, by the way, hope you win." He picked up the phone and spoke into the mouthpiece again.

"It appears I am indeed free on Friday night."

I went out to the living room, where my mom was now home and sitting on the black-and-white couch eating carrot sticks and watching *Wheel of Fortune*. I did my best to put my smile away, though truly I felt like I could float out the window and onto West End Avenue.

"Ooh, carrots!" I said. "Let me get the peanut butter."

My mother shielded the carrots with her hand. "No, Micah. Don't eat peanut butter. It's too late for peanut butter."

It was seven thirty. I would have said that, but it was useless. My mother tended to plant her flag on extremely random hills, and her plants were permanent. *No, don't wear that blue shirt, wear the green one.* Or, when I was younger, *No! Not that teddy bear. That one is so trashy. Get the black one.*

So no to peanut butter, because it was kind of late but not really.

"Were you talking to Deena?" she asked, smiling but not taking her eyes off Vanna White.

"No, um. A new friend. CJ."

"Oh! How nice." She looked up from the show and focused on me.

"Yeah. From the theater. The one I went for a bite with after."

"That's terrific, Micah. I'm so happy to hear you're expanding your circle."

That was clearly a shot at Deena, who my mom felt was using me. I had no idea what she thought Deena was using me for, but *something*.

I paused for a second, thinking about what would happen if I just went one conversational step further. It wasn't like my parents didn't know gay people and like gay people. And it wasn't as if I were the straightest-acting guy in the world.

"He's gay," I said, kneeling on the arm of the couch.

"Oh!" she said. "Good for you, dear. I think it's absolutely darling when straight men have gay male friends. It makes them more sensitive. Like your father with Rick. I wholeheartedly approve."

She smiled and offered me a carrot stick from across the couch, and like a fool I took it, because I'd run out of things to say.

There was no way she'd listen. So I kept the rest of my words to myself . . . though I had a sense that I'd share at least some of them with CJ at a later date. Which made this interaction with my mom different than most.

CHAPTER SIX

STRANGELOVE

October 1987

I waved dramatically from our tiny table in the back of Big Nick's on Broadway and Seventy-Seventh. To say the seating arrangement at Big Nick's was a bit intimate was like saying Sting was kinda handsome. Ten people max could fit in the seating area, and that was about six too many. You basically sat on top of strangers. Still, it was my favorite restaurant. Despite having a cooking area that was only slightly larger than my bed, there was somehow a twenty-page menu, complete with duck, lamb, shrimp, lobster, falafel, pizza, pies, and milkshakes. Anything you could ever crave. The food just sort of appeared out of nowhere.

"Hey," I said as CJ wended his way around bustling servers to our booth in the far back corner. He tried to make himself even skinnier to squeeze past the middle-aged lady sitting next to us. The lady scowled and kept eating her lasagna while CJ shuffled past her, his butt inches from her face.

"Well, this is . . . quaint," he said once he'd sat down. He smiled at me. He was wearing tight jeans and a homemade T-shirt with a pink triangle and the message SILENCE = DEATH handwritten in block letters. I wasn't a hundred percent sure what that meant, but I had a feeling it was related to the governmental silence about AIDS, and how that resulted in so many people, especially gay people, dying. I quickly glanced around the restaurant to see if anyone knew me. Safe for the moment.

"This place is magic," I explained. "I want you to look at the menu and explain to me how they have all those ingredients in this place."

He thumbed through the menu. "Impressive," he said. "Hi, by the way."

"Hi."

I looked at those sleepy eyes of his. They were smiling at mine, and I had to look away quickly. A guy could get lost in there, and doing so while sitting so close to two adults that they might as well be our guardians didn't seem ideal.

We read our menus and I scanned around like a person about to commit murder. The walls were adorned with headshots of actors I'd never heard of, along with, once in a while, an actual familiar face. Like Jerry Stiller, or the guy from the Big Apple Circus. Someday I'd be up there, and I'd be one of the known ones. Not Maggie Stanton, who looked like she'd just arrived from Cleveland and had the perm to prove it.

"Oh, look." I pointed at Ms. Stanton. "I loved her in nothing anyone's ever seen."

CJ looked up, saw the various headshots, and smirked. "She was the best! And Max Brandon! Wasn't he an extra in a gay porn movie once? Was it *Ferris Bueller's Day In*? Or maybe *Cockadile Dandee*?" He pointed to a guy with perfect cheekbones and wavy brown hair.

The woman next to him turned her head and glowered. I blushed. My instinct, as perfect Micah Strauss, son of Ira and Dalia, was to apologize. But there was a new part of me, too, one that was tired of trying to be perfect.

I let that part win for once. Who the hell cared what some frumpy West End Avenue lady my mom's age thought?

"Yes!" I yelled, purposefully not lowering my voice. "But I'm pretty sure it was *Das Booty.*"

"Yep. He was in a submarine," CJ said. Then he lowered his voice into that of a terrible porn actor. "Hello, Captain, I'm gonna fix your submarine REAL GOOD," he said, and then he started humming that tawdry porn music. "How about you lower your periscope right into my—"

"Excuse me!" the woman interrupted. "This is extremely inappropriate!"

CJ turned his body to her and sized her up. He spoke calmly. "Inappropriate is in the eye of the beholder. To me, having a president who took over four years to say the name of a disease that is killing tens of thousands of gay men is inappropriate. But I totally get that for you, it's two fags joking about sex."

It was amazing how quickly she stood and tromped to the front.

It was equally stunning how quickly a manager arrived, and how quickly we were escorted out of the restaurant.

"Oh no!" CJ said loudly as we were marched out, single file, because there was no room for double. "Where will I get a mediocre hamburger now?"

What is this life? I thought as we found ourselves out on the sidewalk. Whatever it was, I hoped it was worth being eighty-sixed from my favorite restaurant. With any luck, they wouldn't remember me the next time I came in.

The sun had set, and Broadway was alive and gearing up for a Friday night. We walked uptown aimlessly. I wasn't sure if any Upper West Side restaurants were ready for CJ. I wasn't sure the streets were ready for his pink triangle shirt. And part of me, for once, didn't care at all. I felt deliciously free, like it was a summer night and school was out, and I could just float on out of the restaurant and up into the sky and never come back to earth.

"My life's dream is to meet Robin Byrd," CJ said after a while, and I laughed.

Robin Byrd was this weird middle-aged stripper lady with a demented smile who danced provocatively in a black crochet bikini on an all-red set with a heart-shaped neon sign that read, *The Robin Byrd Show*. It came on after eleven p.m. and only on Manhattan Cable TV, the low-budget channels that in the late evenings featured mostly phone sex ads. She'd have male strippers come on and sometimes take phone calls. The callers never wanted to talk to her. They were always men and always wanted to talk to the hot guys. It was a terrible, terrible show, and on Friday nights I waited impatiently for my parents to go to bed so I could sneak out to the living room, sit one inch from the set, my hand on the channel button just in case, and put the sound so low I could barely hear it. And in that way, I'd bask in the warm glow of the TV, all senses on overdrive because I was being naughty.

"I think this is a worthy goal. Always set your sights high," I said as we passed H&H Bagels.

"*The Closet Case Show*!" CJ nearly yelled.

"Yes!" I said. That show featured a man wearing a bandana over his face, sitting in an empty room, wearing nothing but underwear and talking in a seductive voice. Sometimes he had guest stars on, again strippers. It deserved many Emmys.

"I watch for the commercials," he said.

"Oh my God. The commercials. They always cut the good stuff out, though," I said. "Do you know I'm seventeen and have never seen a porn movie? Manhattan Cable TV is my only outlet and I have to sneak into the living room and pray my parents don't leave their bedroom for a glass of water or something."

"That's why I go to Les Hommes." He pointed up Eightieth toward Amsterdam.

"Where?"

He rolled his eyes. "Don't tell me you haven't been?"

"What in the world is *Les Hommes*? *The men* in French?"

"Just up the street next to the laundromat. It's this little theater where you sit in the dark and watch gay porn. There's a back area with booths, just big enough for two."

"What?" I stopped walking. I found it a little hard to keep Perfect Micah bottled up with this one.

He shrugged. "Just another part of the gay world. Deny people the right to be who they are and any reasonable outlets for expressing themselves and they will find them or create them anyway."

I stared down the street. All this time, I'd been living six blocks from a place like that without even knowing it. And would I have wanted to know it? Hearing the description gave me a bunch of feelings all at once. Revulsion. Shame. Lots of curiosity. Arousal. And most of all, fear. There was this disease that was a death sentence. Who was going to dirty bookstores during a plague? No way. CJ had to be lying. Was he?

My mouth just about hit the floor. "You've done that?"

"I've dabbled."

"What? Really? How do you even . . . what is . . . how . . . ?"

He laughed. "I'd like to buy a vowel?"

"I just. Is it safe?"

He tilted his head and looked at me. "Define safe."

"Safe like could you get robbed or killed?" *Or could you die of AIDS?*

"I never have. Well, killed, once or twice."

"Okay. Well. Wow." I felt myself being pulled away from CJ, and I hated it because so much was pulling me toward him at the exact same time.

He started walking up Broadway again. "It's okay," he said. "You're new. Also, you have parents, which makes a difference."

I played those words through my mind a few times. *What does that mean? He has Jack, who is a parent, right?* But I didn't want to insult him or seem naive.

"Right," I said.

As we approached the Loews Theater on Eighty-Fourth, I was feeling weird. Who was this person? This person who went to places with back rooms for two? Part of me wanted to run. Part of me wouldn't. Couldn't.

Like he could read my mind, CJ put a hand on my shoulder. "Should we reset?"

I exhaled a huge, incredulous gust of air. "Sorry. It's a lot."

"You really are a virgin, aren't you?"

"Well . . ." I said, not meeting his eye.

He cackled. "I knew it! You're not that naive. No one is."

"My only times were with these two guys. These straight guys from school. Athletes. Napoleon is basketball. Lucas is football."

CJ stopped walking. I turned. He looked stunned. Then he shoved me playfully. "What?"

I blushed and crossed my arms over my chest. "Yeah. I mean. That's what I have available to me."

He put his head in his hands dramatically. "I bow to you! How did you? I mean, older guys, for sure. They all want it, so it's easy. But straight guys, athletes, our age? That's the trifecta! Wow."

For the first time since I'd met CJ, I felt like I had the upper hand. Somehow, I didn't love the feeling.

"Yeah, well, it's not great," I explained. "No kissing. They just, you know. Do it."

"Do WHAT? Micah! Tell me all!"

"Stop it!" I yelled right in the middle of the street. People turned their heads and looked. I lowered my voice. "Jesus. This is a date, right? Why are we talking about having sex with other people?"

He smiled. "Oh, you're young. You'll learn."

Part of me cried inside when he said that. Because I didn't want to learn. And I did. It was all so confusing.

Without any definitive plan, we reluctantly decided to see a movie instead of going to dinner. *The Princess Bride* was playing, and while there was a good-sized crowd, we nabbed a couple seats in the back row. I bought the tickets, and in lieu of dinner, CJ got us hot dogs with all the fixings, the biggest tub of popcorn, Pepsis, and Whoppers. I had no idea how he had the money for all of it. He'd definitely spent more than I had paid for the tickets.

Before the previews came on, CJ turned and whispered in my ear, "I'm sorry. I suck at dating. I want to be better. Reset?"

I turned to him. "Yeah, I'm not so good, either. Reset."

He smiled ruefully. "You're perfect. I'm the problem here."

I stuffed my hot dog in my mouth, so I'd have something to do with my hands and an alibi for not replying. Ketchup squirted onto my green Lacoste shirt, and I groaned. He gently laughed and squeezed my shoulder.

"Bless your heart," he said.

I wiped up the ketchup with a napkin, knowing that a stain was unavoidable. I shrugged and chewed.

That was when I realized: onions.

I hadn't been on a lot of dates, but I could hear Deena's voice in my head, admonishing me. *Three dating don'ts: wine coolers, burritos, and onions.* The first, she said, was *just tacky.* The last two were *dangerous.*

I blotted the sides of my mouth. Once I was done chewing, I put my hand in front of my mouth and inhaled my own breath. Eek.

CJ caught me doing this and smirked.

"Yeah," I said, my mouth still behind my hand. "Rookie mistake. I guess onions are not the ideal date food, huh?"

CJ smiled and sucked in his cheekbones.

"Drink your Pepsi," he said. "You'll taste like the choice of a new generation by the time the movie's through."

Man, was he cute.

The movie was funny and entertaining, and the best part was about halfway through, when CJ put the side of his left pinkie against my leg. My whole body trembled. I hoped he didn't notice. I gingerly snaked my hand down and interweaved our pinkies, and in that way, we held hands. It was unimaginably nice, and I began to think that maybe I could get past the weird conversation stuff from earlier. Maybe.

We were in far better spirits when we left, having just spent a couple of hours laughing together, eating popcorn, and holding hands, which would be the *real* trifecta for me.

"Hello, my name is Inigo Montoya," CJ stated, imitating Mandy Patinkin's character. "You killed my father. Prepare to die!" The character says the line like ten times in the movie.

I laughed.

We crossed Broadway, stopping in the median when the light changed. A homeless man was asleep on the bench, covered by a ratty green jacket. "Although with me, it would be more like, 'Hello, my name is CJ Gorman. You killed my stepfather. Thank you.'"

I laughed again. "Not your favorite?"

"Understatement. And the funny thing is, he kind of *is* my favorite. You know when someone is the best and the worst?"

I didn't, but I nodded. I wondered what CJ would think of my conventional, upper-middle-class, Jewish family. He'd probably roll his eyes and never talk to me again. I prayed he wouldn't ask.

"Is he mean to you? Like, does he hit you?"

CJ stopped suddenly on Eighty-Fifth Street and put his hands on his hips. "Micah. Did you just ask me if my stepfather beats me? No! He's . . . stringent. That's all. God."

We started walking again. A drunk couple, a man and a woman, were approaching. The woman looked at us, pointed, and whispered something in the man's ear. He cracked up. CJ gave them the middle finger.

"Breeders!" he yelled out.

"Be careful!" I said. "I don't want a repeat of what happened after the Tunnel, please."

He snorted. "Yeah. Not concerned. You could probably take the woman, and I know I could take the man. Take him. I'd have him naked in under an hour."

I shot him a look.

"Right, right," he said. "No sex with strangers. God, Micah. You're like my mother."

We wandered to Riverside Park, which was definitely not a place I went at night. But then again, I didn't go *anywhere* at night, unless Deena took me there. I decided to loosen up for once in my life and trust CJ.

The wine cooler he bought me at a bodega helped some. Yes, I was now two out of three on Deena's Dating Don'ts, and I didn't care. Mine was strawberry, and even though it was a little warm, the fizz felt good going down.

"So every time I go out with you I wind up either on a dangerous street or in a park, late at night."

"And your point is?" CJ said. The streetlamps were on and illuminated the path that led to the river.

He took us down this rickety stone staircase that looked like the kind of place where the Son of Sam hung out when he was feeling lazy. We passed several sleeping homeless people, and soon we were wending our way around this rotunda with a stone fountain that wasn't working. Cars whizzed by on the West Side Highway to our west, and just to the south of us, cars exited the highway onto Seventy-Ninth Street. CJ jumped up onto the stone rotunda, put his arms out wide like he was a tightrope walker, and I followed and did the same. My heartbeat sped as he led me under a deserted tunnel that led to the boat basin.

"You're really not afraid of anything, are you?" I asked, a bit envious.

He lightly chuckled. "I'm constantly afraid," he said. "Almost exclusively. Not being afraid and not giving a fuck are two different things."

I didn't know what to make of that. We walked up the narrow path along the Hudson River, where the streetlamps were mostly out. The moon over the Hudson was the only light that kept things from being pitch dark.

The part of me that was my mother's son was by now all jitters. *This is where I'll die*, the voice in my head said. *They'll find me here, and I guess that's how I'll come out? Murdered next to a boy in a T-shirt with a pink triangle?*

"Where did you get 'Silence Equals Death' from?" I asked.

I could hear him shaking his head in amazement. "Did you grow up in a cave?"

"I grew up with Ira and Dalia Strauss as parents. Until, well, about six months ago, there wasn't a single moment my mom didn't know where I was."

He sighed. "Sounds kinda nice, actually."

"Really? I figured you'd hate that."

"Yeah. Probably. But it would be nice to know they cared. Someday I'll tell you about the Italian tourist story. Not tonight, of course, as I've been decreed to not mention any other people in any sort of relational or sexual way, which significantly limits my ability to tell stories, by the way."

"Sorry about that. Maybe you'll get a waiver later. We'll see."

He laughed. "So they pretty much overprotect you?"

"They finally decided to loosen the reins this past summer, but only a little. I was doing delivery for a video rental place on Broadway and then got the ushering gig, and I guess they decided they could trust me. Oops."

"Oops?"

"Well, here I am, in Riverside Park at a very late hour with a boy who is obviously trouble."

We stopped walking and faced each other. CJ's cheekbones were lit by the moon and I could see strands of his hair across his forehead. I wanted his lips. I wanted to feel his lips against mine, and to get to that place again where everything faded away and there wasn't any wall, anything between us. No words, no sounds, no jokes. Just us.

"'Silence Equals Death' is from a new group called ACT

UP. It means that unless we stand up for ourselves and show ourselves, we're as good as dead. It means that Ronald Reagan could give two fucks about whether some faggot dies of a disease. The straights love him, and he quite literally doesn't care if we all die. We need to not be silent. We must stand up and be counted."

He was looking in my eyes. I could see them just a little, and they looked like he was in charge. Like he knew what he was doing.

He reached down and squeezed my groin.

"There are abandoned train tracks," he whispered, and he motioned with his head to a place behind me.

"Oh," I said. The silliest, most unsophisticated word, that. But what did a person say in this situation? I couldn't come up with anything that didn't sound Dalia-ish. *Careful? We'll get caught? What if someone mugs us?*

So I said, again, "Oh."

"Wanna?" he asked softly.

I was picturing a bed. I was picturing music, maybe that Wham! song. *Turn a different corner and we never would have met.* This was big for me. I got the feeling that for CJ, it maybe wasn't. But for me? This was everything.

"Could we go to your place?" I asked.

He looked to the side and quietly laughed. "It's a loft. I sleep in the main room. Like, you get off the elevator, open the door, and bam! My bed."

"Weird," I said.

"Yours is out, I guess?"

"Uh, yeah."

"Our choices are limited," he said. "C'mon."

I think that kind of did it. The tone of his voice, placating and sexy.

"Okay," I said. "If I get killed, tell my mom I love her."

"Will do," he said. "If I die, tell my stepdad it's his fault."

"Do you have condoms?"

"Yes, Mother."

We walked hand in hand toward what appeared to be a beige brick wall, but as we approached, I could see a crevice. I had no idea how CJ knew. But he got us there.

We went inside and it went from dark to darkest. My pulse throbbed and my brain spun and I grabbed his hand tighter. I could feel myself unable to breathe, and when I did inhale, it smelled dank and slightly sour. I grimaced.

Once all the way inside, and once my heart stopped tripping over itself, I felt his breath on my ear.

"My mouth has been declared illegal in three states," he said, a disembodied voice. I got my mouth ready to reach for his in the darkness. I could hear him adjust then, and suddenly felt a hand on my belt. Two hands. I caught my breath.

I needed to be near his lips. I wanted to connect with CJ that way, face-to-face, and I didn't have the words to say no, but even if I did, I wouldn't have said them. I would have said, if my heart could talk, *Slow down. There's time. I need to taste your lips on my lips. I need your nose pressed against mine. Even if we don't open our mouths, because. Scary.*

I had never experienced any of what came next.

The particular sensations below, as CJ rolled a condom onto my erection. How he then used his mouth on me. The warm sensation mingled with the cold of the setting, the fear swirling through the excitement, fear of where we were, fear of a virus.

As if he were reading my mind, he whispered from down below, "Relax. You aren't at risk here. Neither of us are."

Which was weird, and also somewhat nice. And the warmth, too, was nice, and yet, there was no CJ there. I was alone in the sensation, alone in the dark, holding my breath because the air was smoky and stale, and I wondered if I should touch his face while he was down there, or if I should keep my hands to myself, and frankly when it was done, a couple of minutes later, I was relieved.

We walked back into the world in silence, changed.

I wasn't sure if I was the one being distant, or if it was him. I knew that I was feeling disappointment on his behalf, because I had literally done nothing. Nothing at all but stand there, and who does that? I was a dud. A sexual dud. And this was a story I'd take to my grave, I was certain. I couldn't even imagine telling Deena. What was to tell?

"Well," CJ said as we got back up to Broadway and we paused at the subway station on Seventy-Ninth. "That was fun. All of it. Thanks for the movie ticket."

I laughed, feeling too much awkwardness for one body. Again, what was this life? Why were we feeling less close now that we'd been intimate? "Yes," I said. "Thank you. Um. For all of it."

He winked at me and grinned. "Don't mention it," he said.

As I walked home, I felt the streets closing in on me. The eyes of passersby averted from me, and in that aversion was judgment. Not just of where I'd been and what I'd done, but of how I'd frozen up and floated away. I'd had a chance, but now CJ knew what he needed to know. He knew I was a bad lay. And that meant I'd probably never hear from him again. And the taste of regret was like belched-up strawberry wine cooler and onion.

CHAPTER SEVEN

MENTAL HOPSCOTCH

October 1987

When I arrived at Deena's apartment for brunch the next morning, she was already doing five things at once.

"Grab the spatula and flip the pancakes, would you?" she yelled while squeezing oranges into her juicer. Susanna Hoffs was imploring us to walk like Egyptians.

I did as I was told, being careful not to dislodge the chunks of strawberry floating in the half-cooked batter. Deena Robin might have been all about fun, but she was serious about brunch. On Sunday mornings at her place, everything was always maddeningly perfect.

"If you don't watch out, you're gonna become a yuppie."

She ignored me. Even though it was just us, she was showered, made up, and wearing a gorgeous blue-and-red cashmere sweater with shoulder pads with blue slacks. I had eschewed showering in lieu of an extra fifteen minutes of MTV (I'd showered after coming home, obviously), and I was dressed like a ten-year-old who was off to his first day of summer camp: baggy Lee jeans and a tan, off-brand collared shirt from Marshalls. I sometimes didn't know why she put up with me, and I almost always feared that she was judging me. Which she probably was. I was, after all, judging her.

"Are we mimosa-ing?" she asked, glancing over at me. Mimosas were possible because her mom slept in on Sundays. When I nodded emphatically, she grinned. "Brunch with the gays. It's the best."

I replied, "Brunch with the gay, in actuality."

"Yes, but I have big plans," she said. "Big plans to attract at least one more gay guy."

"What am I, chopped liver?" I asked.

"Yes, honey," she deadpanned. "That's exactly what you are."

"Oh good," I said. "I hate chopped liver."

"Oh my God. The self-hating gays. Tragic."

I cracked up. It was funny because in my case it was true. She was arranging two side plates, each with a Zabar's croissant and a pristine berry salad. "So back to my plan to add a gay guy to the posse. And this one will LIKE to shop, and he WILL have decent fashion sense."

"Oh goody," I said.

She exhaled dramatically. "Where is your enthusiasm, mister? And anyway, this should be your job, but you're too busy dating creepy guys and being the football team's mattress."

I giggled despite myself. Once the table was set, we sat down and began our feast. I dug into the fruit salad first. Unlike at home, where my mom had a tendency to allow fruit to grow fur in the refrigerator and then scrape it off and pretend it was fine, I could rest at ease that every blueberry in Deena's salad was plump and fresh.

"So tell me everything about your date."

I swallowed. "Not much to tell, really. We saw a movie. *Princess Bride.*"

"Boring. The good stuff. Did you kiss? Did you do more?" She raised an eyebrow.

I flinched without meaning to. I'd slept for about two hours, because all night I kept thinking about what would have happened if the condom had broken and CJ had given me AIDS. I imagined my parents finding out, and how humiliated they'd be, and also how sad. How all my friends, Deena included, would shun me. It would all be my fault since I should have known better.

I knew I was making some pretty irrational leaps here. CJ wasn't positive. I didn't know what risk there actually could be from a broken condom during oral sex. I didn't know how anyone would react for sure if somehow I got HIV. But my mind was drowning in the worst-case scenarios. And as much as I needed to talk about it, to figure it out, Deena was definitely not going to understand.

"Barely," I said. "Good-night kiss on a side street. After making sure no one was looking, by the way. Peck on the cheek and that was it."

"Oh, Micah. What are we going to do with you? It's supposed to be easier with two boys. Less to negotiate. No one can get pregnant, and you're both guys, which means you're both idiots."

"Guilty," I said, wondering how even Deena seemed to forget about that *tiny little* AIDS thing. I slurped up some mimosa and averted my eyes. "Guilty as charged."

Sunday afternoons were usually when my parents went golfing up at Old Oaks in Rye. For that reason, it was also typically when I'd occasionally play hooky from the theater so that Napoleon Diaz could visit.

The inaccurately named Napoleon had no complex. He had no reason to. He was Puerto Rican, not French, excelled on the basketball court, and quietly let it be known to me that he might be up for hanging out sometime. Just lying back and chilling out. It had started last year, in tenth grade.

We were at Stacy Martin's party. We weren't hanging out together, because why would we? Basketball star and theater nerd? No connection whatsoever. So it was weird when he left right after I did, caught up to me, and asked, "Wanna share a cab to the West Side?"

I was like, *Um.*

"Sure," I said.

We stood there saying nothing as he hailed, and then we rode in silence . . . until he leaned over and said, "Come on over. I wanna show you something."

I was, again, like, *Um.* And a part of me heard Deena's voice warning, *Careful! He's gonna kill you and cut your body into pieces.* But I disregarded that voice because NAPOLEON DIAZ HAD JUST INVITED ME OVER ON A SATURDAY NIGHT, ALONE!

What he wanted to show me, apparently, were his abs. I agreed they were very nice. Then he wanted to show me his legs, which, duh, basketball. Long and nice. And then his butt, which was a surprise, but also quite picturesque. The rest was just as surprising, to the point that while we were doing it, a few times I wondered if it was a dream. But it wasn't. There was no kissing, no sweet talk, no anything else, but who was I to complain? After, he grunted, rolled over onto his back, and said, "See you, man."

I left thinking, *I'm a man now. I, Micah Strauss, am no longer a virgin.* And it felt great! And also, it felt like the biggest letdown I'd ever suffered, because, WHAT? What had just happened? Where were the flowers? Where were the kisses and the hugs and the holding after?

We did it like three times in tenth grade, always at his apartment, and then something must have happened because one day he called me up and was like, "Can we do it at your place?"

Obviously no, we could not, but then I realized that we could, on Sunday afternoons. Which we did a few Sunday afternoons once summer rolled around, when my parents went to Old Oaks.

But then ushering started, and Sunday matinees were important, and while he was entirely unimpressed by that excuse, we stopped. This was only the third time we'd done it again since June.

We watched MTV for a while, me sitting upright on the couch like my parents could come home at any minute, even though they had only left half an hour ago. When Def Leppard's new video "Pour Some Sugar on Me" came on, Napoleon yawned and stretched his muscular arms up behind him, showcasing his six-pack. I felt like the girl in a John Hughes movie.

"Want a soda?" I asked.

He turned his head, his dark eyes inquisitive, his eyebrows arching in a way that suggested, *What are you waiting for? The king has arrived. Do your thing, servant boy.*

I swallowed, my body quivering.

I had so many questions. Maybe that was my problem, I thought, as I narrated the moment to myself as it happened. I wanted to talk. What seventeen-year-old gay boy wanted to talk when provided a perfectly beautiful body to explore and please? A sexual cadaver, almost. Napoleon's attitude was, *Here's my body. Do with it what you wish.* But during, I'd find myself fantasizing about the conversation after.

I was obviously broken.

Staring at my feet, I mumbled, "Feel like lying down?"

"Yup," he said, standing up.

And . . . scene.

After, in bed next to me, Napoleon smelled like talcum powder, which he used religiously after showering. That should have been a turnoff. It totally wasn't. Nothing about Napoleon Diaz was a turnoff. I stared at his rosy lips and the way they stood out against his dark brown skin. I wanted to kiss them, but he didn't allow that.

Thinking back to CJ the previous night, I wondered, *Why is it that suddenly all sorts of guys are willing to do stuff with me, but never kiss?*

I had all sorts of questions darting around my brain. *How do I take this from fooling around to boyfriends? How would that even work, when we've never even had a conversation? I should kick him out. Who kicks naked Napoleon Diaz out of bed? How did Napoleon know he liked that? How does a macho basketball player figure out he likes to get screwed? What does it mean that CJ silently sucked my condomed penis in public? Why don't me and Napoleon do that in private? Why can't we talk? What's a normal thing to say while naked next to another boy?* Or, in this case, half-clothed next to a boy, because I hadn't taken my shirt off. I never did. There was no reason. It was never part of the equation. *Say something! Say! Something! Aargh!*

It was not always pleasant, being Micah Strauss.

I spied the album cover to *Spring Session M*, Dale Bozzio's pink hair and angelic face. I got up and grabbed it.

"Do you know this?" I asked Napoleon, handing him the album sleeve.

He sat up onto his elbows and regarded the album.

"She's a fox," he said.

"Yeah," I said. "Wanna hear it?"

He looked at me with those arched eyebrows. "Uh. Okay, I guess."

I jumped up and turned on the stereo. The record was still on the turntable, on side two. I grabbed the needle and put it on "Words."

He sat there as the music came on, and I found myself hearing it through his ears. Hard rock, which was cool. *You surprise me*, the Napoleon in my mind said, offering me a rare grin. *You're so much more than people know, Micah Strauss. So much more. You're cool. Really cool. This is rad.*

After the first chorus, Napoleon stood. "Gotta jet," he said.

"Oh, yeah. Of course. Cool," I replied.

And just like that, our surreal afternoon of whatever it was came to an end.

My parents returned around four to find me watching MTV. My mother sighed, exasperated.

"Have you moved from there all day?"

Oh, don't worry. I fucked a star basketball player while you were out. Less than twenty-four hours after getting oral sex with a condom while surrounded (probably) by homeless people. I don't know. I couldn't see.

"Barely," I said.

She exhaled and left me alone with The Human League, who felt that the truth might need some rearranging. There were stories to be told. Yeah. Definitely.

Sunday night. The worst part of the week, because it meant the freedom was over. Homework only half done, and not getting done-er. All the floating constellations, pulling me in different directions. They had their shit together. And me? Stuck as the object. Pinballing around the universe while everyone else was the subject, doing. Making choices. Why did it always feel like I had no choices? Like my only thing was to do what was available to me?

What about me? I thought, morphing into a housewife in a Lifetime movie. *What about my needs?*

I sat against my bed, facing the vertical mirror on my closet with the basketball hoop on top. I grabbed the Nerf basketball I didn't even really like and took a shot. I looked at myself as the ball bounced away from the rim.

Really. What do I want?

Sitting there, a few things became clear to me.

Other people might want Napoleon to come over some Sundays, because sex was fun. But there was nothing there. It was like using his body as if it were my hand, and he was using me like a sex toy. Frankly, I would have rather watched *Steel Magnolias* for the fiftieth time. Enough. And Deena, always hurting my feelings. Yeah, we joked, but why was I never enough for her? And if I weren't enough, maybe I'd find friends for whom I was. This one was hard, because it was Deena. I loved her. But at least maybe I could say something.

And CJ. No more. I was not a marionette. He couldn't keep pulling my strings. Yes, I wanted to date someone, but there was no way to date a guy after your first time was . . . that. No way.

Also, the maximum risk for AIDS that I was willing to take was zero. There were only so many sleepless, tossing-and-turning nights a guy could take, and keeping what happened with CJ—which maybe wasn't that risky but maybe it was— from Felicia and Deena was killing me.

So yeah. No more of that until AIDS was over.

I smiled at myself. Some Sunday night clarity. Good.

The phone rang. I hoped it was Deena, because yeah, I was going to tell her to be nicer. And after we had our nice moment of reconciliation, I probably would tell her about Napoleon's visit. Those stories tended to enrapture her.

It was not Deena.

"Hey," CJ said. His voice was a little subdued. I was used to him being over the top. All personality, all the time.

"Hey," I said.

"Do you wanna, um, go to Tower Records with me? Wednesday afternoon? The one downtown?"

I had given him my number during our great phone conversation but hadn't expected him to call, ever. And part of me had hoped he wouldn't, because it was all too much. I was so far out of my league it wasn't funny.

My clarity went out the window so fast.

"Sure," I said. "That'd be great."

CHAPTER EIGHT

WE DON'T HAVE TO TAKE OUR CLOTHES OFF

October 1987

The fourth time I saw CJ, I was standing in front of Tower Records and he was rushing in my direction down Broadway, with boundless energy and excitement. And blue hair. Blue.

"I think I'll dye my hair blue," I said, quoting Dale Bozzio.

He laughed and hugged me like we were old friends. "YESSS," he said.

He grabbed me by the jacket and pulled me into the store, where "Skin Trade" by Duran Duran was blaring. The place was packed, as always. The checkout line was already long and the station to buy concert tickets was busy, too. Browsers occupied the many rows of rock albums heading toward the back, and off toward the wall to the right, I could see that my favorite section, where all the 45s were, was also jammed. There was a pole in the middle of the main floor with listening stations, four sets of headphones. They were all taken, as usual.

"Okay," CJ said, nearly breathless. "Before we go any farther, a task. Meet me back here in ten minutes, okay?"

I nodded. CJ might have been made manic by the

possibilities, but for me, going to Tower Records was a marathon, not a sprint. What rare 45s could I find? Was there anything new from Donna Summer or Nik Kershaw? Many times I'd lost hours in there, and I regretted none of that lost time. Tower Records was like a religion to me.

While I perused singles by Janet Jackson and Jody Watley, I rehearsed in my head what I was going to say to CJ. I'd started this during lunch, when I'd told Deena I was going to see CJ later.

"You're seeing him again?"

"To break up," I said quietly as a senior crossed behind us with her tray of pizza. I didn't point out that it was impossible to break up since we weren't actually dating, but what phrase was there for calling things off before they'd really happened?

"Oh thank God," Deena said dramatically. "I said we needed to add a third, but not THAT third. You can do so much better, Micah."

I was glad she'd said it, but in my brain I thought, *Yeah, probably I can't.*

I rehearsed it over and over while perusing records. *I like you, CJ, and I'd like to be friends. But the other stuff? It's not you, it's me. We're just not on the same wavelength.* I also rehearsed in my head what I would *not* say: *The sex thing? That was weird. And not fun. Let's never do that again, okay?*

Just as I found the old 45 of Sparks and Jane Wiedlin's "Cool Places," CJ grabbed me by the shoulder and just about spun me around.

"Whoa!" I said, regaining my footing.

With a somber expression that clashed with his blue hair,

he presented me a pile of records. Some singles, some albums. It teetered, uneven, and that made me anxious.

"For you," he said softly.

I took them from him. "Thanks," I said.

The first one was "U Got the Look." The letter *U* was circled in pink Magic Marker. I looked up at him, shocked.

"Did you draw on this?"

He shrugged. "It's covered in plastic. Anyway, I'm buying them."

I highly doubted that, since this pile would probably cost a hundred dollars. I turned to the next one, concerned. A pile of record recommendations was not what I needed. What I needed was a way to say what I had to say without hurting his feelings. The second record was "We Are the World" by USA for Africa. The word *Are* was circled. This was the pile:

"**U** *Got the Look" by Prince*
"We **Are** *the World" by USA for Africa*
"The **Great***est Love of All" by Whitney Houston*
"The Bertha **But***t Boogie" by The Jimmy Castor Bunch*
"Infected" by **The** *The*
"**Sex** *(I'm A)" by Berlin*
"Spy in the House of Love" by **Was** *(Not Was)*
"Don't Get Me **Wrong***" by The Pretenders*
"**Let's** *Stay Together" by Tina Turner*
"Wood **Be***ez (Pray Like Aretha Franklin)" by Scritti Politti*
"Friends" *by Whodini*

I looked up at him, simultaneously relieved and beguiled by this person who felt it was okay to defile records he didn't own, this guy who apparently carried around a pink Magic Marker for such occasions. I couldn't help but smile, and my shoulders felt lighter.

"You are the person I would like to be when I grow up. Or down. Whatever," I said.

"The world would be better if there was more me in it, yes," he said.

I hugged him, not caring that it was public. "Friends?"

He relaxed into me. "Friends."

He dragged me to the listening station, and stood way too close behind a yuppie guy who appeared to be listening to Whitesnake. CJ rolled his eyes.

"Ugh. Breeders," he said with great disdain. "This guy is taking up space listening to music that's on heavy rotation on MTV. And of course, he's not worried about the people waiting, because the world was made for him. Ugh."

He tapped the guy on the shoulder. The guy flinched, sized CJ up, and with much dubiousness, removed his headphones.

CJ smiled. "Excuse me, handsome. Do you know where to find the new Communards?"

The guy took off. CJ picked up the headphones, made a dramatic act of wiping them off—"straight cooties," he explained—and proceeded to turn the ear pads around so he could have one and I could have one. Then he scrolled through the choices and found what he was looking for, and soon, the familiar and somewhat unpleasant sounds of Whitesnake were replaced with something I'd not heard before.

"This just came out and I'm DYING to hear it. Jimmy Somerville is my everything. Do you know his band The Communards?"

I nodded. "'Don't Leave Me This Way,' right?"

He shot me a thumbs-up. "Okay, then! That was after he was in Bronski Beat, which of course you know?"

I grimaced.

"Oh dear. Well, consider this the next step in your gay music education. Bronski Beat was maybe the first openly gay pop band. 'Smalltown Boy,' 1984?" When I shrugged, he gave me a dirty look. "It's just so depressing to me that our people don't even know our music. And how would you? MTV barely played it. Somerville left them to form The Communards, and this is The Communards' new album, *Red*. I read the review in *Pulse!* It's supposed to be great."

CJ selected the album and went to the fifth track. "I need to hear this one. They called this one 'haunting.'"

I listened with one ear as I scanned around, still a little afraid who would see me, though less so suddenly, because of CJ. The music started up and the instrumentation was dirge-like, melancholy. I felt chills run up my legs. This was not the kind of music I listened to, but maybe it should have been.

"It's called 'For a Friend,'" CJ said softly. "A friend who died of AIDS."

The chills widened and overtook my body. An intuition wafted through my gut, that this was somehow more personal to CJ than he'd let on. He had a friend who had died, maybe. Maybe even someone he'd slept with.

In the music, I could hear mourning, fear. Then the guy's

falsetto, which was a bit familiar because of the one song I knew. And while I couldn't understand all the words, I picked up the emotion, that he was talking about crying over a friend, and that somewhere else, someone else was crying, too. Then he was watching the sun go down and the world fade away, and I thought of Lorenzo the hair guy, and Walter at concessions, and that guy in the line at Häagen-Dazs, and the old-looking skeleton we saw on Hudson Street who was probably thirty, and for the first time ever, I got closer to the grief, the grief beyond the panic, and I was about to turn my head so CJ wouldn't see my red eyes, but then I caught a glimpse of him and his eyes were red, too, and there we were, in Tower Records, in the Village, in public, crying while listening to a song about a person probably just like us but a few years older, who was dying and there was nothing to be done.

CJ bought the records he defaced, which was just another of the many surprises I'd encounter on a daily basis as we got to know each other. He kept seeming to have money, yet he didn't seem like a kid with rich parents, exactly—he didn't have any of the pretentiousness or world-weariness of the kids at Trinity, kids who had been going to Vail for Christmas since they were six. I was on the less wealthy side of the private school kids, but still, we were very comfortable. CJ struck me as different, like someone who might live in one of those tenements on Ninth Avenue with the redbrick walls and fire escapes zigzagging across, and that, to me, was exotic. I longed to live in a world where things happened, and it seemed like that sort of environment was full of possibility. Meanwhile, I ate dinner every night in my sterile Upper West Side apartment with Ira and Dalia. Not exactly exciting.

We walked down Broadway toward his place. I was excited to finally see it.

"Okay!" CJ said. "So now that we're just friends, that means I can talk about—stuff—right?"

"Sure," I said. "Help me know what I need to do to actually get a boyfriend, because at this rate, I'm gonna be an old maid."

He laughed. "An old maid who gets it on with Napoleon the basketball dictator. Dictate to me, Napoleon!"

"Good memory!"

"When it comes to jock sex, yes. And you're not gonna be an old anything. You'll do just fine. You have no idea of your own cuteness, which is part of your allure, I think." He sighed. "You should never know how cute you are. I, unfortunately, am exceedingly well versed in just how desirable I am, and it's not always a good look."

I cracked up. CJ said stuff no one else said out loud. At least no one I knew.

"So anyway, the jerk from the Tunnel. He calls me. Last week. Out of absolutely nowhere. Glad I picked up and not Jack, because Jack is NOT amused when adult men call me. I think poor Jack has given up on me by now. But anyway, the douchebag calls like he didn't abandon me at a club, dressed in drag, and then not call me for a month. I played it cool. I acted really happy to hear from him, and I told him to meet me at this place called the Pyramid Club in the East Village, which is not my scene, but he doesn't know that. It has the advantage of being right across from Tompkins Square Park, which is like heroin central and a good place to get stabbed at night. And it's also about as hard to get to as possible for him. He lives near Columbia."

We passed Canal Jean Co., where, in seventh grade, Deena used to take me to try to spruce me up. She failed. "So what did you say to him when you got there?"

"What? I didn't. I didn't go. Told him to meet me at eleven thirty on a Thursday night in the middle of the park. Hopefully he died. I dunno."

"You're bad."

"I'm bad, bad, really, really bad," he sang, channeling Michael Jackson. "Oh! I have to tell you about Marshall. Oh my God."

He had more stories from the last week than I'd accumulated in my lifetime.

The sky darkened as he took me east on Houston and then south, which was an entirely unfamiliar area to me. I knew the West Village well, and the NYU area a bit. I never ventured south or east of either, because it sounded too dangerous. A gnarly-looking bum drank from a tall bottle in a brown paper bag. We stopped in front of a mural of a man in a white jacket with a machine gun, wearing a gas mask. In pink letters on either side of him was scrawled *Allen Boys*. The *O* had a gun pointing out of it. The image gave me shivers in the same way the train tracks had, the piers had. Not danger, though there was that, too. But more the sense there was life going on all around me, and I was missing it.

"Marshall is this guy I met at Uncle Charlie's. One of

those forty-year-old guys who dresses like he's trying to pass for twenty. It's like, *If I wanted a twenty-year-old . . .*" He glanced at me and stopped. "Anyway, I'd seen him a bunch of times and I knew he'd seen me, but we were always with someone else, I guess. So this was our time, and he invited me back to his place on Thirty-Third and, like, Tenth, which is basically above the Lincoln Tunnel and gross, but I went because—who am I kidding? I went because I went. And we got there, and he pulls out a toiletry bag, and in it is a hypodermic needle. I was like, what?

"He said, 'Relax. It just loosens me up.' And I said to him, 'So you're a homosexual *and* an IV drug user?' Like, do you get a bonus for being in two high-risk categories for AIDS? And he shrugged. I was like, *This I am not doing.* So I asked him where the bathroom was and I walked down the hallway toward it, then kept walking. Thank God the door locks weren't hard to deal with. I ran down the four flights of stairs, and when I got outside, I look up and he's leaning out the window, naked. I swear to God. And he yells, 'You're gonna make me go all the way back to Charlie's to find your replacement?' I yelled back, 'Crack is whack!' And I walked off. Just as I do, this crash comes. I look back, and there's a mangled, bloody body like right where I had been standing. It wasn't him, it was just a coincidence, but I just ran. Do you want a Popsicle? I have a hankering for a Popsicle."

That was CJ. And yes, I totally had a hankering.

For a story of something that had actually happened.

CHAPTER NINE

LIES

October 1987

We sucked on our red, white, and blue Bomb Pops as the sun went down, and we wended through cobblestone streets toward his place. The sun was nearly down now and the chilly wind coming off the Hudson made the Popsicles somewhat redundant.

"My father was abducted by aliens," CJ said. "Back when I was five."

"I think you mentioned that?"

"Yep. One day he was just sitting on the couch, and next thing you know, this little green man knocks on the door and says to me, 'Sorry, Earthling five-year-old. We must take your father. We must take him for scientific research that includes tons of painful anal probing.'"

"How unfortunate."

"It was. The aliens have not returned him. It's a long abduction, by alien standards."

"Yes. Most abductions are fairly quick, I believe."

"In reaction, my mother became this kind of Supermom. Like the Hulk, but less green and with a Dooney and Bourke handbag. She would leave work after a full day; make a Chinese dinner she learned how to cook God knows where; give me a dry, exhausted kiss on the cheek; ask the neighbor Mrs. Brosnan to hang out while I went to bed; and then go back to work. I honestly don't know how she did it. She probably worked sixteen hours a day, and still she was there at every talent show at school, cheering me on."

"How is that Hulk-like?"

CJ laughed. "I suppose it isn't, though the tightness in her neck was rather Hulk-like, and her pallor often had a green hue."

"I'm sure she'd appreciate you saying that."

He shrugged. "Fortunately, she met Jack. He had more time on his hands to parent, so she went in the other direction. And then . . . the oil rig fiasco, which left her pulseless, which was a shame. That's how I ended up with Jack, who charges me a dollar for every dish or glass I leave in the sink and travels on Christmas while I stay at home alone. Oprah Winfrey says he's doing the best he can, and I think that's wonderful. Just wonderful. It makes me incredibly proud of him and hopeful that one day he will win a parenting award. A for effort."

This was about as real as CJ got, and I averted my eyes, as if looking at him might break the spell. I wanted to hug him. To tell him it was okay to have a human emotion. But I didn't, because his dad had been abducted by aliens and his mom was a possibly dead superhero.

"The good thing about Christmas is that it gives me time alone in the house. Jack went skiing in Vermont last year for seven days. In those days, how many guys do you think I did in his bed?"

I'm sure I visibly blanched. CJ visibly didn't seem to care.

"Forty-seven is the answer. No, fifty-three. Did you know that fifty-three is the number most people will choose if they're needing a random number? True fact."

"Most facts are, in fact, true."

"Nerd."

CJ lived in Tribeca in a dilapidated redbrick building on the fourth floor. The only way in was a freight elevator that opened onto the street. He opened a huge, heavy concrete door followed by a metal gate that accordioned into the wall. Once in the elevator, he cranked this bronze lever all the way to the right, and the machinery whirred to life. Soon we were slowly climbing.

I'd never been in a private elevator that appeared to have been built sometime in the late 1800s before.

I'd also never been in the dwelling of a gay friend before. Because, of course. No gay friends. This was all new.

He needed to use all his might to push the wrought iron gate open on the fourth floor, but once he did, we were in a huge room with a kitchen just to the left, a couch and a TV along the far-left wall next to a door, a desk with a PS/2 computer along the far-right wall, and—smack-dab right in front of us—an unmade bed.

"So here it is. Where the magic would happen if it weren't for a particular shut-in stepdad."

That stepdad then appeared, coming through the doorway at the far wall.

He had curly, light brown hair, a long face with a prominent Roman nose, and a mouth framed by a bushy mustache.

As he got closer, I noticed the iciest blue eyes I'd ever seen.

I wanted to turn around and get in the elevator and never come back. That level of icy.

"Hey, Jack," CJ said. "This is my friend Micah."

Jack approached, his eyes staring into mine. A cool malevolence emanated from them, as if he were shooting rays directly into my eyeballs. I had to look away.

"He's a platonic friend," CJ revised.

I glanced up and those eyes were still on me. Finally, after maybe ten seconds, Jack said, "Hello, Micah."

"Hello."

He turned to CJ. "More records? I dunno, my man. What's with this cash flow? You and me gotta talk. You better not be doin' something that's gonna get you into 'strubble."

Before CJ could answer, Jack grabbed a beer from the fridge, walked back to the TV area, plopped down on the couch, and turned on the set.

I immediately understood how CJ could have such heavily mixed feelings about Jack.

I looked at CJ with wide, horrified eyes. He waved my concern away.

"That's what he calls 'the beam,'" he muttered. "I've seen the beam make people get up and leave a room, many times. He can get people to leave a movie theater. He prides himself on it."

"That's an interesting thing to be proud of," I whispered.

CJ snorted. "He's actually okay." He hurried toward the couch. "Yo, Mr. Jack!"

"Yo, Ceej!" Jack didn't take his eyes off the set.

"Football in the a.m.?"

"Fine 'n dandy."

CJ turned to me to explain. "We sometimes go out to Columbus Park in the mornings, toss a football around. It's our quality time."

I stood there, transfixed. Who was this master of disguises, who dressed as Dale Bozzio and threw a football with a guy who looked a little like the Marlboro Man, and also apparently had fifty-three sexual partners each Christmas when his step-dad went away but not really?

"Ceej?" I asked, not sure how to even begin to figure all of these mysteries out.

He smiled. "Long story involving all-you-can-eat shrimp at Beefsteak Charlie's."

That sounded about as sensible as the rest of it.

"Tell me?"

He rolled his eyes. "So my real name is Jameson. Yep. Jameson Gorman. Doesn't exactly roll off the tongue, does it? And I hate Jim. I'm just not a Jim. Anyway, when I was like twelve, back when Mom was still alive, Jack took us to Beefsteak Charlie's in Times Square. They had this all-you-can-eat salad bar, and there were shrimp on it. I used to love shrimp, so I piled them up on my plate and started eating. Then I went back for more. And more. We kept count. I ate a hundred and eight shrimp. So Jack starts calling me CJ, which stands for, I guess, 'Champion Jameson." That got turned into Ceej for a while, and then CJ, though Jack still calls me Ceej."

"Huh," I said. "A hundred and eight shrimp."

"Yeah. Suffice it to say, I no longer love shrimp."

We sat on the hard concrete floor near his bed because there were no seats anywhere but the TV area. I had that feeling still that I wanted to jet, but I tried to relax into things.

CJ's conversation stayed pretty PG-13 for the most part, with a few forays into sex that were told in more of a whisper. I noticed that when the conversation went from sex stuff to life stuff, suddenly his volume went up, as if he wanted Jack to hear from across the room.

"One time, a couple years back, Jack and I had this throwing competition. Who could throw a football over a brownstone on the next block? We were stupid, because we weren't even close. What happened instead was Jack tossed a football right through a window on the second floor. We ran our butts off, but apparently not fast enough, because on the next block this guy starts yelling that he has a gun and if we keep running he'll shoot. So Jack grabs my arm and says, 'Okay, okay,' and we slow down, and the guy actually does have a gun, and he's pointing it at us in daylight on Franklin Street, and I was like, how New York is this?"

"Whoa," I said.

"It gets better. The guy just wants cash for the window. So Jack takes me upstairs and goes back down with cash for the guy, and the guy cheerfully puts the gun away and that's that."

"That didn't happen."

"Hey, Jack!"

"Yo," Jack yelled back.

"Did we or did we not get chased by a guy with a gun after you threw a football through a window?"

"Truth," Jack said, and CJ's wide-mouth expression was

like *Vindication!* I burst out laughing. How did CJ just throw out a story that happened to be true that was scarier than anything that had ever happened in my life?

"Before he quit school, we had a whole bunch of adventures," Jack called back. "Now I don't see the kid for days and nights at a time and he buys records by the crateful. You know what my stepson does all day and night, Micah? 'Cause I sure don't."

The vindicated look was replaced by one that involved narrowing eyes and grimacing cheeks.

"You quit school?" I asked.

He sighed and spoke in a low tone. "Long story."

I shook my head, not lowering my voice. "Why did you tell me that you were in school? Why not tell me the truth? That was like one of the first things you told me."

CJ motioned with his hands to lower my volume. He spoke very softly. "I didn't really know you then. I guess I was . . . playing a part. Sorry, okay? I don't lie about important things to people I like."

For about the twentieth time in our short friendship, I'd had enough. Yet I sat there on the floor, unable to move. Like I was in front of a puzzle I needed to solve.

Maybe he got that hint, because in that lowered voice he told me a story.

"I've had a variety of jobs. And I don't tell Jack because he's a nosy fuck who will come check up on me and that's not gonna happen. This past summer I worked at Cookie in a Cup in the World Trade Center. Now I'm . . . kind of a waiter."

"Oh yeah?"

"Yep. Pretty boring stuff. Though Cookie in a Cup was pretty wild. Had to sign this proprietary information waiver, because I have the secret recipe now. I could sell it for, like, a million dollars."

"And be the richest person in jail."

"True. My boss was this total closet case. Sometimes in the mornings when I was in the back making cookies, he'd come in and fondle me, and we'd do the wild thing right there on the counter next to the cookie mixer."

"Ew. You're making this up."

His eyes got wide in that CJ way. "We'd use the cookie batter—"

"Ew."

"You're not liking this one."

"I am not."

"Fine. We'd make little cookie houses and set them out for the roaches to move into. Once a family of roaches took up residence in one and overnight, they built six new houses. We came in and there were all these cookie high-rises. We called the head one 'Donald Roach.'"

"I like that one better."

"I figured you would."

The sun had continued to set, and through the slightly grubby windows, I could see the streetlights turning on. I looked around CJ's place and tried to imagine it as my own home. It was hard. For one thing, Jack sat near the TV, not watching us but clearly not leaving us alone, either.

I wondered if it felt like home to CJ.

He sighed and reclined onto his elbows. "This is nice."

"Yeah?" I said, and then I felt bad about the inflection at the end, so I said, "Yeah."

"I honestly can't remember the last time I had a platonic friend over. I was maybe fourteen? Fifteen?" He stretched his arms up over his head and seemed to consider this. "Hm."

"Well, thanks for letting it be me," I said. "I'm honored."

He sat up and smiled at me. "I wouldn't have it be anyone else. Friends?"

"Friends," I agreed.

CHAPTER TEN

HANGING ON THE TELEPHONE

October 1987

"Did you grow up thinking that lanyards were going to be a bigger deal than they turned out to be?" I asked CJ during one of our marathon phone calls. Any night he didn't work, we just camped out on the phone and made each other laugh. Or tried, in my case. It was a Monday night, I hadn't done my homework, and I was as happy as I could remember.

He snorted. "What? No. What are you talking about?"

"I went to this day camp when I was, I dunno, eight? And we used to make lanyards in arts and crafts, and I think I just always expected they'd play a bigger role in my life than they have. To this point."

"Is this deeply upsetting to you?"

"A little," I said, unwinding the tangled phone cord. "I think a world with more lanyards would be good."

"*Buy Micah a lanyard.* Just wrote it down in my diary."

"You have a diary?"

"Oh. I not only have a diary, but I have a diary that will one day be turned into a movie. Like a tawdry gay version of a Jackie Collins novel. *The Twink. The Slut. Lust Boy.*"

"What's a twink?"

"Oh my goodness," CJ said. "Your education is seriously lacking. Probably all that time you spent making lanyards. Do you think it was like child labor? Like they took your lanyards and sold them and didn't pay you?"

This made me laugh. "Yes. I think Camp Maccabee was definitely a scam run by The Lanyard Mafia."

This, in turn, made him laugh. Which I loved. Making CJ laugh was like a drug I had just started to get hooked on. I wanted more, more, more.

"What's the progress report on Operation Closet Extraction?" he asked.

"Oh! New idea. I told you about my dad's friend Rick, right? I think I am going to enlist him."

"What's Rick like?" he asked. "That's a sexy name. Is he hot?"

"Yeah, no. He's probably fifty, first of all."

"And your point is?"

"CJ, that's too old for you. Really."

"To each his own."

"Anyway, he has a combover," I said, lying.

"Okay, not interested. Thanks for that visual."

I laughed.

"Did I tell you my new idea?" I asked. "A twelve-step carnival. All the attractions are for people overcoming addictions and such. Could you just imagine? Start with the Louise Hay Ride, on which you can listen to her tell you to love yourself, amidst all the neurotics scratching their legs feverishly from the itchy hay. Then you have Dunk the Enabler, where you get a chance to dunk a person who is yelling to you, 'Yeah, get another drink. If you have one more, I'll stay and have one more, too.' Followed by the Sexual Compulsive Ring Toss, where you try to toss cock rings onto dildos. After that, it's the Codependents' Horse Race, where you move your horse not by shooting water into a balloon, but by hurling phrases into a microphone like, 'I'm the only one I need, I can find happiness without you!' Then hit the Roller Coaster of Emotions for those new to twelve-step programs. Quickly you speed through the track, from denial to anger to acceptance, greeting each one with hands high in the air and shrieks of pure delight."

"Oh, Micah. You need to get laid."

Was it weird that my new (best?) friend saying that gave me a boner? Because it did. Which didn't make sense, because no way were we fooling around again. We were on way different pages, and I wasn't sure his page was all that healthy, based on the stories he'd told me. But still, my penis responded to his voice sometimes.

He told me about how one time, he used to have a dog-walking gig, and he went to walk a dog for this gay guy who was out of town, and the guy's roommate walked into the foyer totally naked, and they fooled around.

"Is there anything you haven't done, one time?" I asked.

"Probably, but hopefully not for long."

One time had become this mantra for CJ. I don't know if he did it with other people, but really I didn't care. It entertained me countless nights while I lay there in my bed, staring at the ceiling and imagining CJ lying there in his bed in the center of the warehouse.

"You're paying for all this," I heard his stepdad yelling as he walked by.

"Nights and weekends," CJ said.

"You don't know what that even means," his stepdad barked, and I could almost hear CJ rolling his eyes.

"He has such a small penis," he whispered, mock confessional.

"How would you even know?"

"Oh. I'd know," he said, and I got shivers. And not in a good way. "One time, I lost my virginity in East Hampton to a man who was three times my age."

I caught my breath. "What? How old were you?"

"Never mind," he said, sounding annoyed.

"CJ."

"I said never mind. He was an alien who died on an oil rig. It was fine."

"CJ."

"That's all you get until you buy me a fancy, expensive meal."

"One time, I guess I will, then," I said.

Eventually I could hear my parents pacing outside my room, a sure sign they, too, were wondering about their phone bill. They'd gotten me my own phone and my own line, because I'd been crowding up theirs so much. But that didn't mean I wasn't being monitored.

I said goodbye to CJ, and he said we'd pick up where we left off tomorrow.

"You're going to have a permanent indentation in your ear," my mother said, sticking her head into my room after I hung up.

"Yes, yes," I said, lying on my back. "Ear indentation, I know. It'll become a new fad. Dented ear."

She sighed dramatically. "As long as you do your homework, it's fine. That's why we got you your own line."

My mom had always been okay with me talking all night with Deena, or at least as okay as she ever was, so long as I picked up any time there was a call-waiting beep. But this new thing with CJ was one step too much, so a week earlier she had come in to my room, sat down on my bed, and said that she was so proud of me and the wonderful social life I had created, and to celebrate that, here was my new phone, to be placed in my room, to be used whenever I liked. My own line, my own phone number. Part of me wondered if she knew I was gay, if maybe one day when I was talking to CJ in the kitchen I'd said something too loud, and that was why she got me my own line: So she never had to hear that ever again.

As soon as my mother had retreated back to her room, I called Deena.

"Later than usual," she said by way of answering.

"I know, I know."

"I'm not jealous," she said. "I'm just . . . concerned. About your sketchy new friend."

"You really need to stop," I said, my voice box trembling a bit. I'd never countered Deena before. Being friends with CJ must have been giving me new confidence. "He's a good person. I've gotten to know him, rather than just judge him on a few things."

"Micah, you're not always the best at seeing things. Remember the time Jada Kline asked for your math homework and you decided she was now your friend? That wasn't too awkward, when you tried to sit with her people at lunch. And Chip Bennett."

"Unfair comparison," I said.

"Is it, though?"

For a week during freshman year, I'd decided that Chip was my new best friend. He was a popular kid, and one day after school he came up to me and smiled and asked if I could loan him fifty cents for a Snickers bar. I guess I got caught up in my head a little and fell in love with the idea of having a guy friend who was cool. When he went back to ignoring me like usual, Deena had to pick up the pieces.

"I'm just trying to make sure you're not blind to something that could hurt you. That's all."

"And I appreciate that. But how about you just have a little faith that I can make good decisions? CJ is my first gay friend, and I like him. He makes me laugh. I feel, like, alive when we talk. That's new for me."

As soon as I said it, I thought, *Shit.*

An exasperated sigh from Deena. "Gee. I'm so sorry you've been feeling dead when you talk to me. That's disappointing."

"Ugh. That's not what I meant. Obviously you make me feel alive, too, or why else would I be talking to you all the time?"

"I don't know. Apparently I'm this wet blanket who is always judging and bossing you around, so maybe I shouldn't—"

"Stop," I said. "Really. Stop. You're my best friend, Deena. I love you, and you'll always be my best friend, obviously."

This sigh was kinder. "I know," she said. "And, yeah, maybe I'm a little jealous."

Hearing Deena admit she was jealous of me was so novel that I couldn't help it.

"Of course you are. I'm beautiful and smart and perfect and—"

"Don't push it," she said.

On Sunday, Napoleon called and asked if he could come over, and I said yes, because I'd decided to break off whatever this was in person. Certainly not because my stupid hope was that he would say, *That's okay, Micah. Let's just hang out as friends.*

Yeah, that didn't happen.

"Whataya mean?" he asked.

"I just . . . I want a boyfriend. I want someone for—I like this, obviously—but I want someone for more. Like dates." I averted my eyes.

"You don't like what we do?"

"No, I do—"

"Then why stop? You don't have a boyfriend, do you? When you get one, you can stop. But now is just kinda dumb to stop, to me."

"Yeah, I guess, but—"

He unbuckled his belt, and I decided that maybe I would break it off next time.

He was right—it wasn't like I had a boyfriend.

Later that night, Deena called me from a pay phone. It was right after dinner, and I was finally giving my English homework a go.

"You know how my dad thinks Howard Johnson's is, like, fancy?"

"He doesn't think that."

"Not really, but anyway. So, I'm on the corner of Forty-Ninth and Broadway, outside the restaurant, because Dad needs a fried clam plate once in a while, and something just happened involving a certain someone you talk about a lot, and I know you're not going to believe me, but it did."

"Okay . . ."

"Can you, like, come down here?"

"What? It's Sunday night."

"Yeah, but this is, like, super important."

"Can't you just tell me?"

"I think this one I'm gonna have to show you. And bring your fake ID."

My chest filled with tingles. Something was going down and I couldn't help but know it was about CJ. She knew what he looked like because I'd shown her the Polaroid I had of him. My guess was that he was a waiter at some restaurant down there, maybe even HoJo's, and that Deena thought this was somehow shady, but in reality I already knew that he'd left school. So I guess I decided that I'd go down there to stop her vendetta against CJ, once and for all.

Easy, right?

CHAPTER ELEVEN

I CAN'T THINK ABOUT DANCING

October 1987

Deena was sitting at the counter by the window at Howard Johnson's. I was jittery, because Times Square was dangerous—lots of drugs, lots of everything—and while I'd told my mother I was going to help Deena with something, I didn't tell her I was doing that in Times Square. Because that would have ended that.

"Are you ready?" Deena said by way of greeting.

"I have no idea," I said.

She put a sympathetic hand on my shoulder. "I'm actually really sorry about this, and it's at least possible I'm wrong, but I don't think so."

She led me out of the restaurant and around the corner. When I saw the awning and she turned to walk up a couple stairs to a seedy-looking door, I stopped walking.

"Come on," I said. "Stop it."

"Micah, you have to. I'm serious. And I don't actually take pleasure in this."

I wasn't sure I believed her.

"I'm about ninety-nine-point-nine percent sure it was CJ. He looked just like the picture you showed me, and he was carrying a bag, so I don't think he was just going there to look. That boy was there to dance."

Dance. At the Gaiety. A male "Burlesk" theater, according to the huge placard above the awning. The awning read, *Gaiety Male Theater. NY's No.1 Showplace.*

I turned around and walked back toward Broadway.

"Micah!" Deena called. "You know we have to go in."

"I don't know that."

"Really? You don't want to find out if your new friend is a private dancer, a dancer for money . . ."

I stopped walking. I really did want to know. Also, half-naked guys dancing sounded not terrible.

So we walked up the stairs, into a dank landing area, bought two tickets from an old Russian lady who didn't ask to see our IDs, and walked in.

Inside, it was *Saturday Night Fever.* A regurgitation of purple-and-red wallpaper and faux-gold banisters. "Fly, Robin, Fly" was blaring, and when we got to the main area, what we saw was unlike anything I'd ever imagined seeing.

First I saw the stage, with silver tassels as the backdrop and a sole disco ball spinning. Then, on the stage, I saw a guy maybe a couple years older than me was seductively moving his bare torso, his Levi's unbuttoned, a G-string peeking out.

"Whaaat?" I whispered to Deena.

The place was about half full, and it was a big place, with stadium seating in front of the stage. Many men sat alone— probably for good reason—and a few sat in twos. Off to the left was a burgundy curtain.

Deena gingerly took a seat in the back row, far from

anyone. I hesitated in sitting down next to her, unsure what might be on that chair. But then I did sit. The old-fashioned theater seat creaked precariously.

Deena and I stayed there in silence, watching the guy demonstrate his undulating skills and then his prowess with a G-string.

"Where does that string even go?" I whispered. Deena slapped my leg.

After him, a screen came down and a movie came on, and that was the moment at which I could never again say I hadn't seen a pornographic movie. Though I could now say that I'd never seen one except while sitting next to my best girlfriend. I wanted to stare and take it all in, but I couldn't. I had to pretend I wasn't interested, because of stupid Deena.

"Now this. This is educational," Deena said, apparently not having gotten the message that it's rude to stare at gay porn in front of your best friend.

"Ick," I said, lying.

"Such a prude."

All the while, my heart pulsed, wondering if CJ was here, pondering what it would mean for our friendship if suddenly he got up on that stage and our eyes met. Would he be ashamed? Angry? Oh yeah, and what about me? Would this be just another of those things that my friend who "never lies to people like us" was withholding from me? And would this one be the dealbreaker?

Yeah. Probably. I hoped to God it wasn't him.

After an interminable amount of time sitting through porn with Deena, the movie screen ascended and we were left with the silver tassels and a bare stage again. A song started playing, and finally, a dancer appeared.

Tall and thin, self-assured, dressed like a sailor.

Yes. That would be my CJ.

I could feel Deena trying to catch my reaction, but my eyes were plenty busy trying to take this new reality in. This was my new best buddy, who had told me he had a sort of a waiter job. I wasn't sure exactly what he was serving, but. Actually, I very much was.

He danced to "Centipede" by Rebbie Jackson, which I surmised was probably not his choice, since it didn't make much sense with the sailor costume. His lithe fame moved fluidly, with grace, and he seemed totally at home with his body, which was not at all what I had felt back in the park that night, when it seemed like he didn't want me to see it. That thought made my stomach turn, because clearly I made his body uncomfortable. His beautiful, flawless body, which I could not stop looking at. I shrank back into my disgusting, creaky seat, hoping he didn't see me, lest he freeze up again.

His set lasted four songs, during which assorted older men came and stuffed green bills into his purple G-string. The third song was definitely Dale Bozzio and Missing Persons. It was kind of disco-y, with lyrics about not thinking about dancing. During his finale, to Prince's "Kiss," he climbed down from the stage and gyrated atop a balding man's lap.

Deena gasped. "Wow."

I was simultaneously peeved and thankful for Deena taking me here, but mostly I wanted her gone, because I was being pulled as if by a magnetic force up to the stage. Part of it was needing answers. Another part was CJ in a jockstrap. I knew I needed to go up to him, and I didn't want to do that with Deena present. I also knew the likelihood of her giving me space to do that was nil.

After his set, we approached him near the front of the stage. Deena's existence—or maybe both of us, who knows?—seemed to make many of the men uncomfortable, based on the dirty looks thrown our way.

CJ had sat down in one of the seats, next to the balding man, who, from the side, appeared to be maybe forty, possibly older. We stood at the side of the row, Deena behind me, my heart racing. CJ was using his charm, the full smile, the self-assuredness, and it occurred to me that what was happening was a transaction, and that wasn't something I was sure I could take. The lies, the dancing, the creepy place? Those were all things I could imagine him explaining in a way that I would be able to accept. But offering this man whatever he was offering him, for money? That was something else entirely.

And then CJ turned his head and saw me—and he didn't even bat an eye.

"Micah! Oh my God! You came!"

He put up a finger to the man and excused himself, and he pranced over in his jock strap and gave me a full-body hug, which was a lot of things.

His sweaty, bare chest against my jacket. His face, his ear, pushed up against mine. I wanted to freeze time. It was the most contact I'd ever had with CJ, and even with everything I now knew, it was among my top five moments ever.

Ever.

"So this is the famous Deena, I assume?" CJ said, looking behind me and sizing her up.

Deena sized him up right back, gaining the upper hand because she had much more clothing on. "And clearly this is the infamous CJ."

They stared at each other until CJ broke into his toothy grin.

"How come I feel like we're about to have a duel?"

I laughed; Deena did not.

"Come on," Deena said. "Let's go. We've obviously seen enough."

"Stay," CJ said. "Let me show you the dressing room and the back area. Oh . . . the back area!"

I looked from my best friend to my new friend. I went back and forth a few times. I felt the room closing in on me. I began to realize that this was exactly my problem. Other people could do things, could tell me what to do, and I just went along with it. And finally, this was my chance to get a life, make a choice.

"Yeah, I think I'll stay," I said.

Deena's eyes widened and her nostrils flared. I went to her and pulled her aside.

"First of all, thank you. I needed to know this. And I know it now, okay? My eyes are open. And this place is hideous. But this is my friend, and I'm not just dropping him because he's a—whatever. I want this. I want this friendship. Okay?"

She looked down, her feelings clearly hurt.

"I love you, Deena Robin," I said, and then I lowered my voice. "And I'm gonna need you in about an hour, when I get

120

home and my head explodes and I need to unpack all of this."

Her head stayed down but she gave a half smile. "My boy is growing up," she said. "I despise it."

"Love you, too," I said, and I went to hug her. She jumped back. I laughed, realizing this was about her not wanting whatever had been on CJ's body on her own.

"Fair enough," I said.

CJ made apologies to his new older friend, or maybe he just said wait a minute—I couldn't tell. He took my hand and led me back to the dressing room, which was less nice than the dressing room in any movie about a strip club I had ever seen. The gray concrete floors were sticky with who knows what and dotted with spat-out chewing gum. The mirrors were dusty and the chairs in front of them would have been at home on the set of *Sanford and Son*, a TV show about a junkyard. He dressed while he yammered away about the guy before him snorting coke in the dressing room and the balding guy he had been chatting with, and how Deena was pretty.

"She dresses like she watches a lot of *Designing Women*. Like she's not Delta Burke but the other brunette. You know, tall, with shoulder pads. She—"

"CJ," I said, hoping to interrupt. It was my first word in the maybe five minutes we'd been in the dressing room.

He blinked a couple of times. "Yes," he said, going from low to high, singsong style.

"You're a dancer at the Gaiety, CJ."

"Yes." This time, high to low.

"This was information I didn't know. It makes me think you don't care about me."

"Do you really think that?"

I shrugged.

"I spend my nights off talking to you on the phone, despite the increasing threats of Jack the Bully," he said.

"Okay, but . . . this is a big one, CJ. You didn't tell me a really big thing."

He nodded a few times, like this was something he hadn't considered. "Okay, true. But. I have a good excuse."

"Okay." This time *I* went low to high. It sounded artificial to me and I regretted it right away, because it didn't match my growing frustration.

"So, um. I'm shy. And a very private person."

I scrunched up my face, like, *Nice try.*

"I like to be a man of mystery?"

"What does that even mean? CJ. Why didn't you tell me?" He raised his voice in a way I'd never heard before.

"Because I figured you'd leave, okay? Like everyone else, ever."

We stood for a while. I leaned against the makeup table and then immediately straightened up, aware that I really did not want to touch that many surfaces in this place. What he'd said had been real.

"Okay," I said. "I get that. Do I look like I'm leaving?"

His lips went flat. "I'll call you."

"What?" My pulse quickened.

"'I'll call you.' That's what you said the first time we met. Did you call? No. I like you, Micah. But do you think for a moment I believe that this is a forever friendship? No. Because that's not a thing. Not in my life, okay?"

"But it *is* a thing in my life," I said.

He studied my face. I couldn't really tell what he was thinking.

"You are so fucking lucky," he said. "You have no idea."

This time I sat back on the ledge, germs be damned. "That's true. I don't know what you've been through, but I kind of wish you'd just tell me. Instead, you make shit up, you refuse to tell me the truth, you—I don't know, CJ. I don't know how to get you to open up."

He turned his body and put on his coat. He paused, facing the other way. When he turned around, his eyes were slightly red.

"Could you teach me how?"

CHAPTER TWELVE

COMING UP CLOSE

October 1987

I called home from the pay phone and told my mother it was an emergency, and I'd be home late. She didn't sound thrilled, even though I lied and said I was still with Deena. I could tell I was kind of right at the edge of what she was willing to take, that this new part of me scared her and she didn't know how to deal with it. Then I took CJ to HoJo's, where we ate fried clam strips and drank Cokes.

"So . . . real, huh."

"Yup," I said, soaking a soppy French fry in ketchup.

"And how, pray tell, does one do that?"

"You just do it. Talk."

He snorted. "Oy. Okay. So, just talk, right?"

CJ's jaw was tight, and I realized in the time I'd known him, I'd seen him not smiling almost never. I just wanted to reach over and tell him to relax, but then I understood: He was, actually, telling me something real. He was telling me, in his own CJ-ish way, that people had hurt him before. Suddenly I felt unworthy, like my shoulders fell and I thought, *Who am I to tell this person, who has experienced so much, that everything is safe?*

"So when I was eight, my mom left my dad."

"Wait, I thought—"

He put his hand up, and I let him finish.

"My mom left my dad, and he had a good job, but because he had to take care of me, he lost it. We started to get closer, though—that was one good thing. He met this other single parent, and she kind of helped him with me. One time, I ran into her in the bathroom and she was topless and it was awkward."

I laughed, and he gave me an impish, rueful grin.

"Anyway, then my mom came back, and she wanted custody of me, and my dad was like, 'No, you can't do this,' and she was like, 'He's my child. And I love him. I know I left my son, and that's a terrible thing to do. I have to live with that every day of my life.' And everyone started crying, because they realized she was human and not a monster, and—"

"Wait," I said. "Isn't that the plot of *Kramer vs. Kramer*?"

He grabbed a couple of fried clams and threw them into his mouth. He shrugged.

"It might be."

"CJ!"

He threw his hands up. "I don't know what to tell you, Micah. This is me. This is who I am. I'm not sad. I'm not a dancer at the Gaiety because my daddy doesn't love me and therefore I need a new one. I could give two fucks what my dad thinks of me, and my mom isn't here anymore, and Jack is barely a parent. It's all fine, okay?"

I shook my head. "You're unbelievable."

He curtsied in his chair, and I stood up.

"What?" he asked, suddenly all innocent.

"This is me leaving you at a Howard Johnson's."

"Micah. C'mon. Sit." I didn't. "Sit, boy. Sit."

I started to walk out.

He raised his voice. "I didn't tell you because I thought you'd judge me."

I stopped.

"What do you think happens when I tell people I dance at the Gaiety? You think people find that *impressive*? They pity me. They look at me like I'm a speck of dirt. I didn't—I don't want you to look at me that way, okay?"

I sat back down. "Okay," I said.

"So . . . do you?"

"Do I what?" I asked, but I knew what he wanted me to answer. I was just stalling, because I didn't know how.

"Judge me?"

I took a deep breath. "I judge you for lying, CJ. You lie so much. I've never met anyone who lies as much as you."

"Fine, but. For the dancing thing? Am I . . . less, in your eyes?"

I had the urge to make a joke, but he was looking down at his plate in this really vulnerable way.

"I don't know. Not really. I mean, it's a job."

"Are we, like, still friends?"

"Yes. But you have to stop lying to me."

He nodded. "Okay. I promise. By the way, what did you think?" He averted his eyes and grabbed for his soda.

I truly didn't know what to say. For one thing, CJ had been great dancing. Not that I had anything really to compare it to, except the skeezy guy who danced before him, but he'd owned that stage, he'd radiated charm and charisma and mystery, and the truth was I was two different people about it: the one who was sitting here, still weirded out that my friend danced in front of strangers for a living, and the one who wanted a ticket for his next show.

"It was . . . good."

"Ouch." He winced. "That's what you say to your kid when he's played Tree Number Two in the grade school play."

"You were better than a tree."

He snorted. "Oh good. 'Come see CJ Gorman dance at the Gaiety. He's better than a tree.'"

"You're beautiful, okay?" I said this way too loudly, and then I ducked my head as if I could make people not see me.

"Oh!" CJ said. "Okay, I. Okay." I glanced up at him, and his face was a little red.

I had made CJ blush.

It was all so weird. "How'd you get the job?" I asked, hoping to spare us even a second more of this awkward moment.

"A guy at Charlie's came up to me and asked me if I could dance. I was like, this isn't a dance club, but he said he meant stripping, and did I want to, and honestly? At first I told him no way, but then a week later I saw him again and I guess curiosity got the better of me. Also, it's great money. I make a ton of cash every night."

The mystery of him paying for dinner and all those records was now solved, at least.

After a bit of silence, he mumbled, "You think I'm beautiful."

"I will deny having ever said that till the day I die," I said, but his shit-eating grin told me that he wasn't going to forget hearing it.

"Thanks for calling last night, like you said you would," Deena said the next morning in the hallway at school. She was doing her Spanish homework as she sat in the main corridor, under the senior announcements bulletin board.

I stopped and knelt down. "Sorry. It got late."

I could tell from her tight expression that her feelings were hurt, so I repeated my apology.

"Whatever," she said. "So what happened?"

I didn't have the heart to tell her that there was no major fight or reckoning, no dramatic coming-to-understand moment. She would skewer me for having no spine. So I told her a version of the truth.

"He's had it hard," I said.

"Humph," she said. "Gandhi had it hard. You don't see him dancing half naked to Prince."

"Interesting analogy," I said. "I, too, see CJ as a figure likely to bring about world peace."

She looked up from her homework and gave me her full attention. "I just can't believe you have a friend who sells his body."

I looked around to see if anyone walking by had heard her. They didn't seem to. "He doesn't sell his body."

"He dances for money, Micah. What do you think he was doing with that gross guy when he saw us? Getting notes on his performance?"

"I just . . . I like him. I can't explain it. Not like him, like him. I literally like him as a person. He interests me. He's a hard nut to crack, and I'm gonna crack him."

"He may in fact be a nut, but I have news for you, Micah Strauss. You, my friend, are not a cracker."

We sat there thinking about that statement for a while, and then we started to laugh, and quite quickly we both realized that "You, my friend, are not a cracker" would surely be entering our lexicon forever.

I sat down next to her and splayed my legs. "Life is so strange," I said, mimicking the Missing Persons song. Deena didn't seem to know it, because she took me literally.

"Well, not sure you can befriend a hustler and then complain about your strange life. I think that just comes with the territory."

My throat tightened. I hated this feeling. Feeling judged. And I didn't know how to stop it.

"I guess."

She sighed loudly. "I just think you're doing that thing again, where you're super oblivious, and when things fall apart, I'm gonna have to pick up the pieces."

I realized that Deena was judging me and being harsher to me than I was to CJ, and I hadn't done anything except not end a friendship. And that made me wonder: Was I missing something? Should I be judging CJ more?

I truly didn't know.

In the end, the whole Gaiety thing changed just about nothing between me and CJ. It meant that I now knew where he was during the days and on most Thursday, Friday, and Sunday nights, but I didn't press him about it. I told myself I didn't want to know if he was turning tricks. But really, that was all I wanted to know.

"Is there some room you go to with the guys?" I asked. It was the first Monday night of November, and we were on the phone. We had both just bought the brand-new George Michael album and were attempting to listen to it together, like we tried to put the needle down at the exact same moment, and he was about two seconds ahead of me.

"I can't believe George Michael has a song called 'Father Figure.' I think I just died and went to heaven," CJ said.

"I think it's kinda creepy," I said. "Do you have repeat customers? And what do those customers get, exactly, for the tips?"

"I'm gonna dance to this one. It's slow but sexy. I'll wear a leather jacket and aviator glasses."

I flashed back to the outfit he'd worn to the Lortel and considered encouraging him to try a different look. I decided not to do that.

"Repeat customers," I repeated. "Tips get them . . ."

"I think this is where George Michael goes from teenybopper to full-on icon. This song is uh-MAZE-ing. I just orgasmed three times while listening to it. Oh, hi, Jack. No, nothing to see here. Get me a tissue."

"Is he really there?" I asked.

He snorted. "I'm crazy, but I'm not CRAZY. I think he's out drinking with his cop buddies."

"So this would be a good time to bring a trick home, right?"

"I don't bring tricks home, and anyway, youngster, tricks are for kids. You really want to know?"

"I do!"

"Fine, I'll tell you . . . after this next song. Or maybe the song after that. Or side B. I haven't decided. There's a track called 'Look at Your Hands.' Do you think it's about someone who winds up with hairy palms from masturbating? God, I hope that doesn't happen."

Was he protecting me by avoiding the subject, or protecting himself?

I couldn't be sure.

CHAPTER THIRTEEN

I'M COMING OUT

November 1987

Operation Closet Extraction went into overdrive when my mother gave me the news that Rick was going to stay over for a night while his house in Greenwich, Connecticut, was being fumigated for termites.

"He's going to be sleeping in my bed," I told Felicia as we sat in her office after the curtain went up on a Tuesday night. "Friday."

"Whoa," she said.

"Oh, no, no. God no. I'll be in the living room on the extremely scratchy couch."

She smiled.

"So what exactly is it that you think he'll do?" she asked. "Why tell him, and not your parents?"

"I figure he can soften the landing," I said. "They trust him."

"News flash: They also trust you."

Felicia had met my parents over the summer, when we'd comped them tickets to the show on a slowish Thursday night. After the curtain, she'd pulled me into her office and said, "That's who you're scared of? Good grief, kid. Tell your parents. They're like future poster children for PFLAG."

Even though I'd nodded then, I knew she wasn't quite right. They still assumed I was straight, even when I'd never even once said anything about girls, and was into theater, and was hardly John Wayne to begin with.

I ignored her comment and stuck with the Rick plan. "I just have to figure out how to tell him."

"Just let him know you want him there when you tell them. Rip off the Band-Aid, fast. You'll be glad you did."

That advice made me shiver. Maybe for her, coming out wasn't a big deal anymore. But for me? It was the number one fear in my life.

Walter walked in and gave Felicia a kiss on the top of her head.

Well, number two.

"Hey, dear," Felicia said. "How you feelin'?"

"Good," he said, clearing his throat.

"Our prodigal child is trying to come out to his parents."

He turned and looked at me, then cocked his head and smiled. "Aw," he said.

"Yeah," I said.

"They're gonna be fine," Felicia said. "You'll be fine."

"Tell them who you are," Walter said. "In the long run? They'll be glad you did."

I assured him I would get right on that. "When did you come out to your parents?"

He cackled. "I didn't so much come out to them as my pop walked in on me with a magazine."

"Oh my God," I said.

"Yeah. And we're the most Waspy family out there, so

we're all about not dealing with the problem, so my father said, 'Excuse me,' and closed the door, and when I went downstairs for dinner, the conversation was all about my sister's swim meet. I knew he told my mom, because I heard them talking later that night through their door. I didn't hear the words, but I heard the tone, and it wasn't mentioned again for years. Gay apparently hasn't made its way to New Hampshire yet."

Felicia rubbed his shoulder. "But they're here now," she said.

"Thank God," he said. "I truly don't know what I'd do without my mom. Even if the apartment does get a little crowded with her there, she's like my rock." He turned to me. "Tell them. I mean, life is short. Nothing is guaranteed. If they don't know it, they don't know you."

I rolled their advice around in my head for the rest of the night and most of the next day. When I asked Deena about it, she concurred with Felicia and Walter. She knew my parents well, and she thought they knew but were in denial. To my innermost self, I disagreed. If they truly knew, why would they keep acting as if they didn't? Wasn't that bad parenting?

"Just show them how you walk," she said. "That oughta do it."

I gave her the middle finger, and she cracked up.

"How's your insane, slutty friend?"

"Stop it," I said. "Seriously."

She shrugged me off. "If you don't want to be called a slut, don't act slutty."

I wanted to stand up to her for CJ, but it was like I didn't have the energy. Life was too crazy and unpredictable to pick a fight with Deena right now.

"He's fine. He's trying to get me to dance."

She guffawed and her eyes lit up. "At the club? *What?*"

"In general. Like in my room. I told him no way. Or more like I told him no way and then when he played his music I did try a little. I was very, very bad at it."

"Well, that's some improvement, I guess. The first step in becoming a good dancer is knowing that you suck at it."

Luckily CJ understood the gravity of these things. On the phone the next night, he was all about OCE, which he officially coined to make Operation Closet Extraction seem more important.

"As you can see, NOT all seemingly liberal New York parents do great with their kids coming out as gay. As the spokesperson for Gays Whose Vaguely Liberal Parents Totally Snubbed Them, or GWVLPTST, I can tell you that this is a key moment in your life, and how you do this matters. Trust me."

"I think OCE is more catchy than GWV-whatever."

"Agreed," he said.

"How did you tell your mom?"

"Skywriting."

"CJ."

"I rented a plane and had them write, 'Just because your son likes football, don't think for a second he doesn't also like cock.' It was a lot of words, and hence very expensive."

"CJ."

"Fine. About a year before she died. At the dinner table

one night, after a meal. Jack was out with his police officer buddies, and my mom was telling me about this girl in college, way back in the sixties, who had a crush on her. Yeah, I know, my mom used to say weird things to me at the dinner table. I took it as a cue. I said, 'Mom? I'm that girl in college.'

"She laughed and said, 'You have a crush on me?'

"'I have a crush on Tom Selleck,' I said. I figured she'd laugh. It was a funny line, and I chose Tom because my mom clearly had a thing for him from watching *Magnum, P.I.* Also, Jack has that Selleck mustache. She did not laugh. She got all tense and stiff and mumbled something about needing to check the laundry, and that was the extent of my coming out to my mother. And then a year later she died of ovarian cancer, so there's that."

"Oh," I said. "Sorry to hear that."

"Yeah, well, so I tried to come out, anyway. Unsuccessfully."

I was quiet for a moment. I wanted to ask him more about his mom, but he'd changed the subject. "That sucks."

"Yup."

"That's why I'm scared. Why don't they get that? Felicia is like, 'It's gonna be fine,' but how does she know? Deena said I should show them how I walk and they'll just know."

That made him guffaw.

"Thanks. Thanks a lot."

"Sorry. Just joking," he said. "You need to come out. That's the truth."

"But in one moment, everything is gonna change."

"Yes," he said. "One way or another, your old relationship with your parents will be gone in a second. Good or bad, that's guaranteed. Once you tell your folks you like your sandwich with a pickle, the rest of their lives they will be picturing the boy whose diaper they used to change doing stuff with boys' pickles."

"Ugh. You have a way with words and images."

"I am special, yes. Speaking of pickles, I've made a decision. I'm going pickle free."

"You are not," I said.

"But yes I am. First of all, guys are garbage. Second of all, a thing happened."

"Uh-oh."

I expected him to laugh but he didn't. "Did I ever tell you about Mike?"

"Is he the one who gave you crabs?"

"No. He's the clingy one."

"Oh yes, Mike." I remembered something about a weekly rendezvous CJ had with a married guy twice his age.

"So yesterday afternoon, I'm leaving for work and as I walk up Franklin toward the subway, I notice there's a car inching along behind me. I speed up, it speeds up. I slow down, it slows down. Finally, it pulls up next to me, and a hand reaches out the window and hands me an envelope."

"What?"

"Yeah. So the background is that a week before, we were in a hotel near Times Square, and after schtupping, he got all sentimental, and he said, 'I'd like to introduce you to my kids.' I was like, 'Yeah, that sounds, um, grreeat!' And he said he was serious and I said that I, too, was in fact serious, that it didn't make a lot of sense to me to do that, given that he has a wife, and kids, and he said that knowing me had made him understand what he wanted, and what he wanted was a house in the country with me, and to write poetry to me, and to teach me to fish, and to have horses and maybe some dogs, and I tried to lighten the moment by asking whether the dogs might spook the horses or if the poetry would be in iambic pentameter, and he said, 'Don't joke, CJ. I'm serious,' and I said, 'Okay, I'll think about it,' and then, like three seconds later, I said, 'Done.' And he started crying, and I said, 'Please don't cry. I think you're swell and you have a dynamite pecker and a reasonably nice ass for an old guy, but this isn't . . . I mean, we can keep doing this if we keep it just like this, but if suddenly you think you can become my lover and my father, that's not gonna happen.' And he sobbed like a little girl, and it was AWFUL."

"CJ!" I said. "That's . . . did that happen?"

"Yes! And then he handed me a note through an open window, where I couldn't even see his eyes or face, and he drove off. The note said his wife doesn't know what's happened but she knows something's happened, and this is it, and he's willing to go talk to my parents for me, and to tell them how special I am, and how he wishes to show me the world, and even though I'm eighteen, it seems like the polite thing to do, so that everyone's on the same page, and did I know that when I walk I have a subtle limp, and how tasty I look from behind, and he wonders what my bedroom looks like. I honestly didn't know how he knew where I lived!"

"Oh my God!"

"Yeah. So. No more older guys. Seriously. I'll dance for them, I'll take their money at the club, but no more giving out my number or going to Uncle Charlie's to find true love with some thirty-five-year-old stockbroker who shops at All American Boy."

I didn't know where to start, and it occurred to me that maybe I shouldn't start. That story might be true, and it might not be. And what was sheltered Micah Strauss gonna tell CJ about dealing with a stalker?

I changed the subject.

"So Rick is coming tomorrow. He's sleeping over. Like, in my room. I'll be on the couch in the living room, I should explain, for those listening with dirty minds."

"Ooh," he said. "So hot. Could you, like, walk in on him when he's changing?"

"CJ. This is not conduct becoming a person who has just given up pickles."

He cracked up. "True. So you're gonna tell him?"

"I think so!"

"Do you have any gay books?"

"I don't think so? No?"

"Nothing Edmund White? *Dancer from the Dance*? *Faggots* by Larry Kramer? *The Color Purple*, even?"

"No."

"How do you even survive?"

"I have some porn, I mean. I hide it behind my bed."

"Okay! Now we're talking. Take one of the magazines and put it under your pillow."

"What? Why?"

"Because that way he'll know. You won't even have to tell him!"

"Okay, but . . ."

"Micah. Do you have any idea of how awkward it is to come out to a person you barely know for the first time? You said you, like, barely have ever talked to the guy."

"True."

"So circumvent. Leave the magazine. He'll find you and talk to you. If he's a good guy, he'll do it as a mentor. If he's a bad guy, he'll do it in a naughty nurse outfit."

"You're so weird."

"I'm not *not* weird."

I was shivering with nervousness when we got off the phone, but I knew he was right. And with CJ behind me, I was going to be able to do this.

I was eating pepperoni pizza delivered from Big Nick's alone at the dining table when Rick arrived on Friday night.

A whirlwind of greetings, hugs, and "you look great"s spun between my mother and Rick, and then my dad slapped him on the shoulder and said "Hey," like someone my age embarrassed to be having a sleepover. He approached me in the dining room with a kind, slightly asymmetrical smile on his face. Rick was a nice-looking older guy with a slight paunch like my dad. A prominent nose, round face, light brown hair neatly parted on the side. Aging yuppie, maybe. His Lacoste shirts looked appropriate on him as opposed to mine on me, and he wore a brown leather jacket—not the gay wardrobe but maybe gay-wardrobe adjacent.

"Hi, Micah," he said while I was between chews. I covered my mouth and said "Hey" back. Then my mother dragged my father out of the room for who knows what, and we were left alone.

My heartbeat quickened, because this was my chance. Or it would have been, had I not, just fifteen minutes earlier, put a *Playgirl* magazine under his pillow. A *Playgirl* magazine with Mel Gibson on the cover that I'd purchased in the Village over the summer. One that I'd come to depend upon, as it introduced me to Greg Louganis, who was even sexier than CJ, if that was possible.

That magazine had been pulsing loudly, like the lewd version of the Telltale Heart, every second since I'd left it there. *Bud-ump ump, bud-ump ump, lou-ganis, lou-ganis.*

What was I thinking, listening to CJ rather than Felicia?

You listened to CJ if you wanted to know the best way to create a fake passport, or seduce your English teacher. Anything else, Felicia, obviously. Dang it.

"Do you like pizza?" Rick asked, breaking the awkward silence by making it weirder.

He wasn't the most exciting person in the world.

"Yes," I said. "I do like pizza."

And in that moment, I understood fully what a terrible idea I'd followed.

We four sat in the living room, watching *Dallas*. Rick definitely made it funnier, interspersing witticisms about what the various characters should say. Meanwhile, I was trying to figure out how to sneak back into my room, as OCE had morphed to OME (Operation Magazine Extraction). Of course, leave it to my mother, who had planted her flag on not going into my room, as it would be "very rude to our guest."

I was beginning to be afraid that not sneaking in would wind up being ruder.

"Ugh," Rick said. "None of this matters. It's all going to turn out to be Victoria Principal having another damn dream, thereby negating everything."

My dad snorted. "Why are we watching this crapola?"

"Bite your tongue," Rick deadpanned. "This is the best."

"I'll be right back. Need to get something," I said, standing up.

"Honey," my mother responded. She turned to Rick. "Sorry. I've told him. That's your room while you're here. Off-limits to forgetful children."

I tentatively sat down. I stayed fastened to the couch, trying to figure out a way around this. I excused myself to use the bathroom, but the bathroom was within view, and for some reason my mother was very serious about this odd rule she'd made. When I stepped out, I glanced over, hoping she'd be enraptured in *Dallas*, but she was staring straight at me. I walked the plank back to the couch.

"I'm getting tired," my father said as *Falcon Crest* began.

Rick raised his arms over his head in a mock stretch and said, "If we're gonna hit the links early tomorrow, better get some shut-eye." He stood up. "Micah, thanks for the use of your room. I hate to put you out."

"No problem. Could I—"

"Micah!" my mother nearly shouted. Why this one thing had become her obsession, I'll never know. But it was clear: On her watch, I wasn't getting back into my room tonight.

"Okay," I said, trying to figure out how to deal with the awkwardness that was bound to ensue. Was it possible the magazine wouldn't make noise under the pillow? What if it did? Would he think I was making fun of him? Would he tell my parents—and if so, how much worse would it be for them to find out that way than me just telling them?

Damned CJ and his hypnotic ways.

Had I not quite obviously tried to get back into my room twice, the easy time to extricate the magazine would have been when Rick went to brush his teeth in the hall bathroom after my mother excused herself for the night. But because I'd been so weird about it, suddenly my mother was playing warden. Could she know? How?

It was all so weird and confusing, and the stakes felt pretty high.

When Rick said good night and closed the door behind him, my mother kissed me on the head and said, "Just wanting to make sure our guest felt at home. You'll understand when you're older." And what I understood was that when I was older and in therapy for whatever aftermath of this magazine fiasco was, I'd understand that I was raised in a house with utterly bizarre boundaries that were based upon my anal-retentive mother's whims.

I lay on the couch, staring directly at the door to my room, behind which Rick was possibly reading the *Playgirl* magazine I had left under his pillow, or maybe about to find it. I sat up, thinking I should quietly knock on the door. But it was no use. My bedroom was next to my parents'. Any knock would be heard by them.

So instead I went to sleep, dreaming of awkward things exploding at inopportune times.

I woke up at five to pee. My bedroom door was still closed, no sign of Rick having outed me to my parents. I looked in the bathroom mirror after and thought about how much I didn't want my relationship with my parents to change, and how, even if it didn't, even if Rick didn't say anything, now the cat was slightly out of the bag, never to be put away again. I'd never fully know if Rick found the magazine.

I quietly left the bathroom and headed back to the couch for a couple more hours of sleep.

"Hey," a voice said.

It was Rick, sitting on the opposite couch.

CHAPTER FOURTEEN

SIGN O' THE TIMES

November 1987

"Mr. Micah," Rick said by way of hello. He kept his voice down so as not to awaken my parents.

"Hey."

"Is there anything you wish to tell me?"

My face must have been beet red, it felt so hot. "Um. Did you ever take advice from a friend and then realize it was terrible advice?"

He crooked his head slightly and raised an eyebrow. "What's going on, Micah?"

I put my hand over my eyes. "I took some bad advice. I wanted you to know I was gay so that maybe you'd help me come out to my parents."

"Humph," he said, crossing his legs. "Yes, you took some very awkward-making advice, young man."

"Sorry."

"The pillow was quite crinkly, so I investigated. I thought your father was playing a strange joke on me, but then I concluded that, um. He wasn't."

The curiosity got the better of me. "How?"

"Two of the Greg Louganis pages were stuck together."

I hid my face.

"I put it all together. You trying to get back into the room all night. I figured you were sending me a message, and in the name of being a good guy—and not allowing things to get utterly weird with my best friend's son—I thought it best to just ask."

"Operation Closet Extraction is off to a terrible start." I pulled the blanket up to my neck.

He smiled ruefully. "It's okay. No harm done, really. Just. Maybe don't take advice from that friend anymore?"

"Way ahead of you."

He sat up straight and lightly pounded his knees with his fists. "Okay. So how can I help you?"

"I want to come out to Dad. And Mom. Do you think it'll be okay?"

He pursed his lips. "I mean, sure. In the long run, it'll be fine. He might be a little surprised at first. He has mentioned thirty or forty times his dream of grandchildren. Which I suppose he could still have, but it will be more difficult."

I cringed.

"Have you ever said anything to him? To your mother?"

"I've tried, but it's like they're totally blind to the possibility. Even though my best friends are a girl and a gay guy."

"Humph. Denial, sounds like."

"I guess. What do you think I should do?"

He reclined and put his hands behind his head in a stretch. "I think you should tell them. And, if you'd like, I can be there for support. It's going to be something of an adjustment. I do think your parents have it in their heads that you're straight."

I wondered why that was. How, without me ever saying anything about girls, my liberal parents were sure I was interested in them.

"I'm scared," I said.

He nodded and nodded. "I hate that you're scared. We should be further along by now. But clearly we're not. Just know, Micah. In the end it's going to be okay. I think I can promise you that. They'll come around. I'm sure of it."

"Thanks. Your advice is ever so slightly better than that of my friend CJ."

He laughed lightly. "That seems like a really low bar," he said.

"I have never been more embarrassed," I told CJ as we brunched at the Pot Belly Stove on Saturday. "He literally wanted to have the birds and the bees conversation with me. At six in the morning. In my living room with my parents asleep twenty feet away."

"What was he wearing?" CJ said.

I shook my head in disgust. "You are the worst celibate person in the world."

"Not celibate," he said, forking some hash browns into his mouth. "Just awaiting . . . appropriate partners. You know. Under twenty-three, let's say. Twenty-five or -six. Intelligent. Breathing."

"I feel your parameters are getting better but may still be lacking in some areas."

He smiled, but he seemed preoccupied.

I went on about Rick. "He was really nice about it and all. I mean, he had said the pillow seemed crinkly, and he investigated. At first he'd thought my dad was playing a joke on him. That made me laugh, trying to imagine my dad buying a *Playgirl*. But then he put it together, because, apparently, two of the pages of the Greg Louganis spread were stuck together."

CJ hooted.

"He did the math. How I had been trying to get into the room. I'd explained I'd taken terrible advice from a terrible friend."

CJ mugged for the camera.

"He thinks it's really not gonna be a big deal, but he did agree that it will be news. My dad has it in his head that I'm straight."

"Has he met you?"

I ignored him. "He has no idea, so Rick said it might take some adjustment but he will help, which is awesome. He actually gave me his business card so I can call him if I need to."

CJ nodded, staring into space.

"What's going on?" I took a sip of iced tea.

"Nothing. Just thinking about how it's gonna be Christmas soon. Jack is going to Vail."

"Seriously? Without you?"

He shrugged.

"I think that's insane. That's like child abuse."

He grunted. "I'm eighteen. Last year, when I was seventeen, maybe. Anyway, I think you may have a very privileged understanding of child abuse."

I got it, but I wondered if there was part of all of this he didn't get, either. And that's when I got an idea.

"Well, you have plans, too."

"Nah. I'm serious. Older men are out of the picture, so the free-for-all of 1986 is a thing of the past."

"Did you really . . . nope, doesn't matter. I mean that you have plans. With me. You're staying with me and my family."

It was rare that CJ seemed surprised. This, however, stunned him silent. Mouth agape, he just stared at me.

Finally, he said, "Really?"

"Really."

"You know I'm gay, right?"

"Yes. And my mom knows that, too."

CJ looked impressed. "Okay, but. You're gay, too."

"I'm aware."

"I'm not lying to your parents."

That made me laugh. Hard. The idea of CJ chiding me about honesty was a little too much. I nearly collapsed under the table. He punched at my shoulder.

"I'm serious," he said. "No lying. I'd love to stay with you and your family, if I'm really invited. And I'd even consider taking time off from dancing so that it would be more Christmassy, even. But you have to do something, too. Come out, Micah. For me?"

And finally I nodded. Yes. I'd come out. If not for me, then for CJ. And Dalia and Ira would have to stop living in their fantasy world that one day I'd marry a nice Jewish girl.

God have mercy on my soul.

I filled Felicia in on the details during the show. She was excited that CJ was gonna come stay with us. She seemed to have kind of a den mother thing about him, even though she'd never met him. Kids like him, she explained, were far more common than I'd think.

"Also, maybe you'll finally figure out that you love him."

Walter walked in. His eyes had sunk even deeper into their sockets, and his pallor was a bit gray.

"I don't. Or I do, as a friend."

"Sure, Micah." She gave me side-eye.

Felicia was generally quite wise. But on this one, she was way off the mark.

"Whom? Whom do you love?" There was a little energy in Walter's voice, energy that belied how he looked.

"No one," I said, blushing.

"He loves a boy named CJ," Felicia said.

"Ooh!" said Walter, rubbing his hands together.

"Stop," I said, but I didn't really mean it.

"CJ is a piece of work, apparently, but he's age appropriate and he has a job."

I didn't want her to expound, and that made me realize I was still judging CJ. I wished I could stop.

"Condoms, every time," Walter said. "You hear?"

"I hear."

"Go fall in love. Have babies. God knows I need something to smile about."

I nodded. So did Felicia, who put her hand on Walter's bony shoulder. Unsaid was the fact that even if we did that, Walter most certainly wouldn't be around to see it.

It was too unfair to even ponder. Too painful. Walter, not alive anymore. I stood, went up to him, and put my hand on his other shoulder. I felt bone. Skin and bone.

"For you," I said, knowing it was untrue. "I'll do it for you."

CHAPTER FIFTEEN

BIZARRE LOVE TRIANGLE

November 1987

The boiling point of sugar was begging for my attention, but I just couldn't get there.

I was sitting at my desk on Monday afternoon, trying to finish a lab report that was due Tuesday, but caring about the temperature at which sugar boils was a massive stretch.

I mean, things were happening in my life.

I threw my pen down, stood from my chair, and collapsed onto my bed. I let my thoughts go where they really wanted to go.

CJ was going to stay for Christmas break! My mom had agreed. And that meant tick tock, tick tock. I had a deadline. I would have to come out in the next month, or CJ would certainly do it for me.

CJ in my apartment! In my room!

In my bed? *No. Stop. We're just friends.*

Would they have him sleep in another room, even though we were just friends? Would they even allow him to stay over once I came out? What would it feel like, to be out? I couldn't quite imagine that, let alone three steps down the road.

And yeah. He was a friend, only. Felicia was way off. If I had a spark toward CJ, it was just that he was exciting. Life with CJ in it was simply electrifying. Love was something different.

Have babies? I thought about what Walter said and it made me laugh. I tried to imagine having CJ as a boyfriend and us with a kid . . .

Yeah, not quite.

I rolled onto my stomach and hugged my pillow to my body like it was a guy. A guy who made me feel electric inside. Like CJ, but different.

One of these days, I'd have that, too. And then I'd have everything.

When I told Deena on Tuesday morning about CJ spending the holiday with me and my family, she burst out laughing.

"Micah! How on earth is that going to work? You're doing that oblivious thing again."

"I am not."

She closed her locker and turned to face me. "So, your thought is to put your anal-retentive mother at a dinner table with CJ the exotic dancer? What exactly are you expecting will happen?"

I stared at a poster for a holiday bake sale. "I don't know, okay? I haven't thought that far ahead. I'm going to come out first."

"Good. That's good, Micah. But you need to get your head out of the stars and stop making awful decisions. And I'm telling you: Introducing him to your family? You can't do that."

"Will you stop telling me what to do?" I stomped my foot. "It's so annoying. I'm not a child."

"Then stop acting like one."

I looked Deena in the eye, and what I saw there wasn't my longtime best friend; it was a scared stranger who didn't understand me. Not in the least. I shook my head and walked away.

After school on Tuesday, I did my homework in the library and went straight to the Lortel to usher. I was thinking about telling my parents I was gay. I hadn't figured out how quite yet. A small part of me thought drama. Like tell them to meet me in the hallway, and I'd have been hiding in the closet and I'd just come out. Psychodrama, sort of—

My thoughts were interrupted by a vision some twenty feet in front of me, on the corner of Sheridan Square, in front of the cigar shop. It was CJ, with his hand on the shoulder of a man my grandfather's age—a man with wrinkly white skin and a bad gray toupee poorly balanced on his clearly bald head. CJ's hand was rubbing, massaging that shoulder.

Speaking of sugar boiling over. Just two days ago, CJ had vowed to give up older guys. And here he was out on the street with someone my grandfather's age, who wasn't even attractive, and—to hell with all the things Felicia and Walter had said about me having feelings for CJ. I was done. Done.

I rushed toward them. "Are you kidding me with this?"

"Micah—!"

"CJ. I thought you were through with older guys?"

"What? No!"

"Seriously," I said, and for some reason I turned and addressed the old guy. "Yes, my friend has the most intense daddy issues ever. But could you maybe find someone your own age?

This is really pathetic. He's eighteen. Are you sixty?"

"Excuse me?" the man asked, but CJ gently stopped him by squeezing his shoulder.

"I'll get this, Winston," CJ said. Then he turned to me, as angry as I'd ever seen him.

"Any other true feelings about me you wish to get off your chest? Inappropriately, I might add? This is not a date, Micah. It's not anything you're assuming it is."

"Right," I said, steaming, while just a sliver of doubt started to enter my brain. It felt ice-hot, painful. "You're rubbing the shoulder of a guy on Sheridan Square who happens to be fifty years older than you—"

"Hey," Winston said. His voice was sandy. "Enough with the age crap. I'm standing right here, and I'm a person, with feelings, who has been through more shit than your profoundly immature brain could even comprehend."

"Sorry," I said. Then, overwhelmed by how outmatched I was by the situation, I turned around and walked toward Christopher Street.

CJ called after me. "Micah! You mind if I tell you who this is?"

"I don't care!" I called back.

As the show went on and I sat in my usher chair by the side curtain, my mood turned dark. The crowd was laughing at something Ouiser had said, and I just wanted them to shut up, because I was hurting. Someway, somehow, CJ had lurked his way into my heart. I cared about him, and caring about someone you couldn't trust was the worst. My stomach hurt. My head buzzed. I was imagining him in bed with Winston.

I couldn't unsee the image in my head, of CJ massaging his shoulder on the street. I couldn't stop thinking of who Winston thought CJ was, because he was always someone else, never himself, and I hated him for that.

Also I maybe loved him for that. Or I had, at one time. Okay, maybe. But I couldn't now, because here he was again, choosing some old guy over me. Fine. I didn't even care anymore. He could do what he wanted. But then I pictured CJ's smile, and my heart hurt again, and I couldn't wait for intermission so I'd have to do something and I could get my brain to stop spinning.

When I got home, in my room, the thoughts continued to jump around in my head. I wasn't sure if I still needed to come out, as I'd promised that I would to a liar.

And . . .

What if I never saw him again? And what if he wasn't lying for once?

I'd never had a CJ in my life before. I'd never had someone come into my life and totally rearrange it, and change me to the point that I wasn't even talking to my best friend, and I didn't care because I had CJ, CJ, who—

Shit. Maybe Felicia was right? I did love him, in a way?

Maybe I lost it not because he was lying, but because I was jealous? That made me laugh. Jealous of an old guy? But I was, wasn't I? If I wasn't jealous, why was I so angry about seeing him with someone else?

Sitting in my desk chair, I tried to put the entirety of CJ's story out in front of me. All the things he'd told me about who he was, and how he'd said he'd stay at my house and seemed excited to do that, and the fierce denial, which was new; he'd never fiercely denied anything to me before.

Shit. Maybe somehow he wasn't lying. And maybe I did sort of love him. Which wasn't going to work. It just couldn't. We were friends. And it sucked to maybe be in love with your first gay friend. I would have to put those feelings away forever.

Even though it was around ten, I picked up the phone and tentatively dialed.

"Connell/Gorman residence, kindly start speaking."

"Hi, Jack. Um, this is CJ's friend Micah."

A loud sigh. "It's late," he said. "Just a sec."

I tried to steady my breathing as I rehearsed what I was going to say, only to realize I hadn't given myself time to figure it out.

"Hey." CJ's voice was flat.

"Okay," I said. "Just tell me. Who was that?"

He sighed and the line was quiet.

"CJ?"

"He's my delivery buddy for God's Love We Deliver. We deliver meals every Tuesday and Thursday lunchtime to people living with AIDS."

I closed my eyes and took a deep breath. Without giving my embarrassment a chance to take hold, I just spoke up.

"So you know that if this is a lie, this is your worst lie ever, right?"

CJ's voice was a mixture of annoyance and enjoyment. "It would be. We finished our rounds and we grabbed a meal and were, gasp, talking."

"You were rubbing his shoulder."

"Because his lover, Louis, just went into the hospital with pneumocystis pneumonia."

That term I knew because of Walter. It was the opportunistic infection that killed most people with AIDS. "Shit," I said. "You swear?"

"Yes, Micah. I swear. I didn't make up that a man's lover is in the hospital with AIDS."

I winced. I had really screwed up. Royally. How could I even come back from this level of wrong? "I'm sorry, CJ. How do I fix this? Or do I? Or do you never talk to me again?"

CJ said "Hmm" in a way that sort of pissed me off, because it wasn't as if I had no reason for thinking he had been lying. But I knew that if we were to remain friends, I probably had to put that away. Also, I had to put away any stray feelings I had for CJ. Forever. I closed my eyes and pictured the feelings as a piece of paper in my chest, and I visualized it coming out and me crumpling it up and throwing it into the wastepaper basket by my desk.

Finally, he said, "You fix this by coming with us on Thursday."

"I have school," I said.

"Skip."

"I've never skipped."

He paused, then said, "You told me you skipped once because you wanted a day to just watch MTV."

"I've never skipped for a non-television-related reason."

"You kind of owe me," CJ said.

"Fine," I said. "Thursday. Delivering meals to AIDS victims."

"Oh dear. We have so much to teach you. You don't say AIDS victims, for one thing."

"Why not?"

"Because people with AIDS don't want to feel like victims."

I didn't really get it, but I got that it was something I couldn't really understand. "Okay," I said. "People with AIDS."

"Attaboy."

When I got off the phone, I felt relieved. I had almost lost my friend CJ over something really stupid that was totally my fault. But now I had a second chance, and I could do my best to do better.

And, as I stared at my math textbook, I felt the dread of what was coming in two days.

I would be going into the apartments of people who were dying. I tried to imagine Walter's apartment. I had a weird fantasy where we delivered a meal for Walter, and then I had the dreaded thought that Walter could get his own meals. No, these people were going to be sicker than Walter, and my blood chilled. Not that AIDS was transmitted through the air; I knew more than that. But who was to say? This was where people lived, and if they were sick, could their fluids be around? What if—

I shook my head and clicked my fingers on my textbook. Clearly this wasn't a rational fear.

Plus, I had more down-to-earth, immediate fears to focus on.

Those fears were sleeping in the next room.

I THINK WE'RE ALONE NOW

November 1987

It was so important to me to find the right moment to come out to my parents.

It was after school on Wednesday. I called Felicia to say I wasn't ushering and I told her I was about to do it.

"It's gonna go great. I promise," she said.

In preparation, I played the Missing Persons album on a high volume to hype me up, and I took out of my knapsack *On Being Gay*, the book of essays I'd bought on my first-ever trip to the Oscar Wilde Bookshop in the Village over the weekend. I'd read the book in one sitting, because I was so amazed to be reading stuff written by a gay person, about people like me. There was this one essay I thought would really help us talk about it, and I thumbed through to the page I wanted to show them.

And then nature called.

I went into the bathroom and sat, thinking about the conversation we would have, and what would happen, and what the world would be like after.

"Micah?" I heard my mom knocking on my door. I was in the bathroom off my bedroom with the door closed, but I could still hear.

"Yeah?"

"What?" she yelled.

"I'm in the bathroom!" I yelled, but the music from my bedroom was too loud.

"What?"

"I'll come out in a minute!"

"I'm coming in," I heard her yell. "I can't hear you over that music."

My heart sank, thinking about the book on my bed. "Noooo!" I screamed, behind the closed bathroom door.

I heard the door squeak open, and her saying, "Oh, you're in the bathroom," despite the blaring music. I closed my eyes, well aware that if she ventured in even a bit more, my "right moment" to come out was going to be exceedingly wrong.

I wanted to open the door, but I couldn't. There were other things I had to attend to.

"Micah?" my mom yelled.

"Mom. Get out, please. I can't talk right now."

"Micah, what is this book?"

"Get out!"

"Is this for your gay friend?"

"Please leave my room!"

"Is it, Micah? It's for your friend, right?" she yelled. Dale Bozzio sang "Life is so strange" over the opening notes of "Destination Unknown."

"I'll be out in a second!"

"Just tell me, Micah. Is this for your friend, or are you . . . ?"

"I can hardly hear you. Can you please give me a moment?" I shouted.

"Tell me now, Micah Strauss. Please tell me now."

"Mom!"

"Are you a homosexual?"

I put my head in my hands.

"Are you?" she shouted. "Are you a homosexual?"

"Mom, please give me a minute!"

"I need to know, Micah. It's not as if we don't have homosexual friends. But this isn't . . . I didn't think . . . I'm coming in."

The door, left unlocked because who enters the occupied bathroom of a person who has thrice shouted *get out*, opened.

"Oh, Micah," my mom said, standing over me.

"Mom! Boundaries!"

"Oh please. I changed your diaper for years."

"Get out!"

"So you're homosexual. Okay, okay."

"Mom!"

"I just need to digest this."

"Mom!"

She scurried off, slamming the bathroom door behind her. And then there I was, stunned and flushed, and in need of flushing. Never to be the same again.

Later that evening, after curling up into a humiliated ball for what felt like several hours, I sat with my parents on the living room couch and we talked it all out.

"Okay, okay," my dad said. "Okay."

"I just don't understand why you didn't tell us!" said my mother.

"I tried."

"Well, you should have tried harder. After all, you know us. We're reasonable people."

"Even reasonable people can be unreasonable about gay stuff."

"Okay, okay," my dad said, still at step one. "Okay." He grabbed for a tissue and wiped his eyes, which were rimmed red.

"This is my fault," my mother said, joining him in tears. "I did this. I'm overbearing."

"Mom! This isn't your fault. Nothing is your fault. This is just who I am."

"Okay, okay," my dad said. "Okay."

"Do you think you need counseling? Maybe we should have you see someone."

"Mom . . ."

"Macy Gardiner is a therapist. That's Tara's mother."

"Mom, I'm not going to see Tara's mom."

"Well, we have to do something," she said as a tear ran down her cheek.

"Okay, okay," my dad said. "Okay."

I felt so guilty for making them cry. I wanted to disappear, back into my bedroom, back into my own little world, which didn't include crying parents who kept saying the word *okay* over and over.

CHAPTER SEVENTEEN

GIVE

November 1987

This story made CJ feel gleeful when I told him the next day. We were standing out in front of his place, waiting for the God's Love We Deliver van.

"So, *it* was coming out while *you* were coming out."

"Stop."

"You were both digesting," he said, giggling.

"Really. Stop."

"Coming out of the water closet."

"Ugh. I hate you."

"What did Deena say when you told her?"

"I didn't," I said. "I will, probably. But not that version. That one is going in the vault."

CJ laughed.

My mom hadn't really fought me much when I told her I was sick that morning. She felt I needed a day off to "process" what happened. I was grateful, but really I thought she was the one who needed to do some processing.

The van arrived. Winston rolled down the window and yelled, "C'mon. We're running behind."

We slid into the front seat, me in the middle. The van

smelled like cigarette smoke, and there was a cigarette recently put out in the ashtray in front of me. The radio was on a talk station.

"Micah, CJ," Winston said in his gravelly voice by way of greeting.

I winced, having dreaded this moment. "Hi, Winston. I'm so sorry for the things I said the last time. That was way out of line. Can we start over?"

He started the van. "That's okay. You weren't thinking straight. My lover, Louis, brings the same sort of fury out in me sometimes."

The analogy made my face redden, and I hoped CJ wouldn't see. He asked Winston for the update on Louis.

"He's stable for now," Winston said, sighing.

"I'm really sorry it's not getting any better," said CJ.

"Me too," I said.

"Nothing to be done," Winston said.

CJ changed the subject. "Micah here came out to his parents yesterday."

"Oh!" Winston said. "And how did that go?"

"My mom cried because she thinks it's her fault for being overbearing."

"Is she?" CJ asked as the van pulled off the West Side Highway.

I pictured her towering above me while I was on the toilet.

"Possibly," I said.

We parked on a cobblestoned street deep in the West Village, a few blocks south of Christopher. Winston opened the back of the van and handed CJ and me two bags each, and he took two himself. My heart pounded, because I wasn't sure how this was going to go or what was expected of me. Did we talk to them, or did we just drop off the food and go? I wasn't sure I would know what to say, or what to do, and I didn't want to embarrass myself.

We approached a redbrick apartment building on the corner of Barrow and Washington.

"On this first one, why don't you just let me and CJ do it so you can see how it goes?" Winston said.

I nodded. We took the elevator up to the eighth floor. We were each carrying two plastic bags filled with containers of freshly made meals featuring things like tomato soup, sautéed broccoli, and roasted carrots. CJ had told me a nutritionist consulted with each client, as each client's needs were different. Somehow, though, broccoli was pretty much something they all needed.

Our first client was named Brian, and though I'd steeled myself, I wasn't prepared at all in actuality.

Brian sat motionless in the living room, staring at a soap opera on a small television. Two friends, a man and a woman, talked to Winston and gave him an update about how Brian was doing as if he weren't there. Brian was a tall skeleton with stringy orange hair, an emaciated, sweaty face with eyes so deep in their sockets that he looked barely alive. I couldn't look away, but I knew I had to. And once I looked away, my heart started to register just how sad this was. Whether he ate the meal we brought or not, Brian wasn't going to be here in a month, probably. I couldn't look back. Or blink. Because if I blinked, the tears would start coming. I held my breath and stared at the floor.

Juan was next. He lived in a dark room with the shades pulled down, in a three-story walk-up on St. Luke's Place. While he was less skinny than Brian, his entire face and neck were covered in the purple splotches.

"Oh my God, thank you, thank you," Juan said. "It's like the Easter Bunny, or Christmas."

"I do a fantastic slide down the chimney," CJ said, and Juan laughed until he coughed. "How are you doing?" CJ asked. "Last week you said you were fighting with your mother."

Juan groaned. "She's impossible."

CJ groaned back. "I hear you. My mother won't stop badgering me about college stuff. It drives me crazy."

"Right?" said Juan. "There should be some sort of gays with crazy moms support group."

"Good-looking gays with crazy moms," CJ corrected him, tickling his neck.

"Oh, you," said Juan. "Such a tease."

I was totally amazed. CJ was such a natural, and it was like he knew how to alter himself to the person to be the most likable version of himself. Sure, he'd lied about his mother, but I could see that really it was a lie with a purpose. Connection.

CJ sat with his arm around Juan while Winston asked some questions for a form he had to fill out. I stared at the floor, feeling useless.

I couldn't stop thinking the worst thought. That each of these people was dying because of sex. And I couldn't help it, but I found myself imagining them doing it, and then I felt truly ashamed of myself, because they were just like me, and I liked those kinds of sex, too, so why was I judging? And was I? It was incredibly confusing, and the sadness twisted my gut.

Our third client was a rail-thin Black woman with thinning gray hair. She had huge circles under her eyes, like she hadn't slept in a while, and she was wearing a tattered nightgown.

"Hi, Anita," CJ said, and the woman seemed to smile in spite of herself.

"Not hungry," she said, sitting at the kitchen counter.

"But you have to eat. Here." CJ started to unload her bag, which included a plastic container filled with what appeared to be beef stew. "Just have this. You don't have to have the vegetables if you don't want to."

"Nooo," the woman said.

"C'mon. You have to eat something. I'm worried about you. I was thinking about you the other day and wondering if that Rodney was still coming around."

This got Anita talking, and while she talked, CJ nodded and spoon-fed her occasionally, responding to her while she chewed. Winston put his hand on my shoulder.

"You want to do this intake?" he asked.

My nerves were shot. "Okay, I guess," I said, and after CJ had finished getting her to eat the stew, he waved to me to come sit with them.

"This here is Micah. He's my bestest friend in the whole world."

Anita smiled at me. Her teeth were falling out. "Any friend

of CJ's is a friend of mine," she said, and though I stammered through the first couple of questions, by the end I was feeling more at ease and able to do the job.

CJ hugged Anita goodbye, and I stood there, not sure if I was supposed to hug her or not, but when she looked at me, something in her eyes pleaded with me for contact, so I opened my arms to her and held her.

I would probably never see this person again, I thought as she held on for dear life, and soon I was holding on, too, not able to let go.

"C'mon, you lovebirds," CJ finally said, prying us apart. "See you next week, okay?"

"Thanks," she said. "See you."

We wandered north, entering arbitrary buildings, and it struck me just how random this disease was, how just like we were skipping certain brownstones and apartment buildings, others we weren't, and AIDS wasn't like a bomb going off and taking out an entire structure, but more like a precision attack, decimating one while leaving another totally unscathed, and I wondered whether there was any unscathed apartment building anywhere in the city, if maybe this was just a few people, but most people were okay, because God knows no one at my school was talking about a deadly virus that was leveling Brians and Juans and Anitas throughout the city, but that's what was happening, and in most apartment buildings there was probably at least one person wasting away in bed, weighing half what they used to. And I thought: *They all have families.* And it was like a huge, awful tidal wave, and tomorrow I'd go to school and no one would be talking about this thing that was happening. Mass death of mostly gay men. No one. Because the dying were less-than-people to them. I was a less-than-person to them. That's how it felt.

"You okay?" CJ asked.

I nodded, unable to speak because of the tears behind my eyes and the unuttered sobs climbing up my torso and tensing up my neck.

He lowered his voice and put a hand on my back. "The first time is really hard. It gets easier."

I didn't want it to get easier. I wanted it to magically go away.

And I had a terrible feeling that it wasn't going to go away anytime soon.

CHAPTER EIGHTEEN

SOMETHING SO STRONG

December 1987

Thanksgiving flew by, and suddenly the extended Christmas season was here, and every store put up holiday decorations, and Deena started with her daily questions about Chanukah, knowing full well that even though we had a mezuzah by our door, my family didn't celebrate Chanukah in any real way, and therefore I had no idea when the holiday began and ended each year. I think she just liked admonishing me for things, and every early December this was low-hanging fruit.

"I'm pretty sure you missed Sukkot this year, too," Deena said to me on the phone one night in early December.

"Suck-ot," I said.

She ignored me. "You don't even know which one that is."

"That's the one with the gourds, right? Harvest or something?"

"Yeah."

"Yeah, and when you sit on the gourd, the payos come out, and then you pull on the payos, and the wheel on the slot machine spins, and if three bells come up it goes 'ding, ding, ding' and you win fifty dollars."

She laughed. "I think you got it."

Meanwhile, CJ got busy at work and I got busy with exams, and suddenly I wasn't seeing him that much. But we were having epic phone conversations nightly, ones that were often punctuated by my mother's tight-necked "Chatting with your boyfriend again?" She could not seem to understand that two gay boys could be friends, and while she and my dad were okay with him staying with us for the holiday, she had staked her flag on us never being in a room together with a closed door.

"It would be the same if it were Deena and you were heterosexual," she said, not meeting my eyes, and I nodded, pretending to forget that Deena and I had been in my room with the door closed probably hundreds of times.

After our God's Love We Deliver day, the conversations with CJ had shifted. I hadn't gone back—school, after all—but he kept me updated on Juan and Anita; Brian had died a week after we'd seen him. Now, after days in school in which AIDS didn't seem to even exist, it was front and center.

"I think I'm going crazy," I said to him one Thursday night as we began the second hour of our nightly talk.

"Short drive," CJ said.

"'Digging Your Scene' by The Blow Monkeys—that's a song about AIDS, right? Like clearly?"

"Oh God, yes."

"'I know I'll die . . .'" I sang.

"Yep."

"This jock, Tony Calabrese. He would literally kill you if you looked at him and he thought you were a fag. He's walking down the hallway singing that song."

"Welcome to Planet Gay. They steal our culture. Same

with what the straights did with the Village People. You know 'YMCA' is about hooking up at the gym, right?"

I kind of knew that.

"They play that shit at Yankee Stadium every seventh inning. That's what they do. They steal our stuff, they make it their own by stripping out the true meaning, and they don't give a flying fuck if we die."

"I'm beginning to think that's true," I said.

"You're beginning to wake up to the truth. AIDS is what they've always wanted. You hear that guy Pat Buchanan? He wrote an essay about how the homosexual declared war on nature and now nature is getting its revenge. He works for Reagan now. Watch. Someday he'll be their king, and we'll be in prison camps."

I shut my eyes and shook my head, hard. My parents had always been liberal, but politics hadn't ever meant that much to me. All of a sudden, it meant everything, and I didn't even know where to put my feelings about it. They were so big.

"By the way, it's tertiary syphilis," CJ said, waking me from my angry haze.

"What is?"

"AIDS. Tertiary syphilis. That's what the *Native* says."

The *Native* was New York City's gay newspaper, and CJ was an avid reader. He said it was basically the only place you got coverage on AIDS. Or, according to their publisher, "so-called AIDS." They'd been digging into things a bit, and now every week there was a new conspiracy theory.

"He says it's basically untreated syphilis."

"That doesn't sound right."

"Yeah, I think he's lost it. Last month it was swine flu. Now it's syphilis. Next month, who knows? Runner's knee."

"Untreated scurvy," I said, and he laughed.

"A side effect of being chased by Frank Perdue," he said.

"Undoubtedly," I said.

The answers to *Why did the chicken cross the road?* had become part of our banter. *To get to the other side. Because Frank Perdue was chasing him. To keep his pants up*, which I guess was the answer to *Why does a fireman wear red suspenders?* These became the interchangeable responses to any question to which neither CJ nor I had a correct answer.

"Why is it that our president refuses to spend the money to find a cure for this disease?" CJ asked.

"To keep his pants up," I answered.

"And Nancy Reagan. She goes on *Diff'rent Strokes*, interrupts a perfectly good episode in which Willis is about to get high for the first time, and encourages us all to 'Just say no.' *Just say no*. Like that's going to make the drug epidemic disappear. Why even do that?"

"Because Frank Perdue was chasing her?"

"Probably. He's probably behind this whole 'Just say no' movement. It's like a drugs-for-chicken trade-off he's trying to popularize. Get all the people who smoke crack to switch to Chicken McNuggets and make a killing."

"Maybe Ronald McDonald was chasing Nancy Reagan?" I added.

"Maybe he was," he said. "That's probably it."

"We've solved the world's problems, yet again. Why are we so damned brilliant?"

"To get to the other side. Did I tell you about Matt?"

There had been a lot of "did I tell you" stories.

"I have no idea."

"He's the one, we met at Les Hommes earlier this year and we took a walk, and he was so, so nice. Like he really cared about me, like he asked questions and we didn't just talk about sex. And he was young! I mean, for me. Like, twenty-six."

"Almost a baby," I deadpanned.

"Exactly. Well, anyway, we walked to Riverside Park and we stopped on Riverside Drive at this angel statue on Eighty-First. We were talking about the plague and I don't know what made me say it, but I said, 'If this thing ends, how about we meet here. Like the next day?' And he hugged me right there on the street and said we would. That was in the spring. I'm just . . . I'm tired of waiting, is all."

I didn't say anything, because I got it. I hadn't been waiting as long as CJ, but it seemed so long already. When would I get to experience life without AIDS looming over everything?

He changed the subject. "How's the incorrectly named Napoleon?"

I groaned and took a sip of juice from the cup I left on my nightstand. "He literally won't take no for an answer. He came over last Sunday again. I told him no, but he was like, 'I'm coming over,' and even then I said, 'We're not going in the bedroom. This is not a thing that's going to happen again.' And we wound up there. He knows how to get me in a moment of weakness."

"Was it fun?"

More than anything, I wanted CJ to feel jealous. It was totally maddening that he didn't.

"It was okay."

"Just okay?

"Just okay, okay?"

"Okay!" CJ said. "God. Some people are so unwilling to kiss and tell."

I got off the phone a little after nine, and when I went out to the kitchen for a glass of juice, my father stopped me.

"Got a minute?" he asked.

"Sure."

We sat down at the kitchen counter and I put my feet up against the side of the refrigerator, which always bugged my mom when I did it.

"I just . . . how's it going, Micah?"

"It's going okay. Why?"

"I mean this gay thing. I worry about you. I know from Rick that it can be hard to be gay, and I just don't want you to struggle."

I stared at a photo of my grandfather holding me as a baby. The side of the fridge was covered in stuff like that. I looked happy. He looked happy. Would we look as happy now if he were still alive and he knew?

"I haven't told anyone, and I don't think I will. At school or anything."

"I think that's probably a good idea."

"Yeah."

We sat quietly for a while. I was thinking about my father saying it was probably good not to tell people. Because maybe he was right, but basically that was my father telling me to be dishonest. I thought about what CJ had said about people wanting us to die, and I wondered what my father would say if I told him that. We were tiptoeing around each other, making sure not to say anything that might rock the boat. And that made me think about what CJ had said, about how one way or another, telling my parents would change the relationship forever, and I wanted to go back. Back to before conversations with both of my parents got so damn awkward.

He broke the silence. "Do you think—"

"What?"

"I don't know. If I had played more sports with you?"

I laughed. "I don't think that's how it works."

"Well, I know, but. I mean, Rick plays a pretty good game of racquetball, but, like, team sports. If we had thrown around a football sometimes."

"Dad. That's not it. CJ plays catch with his stepdad all the time, and he's almost too gay. Don't think there's a correlation there."

My dad nodded absentmindedly, like his fears weren't really quelled by my words but he wasn't going to push it.

That Friday night, CJ took me to my first gay bar.

The Works was on Columbus Avenue at Eighty-First Street. The sign was a water faucet, and the front was entirely black glass, so you couldn't see inside. I'd always wondered, every time I took the crosstown bus and passed it, what it would be like inside. I imagined it would be more modern and cleaner than Badlands.

I clutched my fake ID as we walked inside, and found I was right. Way more modern. No bouncer stopped us, and we walked the narrow floor opposite the mirrored bar, which was adorned with neon-blue lighting. Above the bar were huge video screens, playing the video for "Head to Toe" by Lisa Lisa and Cult Jam. The floor below thumped with the beat. We brushed past a tall, pudgy, middle-aged guy with a mustache, who smiled at us.

"Well, hellooo, Peter Pan," he said. My shoulders clenched.

Toward the back, a few guys were playing pool, but most of the men kept their eyes on the video screens on the upper walls.

"Total Stand and Model," CJ whispered to me, and I grinned self-consciously.

Across from us stood an older guy with freckles wearing an honest-to-goodness raspberry beret, like the Prince song. CJ pointed and said to me, "Look, it's the kind you find in a secondhand store." I smiled. The guy became animated, seeing that we were talking about him and deciding, incorrectly, that this was a good thing. I looked away, not wanting to hurt his feelings.

"Drinks on me," CJ said. "No wine coolers."

"Finally, you and Deena agree on something. Well, that and my jacket." I pulled on it, as of course I was wearing it again. "A beer?"

"How manly," CJ deadpanned. "You got it."

He went back to the bar and I kept my eyes on the videos, scared to death some old guy was going to come over and talk to me. What would I say? The year before, the drinking age had been raised from nineteen to twenty-one. I wasn't even close to being old enough to be there, and I was afraid someone would catch on and have us kicked out. Or at least me.

I couldn't imagine CJ got kicked out of anywhere, ever.

He returned with my beer, a Rolling Rock, and we clinked bottle heads. The bitter liquid curled my tongue as I swigged it. Man, did beer suck. *Give me a strawberry wine cooler any day*, I thought. But I knew not to say it to CJ.

"Basically, you just gotta look bored."

"I'm thinking that's gonna be kinda easy."

"Just look bored and wait and see what you catch," CJ said into my ear, over the thundering base of "Some Like It Hot" by Power Station.

"I'm guessing herpes," I responded, and that made CJ laugh, which was always good.

The man in the raspberry beret tapped CJ on the shoulder.

"You are soooo cute," he said, and even though I had less-than-zero interest in him, a puff of jealousy spread across my rib cage.

"Thanks," CJ said. "Just out of prison."

The guy laughed like this was the funniest thing ever and leaned in toward CJ. I couldn't help but lean in, too, not wanting to miss anything over the loud music.

"You should know: I'm anally oriented," the man said.

CJ took this information in, seemingly impressed. "Well, that's great. You must keep a very clean apartment."

This did the trick. We were left alone, and CJ sighed dramatically.

"Have you ever wanted to live somewhere where there are actual young people?" he asked over the blaring music, something by Eurythmics. In the video, Annie Lennox wore a blond wig.

"What do you mean? We're young people."

"Yeah, no," he said. "We're young adults. As kids, we got teddy bears from Pottery Barn. We eat Tofutti instead of ice cream. We schtup adults because that's all there is. I mean, like, let's go where there's a Dairy Queen and a mall. Manhattan is too expensive for people with kids. It's just the very rich kids, who hang out Friday nights smoking pot outside on the steps of the Met, and the very poor kids, who hang out in Times Square or on the piers. The rest of us don't exist, Micah. We're figments of others' imaginations."

I didn't answer, because CJ was obviously just rambling. When he realized I wasn't answering, he started a roiling game of *Who's been to prison and for what?* and we found ourselves laughing so hard that I teared up. Then the DJ came down from his cage and gave CJ a warm embrace and kissed him on the cheek, and soon CJ was holding court with a circle of men, regaling us with stories of trips to Spain he'd certainly never taken, and wealthy lovers he'd probably never had, and annoyances with his stepfather that were almost certainly true. Everyone wanted him, and the jealousy I'd felt earlier faded because who could blame them? Drinks kept arriving, and I kept taking them, and soon the place was spinning, and it felt so out-of-body. Unlike at the Tunnel, I didn't want to be home watching MTV. I wanted to be right here, right now.

And maybe the guys weren't all over me, but did I want them to be? There wasn't a man in that bar within five years of me, and most of them were at least a decade older. CJ left with several new phone numbers and the hearts of at least two admirers in his pocket. And I realized, when we left, that I hadn't looked at another man the entire night. Not like I was interested, anyway. My eyes had stayed on CJ.

I got home around one in the morning, and I expected my parents to be asleep. I was wrong.

"Let me smell your breath," my mother said. She had placed a rocking chair in the foyer, facing the door, and now she stood up and came at me, leading with her nose.

I hadn't planned for this.

"Are you drunk?" she asked, frowning. Her nose confirmed for her that indeed I had booze on my breath.

"Not really?" I said unconvincingly. My mother's frown lines grew to epic proportions.

"Micah," she said. "I don't even know who you are anymore. Grounded. For a long time."

Grounding included the loss of my telephone, and the next day I couldn't even convince my mom to let me call CJ so he'd know I was alive and grounded. I slammed my door to voice my disagreement with this policy, and I put on *Spring Session M* as loud as I could, until our downstairs neighbors started to thump on their floor. After I turned it down, I sat there on my bed seething, my head and heart pounding, feeling utterly changed and misunderstood and maybe even a little bit proud.

I think my mom knew this wasn't the time to mess with me, and all I could do was wait until it was time for work.

"You'd better be back right after the second show, you hear? I can't monitor you, but if you're not back, there will be repercussions beyond anything you've seen. You have your backpack?"

I nodded, tight-lipped. She'd strongly suggested I study during the break between shows. I took the elevator down to the basement rather than the first floor, and I dropped my knapsack in the super's office and asked if I could grab it tomorrow, because you know what? Screw that.

Grounding was for people who gave a crap.

CHAPTER NINETEEN

LOST IN EMOTION

December 1987

Felicia listened patiently while I breathlessly told her about my night—all of it. Her expression didn't change when I shifted from the Works to the ramifications with my mom. Even when I told her about leaving my bookbag in the super's office and that I hoped it would be okay if I missed the second show, her face remained passive. Walter stopped in with the cash box from concessions; it looked like he'd lost another ten pounds, and he was walking stooped over. He kissed her on the cheek and said he was heading home, and she said, "Okay, baby." As he left, I winced, wishing I wasn't bothering her with what suddenly seemed fairly unimportant.

"This is what makes you unique," she said finally.

"What?"

"You're knee-deep in your first-ever rebellious phase, and you tell your boss you're going to play hooky. Go. Have fun. Be safe."

The box office at the Gaiety was empty aside from a bored-looking woman who barely raised an eyebrow when I slapped my money down. I felt like an adult in a glorious way, painlessly, dangerously free, and I wondered who I could be if I just let go.

I paused before going in. "Are you hiring dancers?" I asked.

She crooked her head to the side and looked me up and down.

"Wrong type," she said in a thick Russian accent.

I cataloged that interchange as something to discuss in therapy when I was an adult looking back on my childhood, and I entered the club.

A skinny, dark-skinned guy with a sideburn-free mullet gyrated to something I couldn't recognize and didn't like. The theater area was about as crowded as last time, and I felt the rush of excitement that came from possibility. I could do whatever I wanted, within reason. If I wanted to play around, I could, because I was free. Scanning the middle-aged crowd, I quite quickly disabused myself of that notion.

Older guys. AIDS. No thanks.

CJ was the third dancer to come on, and I moved down to the front row for his set. His face lit up when he saw me, and he gave a goofy smile before swallowing it and going back to the persona of a macho guy dancing to "The Glamorous Life" by Sheila E. He writhed his lanky body and he shook his skinny butt, and I sat there, trying to ignore how turned on I felt, and totally transfixed by how amazing CJ was, how he just fit into every situation, including some incredibly weird ones. I wondered what it was like to be the center of attention, as I'd always lurked around the sidelines. Of course I wasn't the right type to become a dancer. How did a guy become worthy of that sort of attention, and did I even want it?

Yes, I realized. For a minute or two, maybe. To have guys look at me like I realized I was looking at CJ.

My heart twisted.

After, backstage, I told CJ about getting grounded and ditching my ushering job for the day, and his eyes lit up.

"Well, well," he said. "Look who's allowing himself to be mentored by the worst."

We both laughed.

"Don't worry, kid," he said. "Stick with me, and in a few months, you'll be living under a bridge."

But happily, I thought. *Happily and freely.*

As if to prove his point, CJ came down with a quick flu (*ha-choo, ha-choo*) and we wandered up to Central Park, taking a pit stop at Rockefeller Center to look at the humongous Christmas tree. It towered over us, dressed up in red, white, and green lights with a white star on top.

"Did you know that elves created that?" CJ asked. His breath was visible in the chilly early-evening air.

"Elves?"

"Yes."

"It's very tall. Elves are very short. This seems like a poor match."

"Well, it's for their self-esteem," CJ explained. "Occupational therapists have created a program for elves to build tall things. It's really a win-win. They do beautiful work, and they come out of it feeling really great about themselves."

"Awesome," I said.

Once we got to Central Park, we beelined to the skating

rink, which was not a destination I normally would have chosen, but when a friend offers to pay and you would do just about anything with that friend, it's not the time to tell that friend that you last skated when you were six.

The blades felt comfortable right away, and maybe having thick ankles is good for something, because within minutes it felt like I'd been skating forever.

"You're good!" CJ said as we glided in a circle, our arms bumping into each other.

"What, did you think I'd suck?"

"Kind of, yeah." The song "Make It Real" by the Jets began.

"So you wanted to lord over me yet another thing you're better than me at?"

"Duh," he said, and then he glanced over at me. "I don't think you have any idea how good-looking you are. You're chunky, yeah, but you're classically handsome. Swarthy. You have no idea, do you?"

I shivered all over. Was he lying to make me feel better? I knew my mom thought I was good-looking—at least she did before this new phase—but really no one else had responded to me like that. Napoleon and Lucas wanted sex with me, but I was pretty convinced that they were just looking for someone who was willing, and I was the guy they saw as gay. Sometimes when I stared in the mirror in the bathroom, I came up with a good angle that wasn't hideous, I guess.

When I didn't answer, he smiled and skated ahead of me. I watched his brown hair blow in the chilly evening breeze, and I allowed the song to blow through me. I thought about moments in my life. And how if I told Deena that I had a moment while that song was on, she'd laugh at me, because she thought it was funny that I liked such cheesy songs. But I did, and the moment unfolded in that way where time slows and you know that you're making a memory that will never fade, like a tiny night-light in the corner of your brain that will stay bright for eternity.

After a late dinner at Gray's Papaya, we wandered up to the Planetarium and watched "Laser Genesis," which paired a psychedelic light show with the music of Genesis, Peter Gabriel, and Phil Collins. We sat in a round auditorium, all of us looking up at the domed ceiling where lasers danced along to "In the Air Tonight," and then "I Don't Care Anymore."

"This would be better stoned," I whispered to CJ. I'd never been stoned, and this almost made me want to try.

"I love it just like this," CJ said, and I turned my head and watched as he took in the jumping laser patterns with wide eyes, like a child, almost, and I had this weird urge to kiss my best friend.

"Yeah, me too," I said.

The show let out at midnight, and I knew I was going to be in big trouble at home, but also I didn't care. For once, I was living. For once, little Micah Strauss was peeking out of his bubble and seeing the world as it was, and I wanted more, and I wanted immediacy, and I wanted it to never, ever end.

"Do we need to get you home?" he asked.

"Nope," I said, and that was good enough for him.

We subwayed downtown, and CJ took me to what he called "THE bar." On the subway, I watched as he clearly was getting excited about whatever was going to happen there, and soon I couldn't wait to check out "THE bar," either.

Uncle Charlie's was on Greenwich Street, a diagonal street I'd traversed to get from Sixth to Seventh Avenue a million times. I'd never known that I'd been walking past the apex of gay life, but apparently, according to CJ, I was.

Also according to the size of the crowd, which spilled out onto Greenwich.

Inside, shirtless bartenders with bow ties served drinks to a wide array of men, many of them preppy. My heart thumped because there were so many good-looking guys, and this was the first time we'd been somewhere where I'd seen that. CJ, in character, hugged several guys old enough to be his father, and I, a bit out of character, tried to catch the eye of a guy around our age. He wore a bright blue sweater under a burgundy down jacket, and he had dark blond hair. He either didn't see me or he wasn't interested, because I couldn't catch his attention.

"You're cruising," CJ yelled into my ear.

I looked at him, smiled impishly, and shrugged.

"Good boy," he said. "They're gonna eat you up."

A tremble shook my body when he said that. Did I want to be eaten up? There was a disease that was metaphorically eating people up. How could I possibly be sexual when the outcome could be death? And then, as I looked at some of the guys there, I kind of got it. How could a person NOT be sexual?

Sex defied logic. It was biological, and when sex happened, it was like a screen came down and blocked out all semblance of reason. I knew it because of Napoleon. None of the things I'd done with Napoleon made sense, exactly, except that in the moment they totally did. It was a question of context. Two men screwing was—at best—bizarre out of context. But in context, it could be absolutely beautiful. I could imagine, anyway. With love involved.

I had never had that thought before.

I broke free of my deep thoughts to find myself lost in a sea of gay guys, and I couldn't swallow or breathe because it was so immediate. Sex and life and death and joy and sadness, and suddenly I understood opera, and those big moments those singers have, because I felt like singing out all the pent-up energy inside me.

Who even was I tonight? And could I be whoever this was without being unsafe, so that I could wake up tomorrow unscathed, even if I were in trouble with my parents?

We found ourselves in a circle with a college guy named Art from NYU, who wore a black peacoat and eyeglasses that made him look like a hot nerd, and Sammy, who was probably thirty-five and dressed about fifteen years younger, with shiny, Dippity-Do'd black hair and a tight white All American Boy T-shirt hugging his large chest and thin waist.

Art was talking about taking classes in creative writing, which I thought was cool, and I asked him a lot of questions about what college life was like. He asked questions back, and, taking my cue from CJ, I became someone else.

"I'm Carter," I said.

"Hey, Carter. You in school?"

"In college, but. Taking a year off. I'm a . . . paralegal," I said, looking at CJ for guidance. "I have my own apartment, but. Also a roommate, so we couldn't go there, even if you wanted to."

CJ rolled his eyes, gave me a sarcastic thumbs-up, and went back to Sammy, who seemed to bring out this part of CJ that was doting and solicitous, as if he were auditioning for a part, and trying to figure out exactly who he had to be to get it. It was a little fascinating, but I didn't want to be rude to Art.

"Do you come here a lot?" I asked.

"And other pickup lines from the seventies," Art replied.

"If I said you had a beautiful body, would you hold it against me?" I asked.

He smirked. "What's cookin', good lookin'?"

I leaned in. "I'm terrible at this."

"I know. You're in high school."

"How did you know?"

"The weird paralegal thing. Smacks of someone who has just about no street smarts and lives at home with his parents on the Upper East Side."

I smiled sheepishly. "West."

"Close. What's your real name?"

"Micah."

"Hi, Micah. I'm actually Art."

"Sorry, Actually Art. I have what is known in the business as a TERRIBLE mentor," I said, raising my voice so CJ could hear the important part, but even though he gave me another thumbs-up, I could tell he had other priorities. I wanted to reach out and grab him. To shake him and tell him to pay attention to me, but I couldn't.

Art and I went and sat on a bench in the corner, in a place where I could keep an eye on CJ. We talked about writing and books, then music. He was bullish on George Michael's new album, and expounded on Wham!'s *Make It Big* album, both of which I loved.

"You like him," Art observed.

"Who? George Michael? Yeah."

"Your friend," he said. "You can't take your eyes off him."

"What? No . . . I just want to look out for him."

He chuckled. "Sure. You're a cute guy, Micah. But seeing as I want to take someone back to my dorm room tonight, and I don't feel like competing for your affections, I think I'd better take my leave."

I looked at him, ready to refute, but something in his eyes was final. He smiled and kissed me on the cheek. "In the next lifetime," he said, and the crowd swallowed him up as he walked off toward the back of the bar.

I sat there feeling the wetness of Art's kiss on my cheek, trying to douse out the part of my brain that was illuminating that saliva, as if it were a death kiss. That wasn't how you got it, but. Didn't matter. I took my mind off it by watching CJ's illuminated face from across the floor, and I wondered if what Art said was true.

How could it be? We definitely didn't do sex well together, and that was important, right?

But also, CJ. Who made me light up every time I talked to him. Who everyone important called my boyfriend. Everyone except me. And him.

"What's your sign?" a voice asked, and I smiled, because I was looking down and I'd lost track of CJ, and this was just the kind of cheesy line he'd give me.

But it wasn't him. It was a guy with a grizzly mustache and a ponytail. I was barely able to hide my lack of interest, and then I remembered things I'd heard CJ say to guys, and I realized I didn't have to.

"Yield," I said, and that did the job.

I rejoined CJ and Sammy, and I kept my eyes averted from CJ, lest he realize that I was fawning over him.

CJ smiled widely when he saw me. My heart jumped.

"Did you at least get a number?" he asked.

I shook my head, and both he and Sammy booed me.

"He wasn't the one," I said.

CJ guffawed. "The one? Mr. Right? This is Uncle Charlie's. Sometimes we settle for Mr. Right Now."

Sammy said, "You're young and cute. You know how many guys are looking at you?"

My shoulders tensed. I did not.

CJ and Sammy kept their flirting going, with CJ touching Sammy's arm repeatedly and Sammy throwing his head back and laughing even when CJ said stuff that was less than his typical A-game material. I decided I hated Sammy. I decided Sammy probably spent hours in front of the mirror, making sure he looked just right, and that in reality he wasn't really that good-looking, and also he was old, and at some point, someone was gonna have to tell CJ to cool it with the old guys. There were guys his age, guys who got who he really was inside, not whatever bullshit he was putting on to get whatever he thought he wanted.

Guys like me.

"Can you excuse me?" I asked. "Gonna go find the bathroom."

"Shake it more than three times and you're playing with it!" Sammy called out, but I kept my eyes hidden from them, because in a flash I realized that everyone was right.

I loved CJ. Messed up, occasionally extremely dishonest CJ.

Because he alone shined bright in my galaxy. Because there were so many guys there who were just fine, and I guess if I'd wanted sex, I could have made that happen.

But I didn't want sex. I wanted CJ. Whatever that meant. And yeah, at some point we'd try again, if he'd let me. That was what I wanted.

And the need in me pressed against my rib cage and shut out every other man in the place, and no one's eyes on me mattered, because I just had to get back to CJ.

Who wasn't there when I got back.

I looked to the door and I started pushing my way through. Why would he leave without—

"Micah? Where are you going?"

CJ had grabbed my shirt collar from behind. He was standing with Sammy, and I realized that I'd been looking in the wrong place. He'd been there all the time, and I chalked it up to the beer.

"Can I talk to you for a sec?" I asked.

He looked to Sammy. "Right now?"

"Yep."

"Where?"

"Outside."

"Um. Okay. Sammy, meet me outside in five?"

Sammy winked, and I wanted to claw his stupid eyes out.

We went outside, where a frigid wind gusted up the avenue, which was emptying of people, as it was now two. I had never been out this late before.

"So," I said as we huddled near the wall of Uncle Charlie's.

"So. Not to be awkward, but I'm gonna—"

"Don't," I said, my voice pleading.

"Micah."

"Don't, because you don't know him. And he doesn't know you, okay? It's dangerous. And . . . I just. He doesn't know how great you are. He never will."

CJ averted his eyes from me, and I moved my head to try to search them out again, to no avail.

I kept going anyway. Maybe it was easier not to see his eyes.

"I know we did sex badly, but. I love you, okay? You should be going home with me, not some old guy with Dippity-Do'd hair."

CJ looked me in the eye again. He held my gaze for a few seconds and then dropped his eyes to the ground.

"Micah," he repeated softly.

"CJ," I said, matching his tone.

"I love you too, kid. And I'd give this all up for you. But you don't want that. I'm damaged goods."

"No, you aren't."

His voice, when he responded, lacked a certain pretense that had always come with his voice, every single time he spoke. It was like this was the voice under the bullshit. "Yeah, I am. And it does no good to pretend that I'm not." He crossed his arms over his skinny chest.

I wanted to tell him that I knew. That I didn't understand fully, but I knew. And I loved him anyway. And I wanted to save him, save him from himself. I wanted to be the one who tamed CJ, who took that wild fire in him and didn't tamp it out, exactly, but more like focused it into something brilliant, a diamond that shined in a way that could be seen by everyone, by more than just me.

"I don't care," I said.

He blinked several times and chewed his lip. A cab rolled down Greenwich. Across the street, a woman with a buzz cut leaned down to pick up after her poodle.

"I don't know how," he whispered, his voice still painfully un-CJ-like. "If I knew how, I would. You don't know the whole story. Really, Micah. Go find yourself someone who isn't me. Who hasn't—who likes himself, okay?"

Sammy came out then, and CJ's entire demeanor changed. Quickly he said to me, "Call you tomorrow, buddy?"

I wasn't CJ. My demeanor couldn't just shift on the spot. So I said nothing. He gave an imperceptible nod that I took to mean *I understand you can't play this game.* And then they walked off toward Seventh Avenue.

As they walked away from me. I watched their silhouettes retreat in the distance and it felt like a part of me was splitting off.

When I could no longer see CJ's skinny frame in the distance, I had this feeling that it was like a mirage had come and gone. Like I'd never see him again. And I wondered if that were true, if I'd be able to handle it.

CHAPTER TWENTY

SILENT MORNING

December 1987

When I got home, it was nearly three a.m., and my mother was waiting in the same chair as the night before, my knapsack in her lap, her face a mask of fury—lips so tight they could rip apart, eyebrows so high they were almost cartoonlike.

"We came down to the theater to check in on you," she said.

"What? Why would you do that?" I marched right by her and she popped up from her chair and followed me into my room. Their bedroom door was closed. Dad must have been asleep.

"You reek of cigarette smoke. I did it precisely because of this. Because ever since your little announcement, you've been impossible. Are you becoming a drug addict? A—a—*smoker?*"

I wanted to laugh, because the way she said it made it sound like the second was worse than the first, but I held my tongue.

When I got to my room, I turned around and told her, "I'm becoming a person, Mom. I'm becoming someone who doesn't live for his mommy and daddy, and I like it, okay? I'm not twelve anymore."

"Well, you can certainly count out having your little friend stay here for Christmas."

"What? You can't do that!"

"The hell I can't. I never want you to see him again, because he's breaking you."

"HE'S FIXING ME!" I yelled, not worrying about waking up my dad. Someone else had taken over my mind and my body and I loved it so much and I hated it so much. I wanted to go back to before, and I never wanted to go back there ever again.

"You weren't broken," she said, lowering her voice. I could tell she was really upset by the dispassionate way she was speaking.

"You wouldn't know. You don't have an f-ing clue, Mom, if I was broken or not. You just think you know exactly who I am, but you didn't know the biggest thing, so maybe you didn't know me at all."

"Well, if this is you fixed, give me broken."

I slammed the door in her face.

The next morning was a Sunday, and I stayed in bed until ten. My head hurt from the combination of alcohol and screaming and broken heart. I didn't want to deal with my mom or my dad. I didn't want to think too much about CJ walking off with that Sammy guy. I didn't want to feel anything that I was feeling.

I would have called Deena, at least, but my phone was gone, of course.

I put on the second Missing Persons album, the one called

Rhyme & Reason. I hadn't listened to it yet, but CJ had told me it was more somber and mature, and the black-and-white cover—Dale draped over a piano holding a microphone—made that pretty clear. I placed the needle at the start and got back into bed, snuggled up under my navy blanket. From the very first note, I could tell the songs featured more heavy drums and guitars than the first one, and the magical, colorful tone of the first album had been replaced by something more adult, more pensive and introspective. Lying there listening to the songs, I felt for the first time in my life acutely like an adult. My shoulders felt strong and manly. My legs felt powerful.

Even though being grounded wasn't a very adult thing, being in love with someone who thinks they're too screwed up to love you back felt like it entered older territory, and I wondered if all my adulthood would feel like this, if I'd have this fire in the pit of my stomach always, or if this was just a transitional phase.

The first song I really liked was "Surrender Your Heart." Ethereal keyboards drifted through my room from the speakers sitting on either side of my stereo. The tempo was slower than anything they'd done off the first album, but it was mellow, a little melancholy, which was perfect for today. Not to mention the lyrics:

> *Surrender your heart.*
> *I don't know why but you never give in to me.*

I wanted to call CJ and talk to him about it. I wondered if he loved this album as much as the first. I couldn't imagine that I ever would, but I admired the artistry just the same. But if he said he did, maybe I would learn to love it that much, too.

I'm damaged goods.

He'd said that. What did it mean?

What had happened to CJ? And would he ever tell me about it?

When I was a kid, I saw this episode of *Gilligan's Island* after school one day. Or I saw the first part of it. It seemed like they were finally going to get off the island, and I was riveted. And then my mom made me go do my homework. I pleaded with her, to no avail. And I never saw the rest of the episode, and though I know they never got off the island—at least I think they never did—I wanted to know what had happened to keep them there.

This was like that, times a thousand. My mom was canceling a show that I needed to see the end of, as if my life depended on it. And there was no way she was going to understand that.

When I finally ventured out of my room, my mom and dad were sitting on the living room couch, waiting for me. I trudged in and sat opposite them on the chair where Rick had sat the night he'd stayed over.

"Well, first things first," my mother said, her forehead creased more than I'd ever seen it. "You're going to call the Lortel right now, and you're going to quit."

"Mom! No!"

"Micah. Yes," she said, dead serious. "You clearly can't be trusted, and I don't think they've been a very good influence on you. We spoke to your boss, Felicia, yesterday, and I think what she's been doing with you is . . . unfathomable. It's proselytizing youth."

"Mom!" I looked to my dad, who was slouched on the couch and not speaking. Proselytizing? That was what churches did. That was homophobic, and I knew it, and I thought he knew it, too. Rick was gay and his best friend. He had to know that Felicia was being my support. Right?

If my mom could only have seen the number of times Felicia had counseled me to use condoms, how she'd steered the college kid away from me. If anything, she should have been praising Felicia for her role in my life.

But I couldn't imagine how I could get that point across. My mother had planted another flag, and it was as good as done.

So in front of my parents, I called Felicia at the theater.

"Hey," I said. "It's Micah."

"Hey there. Are you coming in today or are you grounded until the next millennium?"

"I'm not coming in ever again, apparently. I'm sitting here with my parents and they're making me quit."

"Oh, Micah! No. Are you okay?"

"I don't know. Not really, not at the moment."

"You call me. Anytime. Hear? And you're okay just the way you are—don't let them tell you otherwise. Right?"

"Right."

"You sound really sad."

"I dunno. Gotta go."

"Call me, Micah."

"Okay."

When I got off, my mom explained that until winter

break, my life was going to consist of going to school and coming home. There would be no telephone. There would be no going to Deena's. And if I even thought of breaking the rules and going to see CJ again, I would begin to understand just what being grounded for an entire school semester felt like.

"Do you hear me?"

Do you care? I thought, finishing the line the way Dale Bozzio did.

"Yes," I said, pushing down on the scratchy couch fabric with my thumb. I wished I could tear the whole thing apart.

The rest of the day was spent in my room, where my feelings darkened and spread. I felt in my throat this twinge of remorse, for stepping too far over the line, and humiliation seized up in my chin from the grounding, and down lower, in my legs, I felt like kicking something, because even if I couldn't explain what it was, something good had been happening there. Yes, maybe I'd gone too far, staying out so late, but also there was something necessary in me standing up for once, in trying new things. And my mom was thwarting something essential, and there was no way to make her understand that this was in a way killing a part of me that couldn't be killed. And behind my eyes, so much panic, fear of what CJ would feel when he tried to reach me and I didn't pick up. The idea that he'd think I was leaving him, which I'd promised not to do.

It was much too much to deal with.

Somehow all the feelings got lost in translation when I told Deena at school the next day.

"They took away your phone?" she said. "Seriously? But you just got it!"

We were hurrying toward homeroom. Hurriedly, I told her, "I literally can't do anything. Home and school, home and school, that's all."

"Well, I guess there's a downside to befriending some hustler. Two downsides, actually, because befriending a hustler in and of itself is one."

I didn't bother to defend him to her.

There wasn't any point.

I planned on calling him from a pay phone on my walk home from school.

But when I walked outside after the final bell rang, I found my mother waiting for me.

She didn't trust me at all.

The whole walk home, we didn't say a word. If I was going to be forced into silence with CJ, then she'd get my silence as well.

As the week went on, I was forced to break that silence, and the conversations at home got a bit repetitive.

"You have to let me call CJ. He's gonna think I'm mad at him," I said on Tuesday.

"Absolutely not," my mother responded.

On Wednesday: "He probably thinks I hate him."

"Perhaps he will take this hardship, this lack of knowing, as an opportunity for growth."

On Thursday: "What if he thinks I'm dead?"

"It seems as though CJ may be jumping to conclusions, if that's what he thinks."

On Friday: "Please? Pleeaasse?"

"No. Noooo."

On Saturday morning: "Just one call. You can be in the room. I really just want him to know I'm okay."

She sighed. "Fine. One call."

I jumped off the couch, where I'd been sitting, and ran into their bedroom to get the phone. Dad was on the rowing machine, getting his daily fifteen minutes in.

"You wore her down," he observed as I grabbed the phone.

"I did."

He kept rowing. "You gotta be smarter, Micah. Going out late isn't a crime. But after she was already so upset?"

I put up a finger as if to say, *one minute*. But really I just meant that I needed to make a call, and anyway he didn't really have that kind of authority over me. Mom ruled the roost.

I pulled the phone into the living room, where Mom was sitting.

"Connell/Gorman residence, kindly start speaking," Jack said, his voice softer than usual.

"Is CJ there? It's Micah."

"He's sleeping."

"Well, wake him up. Please."

"This should be fun," Jack said. A few seconds later, I heard mumblings of a conversation and then the phone being picked up again.

"Hello?"

"Hey," I said.

"I'm sorry, who is this? I'm not familiar with this voice."

My heart sank. "Ha ha," I said. "I'm sorry."

"It's totally fine. I mean, I thought you were the one person I could count on to stick around, and I guess I was wrong. Oh well. I'm wrong a lot. Not a big deal."

I suddenly hated my mother with a passion.

"I was grounded. I'm still grounded. My mom is right here with me, but I finally am allowed one phone call. Believe me. I wanted to call you."

He snorted. "Ever heard of a pay phone?"

"You have no idea the level of parental surveillance that's involved at this house. I was walked home from school."

He chuckled lightly. "You poor thing."

"CJ," I said. "Come on. Are you okay?"

"Oh, Micah. I'm always fine. You think not calling me for a week is gonna upset me? Please. Nothing upsets me at this point. I'm okay, you're okay, we're all totally okay. It really makes no difference to my life whether you're in it or not."

I was stunned silent.

He exhaled. "That was unkind of me. Sorry, Micah. This has been a really shitty week, and I have something I kind of need to tell you, and I can't tell you over the phone, and you're grounded, I guess, so I guess I'll have to hold on to this for a little longer, which sucks, but what's new? Lots of things suck."

I was still not ready to talk, but I worried if I didn't say anything our friendship might end.

"It's okay," I said, lying. "I know you didn't mean it."

"I never mean anything, apparently," he said.

Before I could reply to that, my mother said sternly, "Time's up. He knows you're alive."

"I heard that," CJ said. "Give her my love. I'll see you on the other side."

He hung up before my mom could force me to do it.

"Feel better now?" my mother asked.

I didn't give her the pleasure of admitting that no, I did not.

CHAPTER TWENTY-ONE

TRUE COLORS

December 1987

The next day, my mom thought long and hard about whether she and my father would be going up to an annual Chanukah party at Old Oaks. In the end an accord was reached. They would go, and Rick would come into the city and watch over me like I was a child.

"Are you going to do this the rest of my life? Just not make plans, or hire a babysitter?"

"Just till Christmas break," my mother said. "Just another couple of weeks."

Rick showed up around eleven in all his Rick-ness, looking like the straightest gay guy in the history of the world. He wore a white Lacoste shirt with the arms of a pink sweater tied in front of it, his hair parted in the middle. My face got tight seeing him, as if it were seeing an uncomfortable vision of where my life was heading if I didn't break out, and soon. And at the same time, I was so grateful, because I had a plan, and Rick was going to be much easier to persuade than my mom or dad.

"I heard you came out," he said as he made himself comfortable on the chair opposite the couch.

My shoulders tensed. I prayed he hadn't gotten the whole story.

"One day, when you have a lover, he's gonna love the story of you coming out on the john."

I turned bright red.

He laughed. "C'mon, it's funny. But the bottom line—no pun intended—is it sounds like it went well?"

I shrugged. It was hard to think of anything as okay right now.

We talked about nothing for a bit, and I waited about fifteen minutes until after my parents were gone to bring up the subject.

"I need your help," I said.

Rick automatically shook his head. "Oh no. I promised your parents—"

"This is a very minor thing, but it's a huge deal to me. It's my friend CJ."

He frowned. "This the boy who's been causing all the strife around here?"

"It's not his fault. In fact . . . never mind. The point is, something isn't right with him. Rick, if I tell you something, do you promise not to tell them?"

He laughed. "No."

"Okay, I get it. But let's just say CJ is in a bad situation. And he's my best friend. Yesterday when my mom finally let me call him, he got all mysterious and said he needed to tell me something. It was really weird, like he didn't sound okay at all. I'm afraid he's in trouble." I pursed my lips and my eyes searched the room. It was a bit of an acting job, to be sure. I just needed to see him.

He shook his head. "What are you asking me to do? Because I'm not allowing you out of my sight."

"You don't have to. I just need to call him, and what if I tell him to meet me in Riverside Park? You could watch me from the window. I'm serious. This isn't me running. I'm just trying to make sure my friend is okay. He's not that okay to begin with. He's seen some things. I worry about him."

Rick furrowed his unibrow. "What are you doin' to me, Micah? I don't want to piss off your mother."

"You'll see me the whole time."

He took a deep breath and walked into the other room, returning with the telephone. "Worse than that," he said. "I'll be there. I'll give you privacy, but you're not leaving the apartment without me."

That was good enough for me. I grabbed the phone, called CJ, and within a minute, a plan was hatched.

I don't think I had really taken a full breath since I'd last seen CJ, because when I saw him ambling down Riverside Drive from Seventy-Ninth, my whole body felt reenergized. Even with the thing he'd said on the phone the day before, it took everything I could not to dash off and hug him and run off with him. But I wasn't going to do that to Rick.

CJ wore a smirk and a new platinum-blond crew cut. "You're a sight for sore eyes," he said.

"No kidding," I told him, and we hugged slightly awkwardly.

"Is that him?" CJ pointed toward Rick, who was sitting about fifty feet away on a park bench, reading the Sunday *Times*.

"Yep."

"You're right. I *don't* want to sleep with every old guy."

I laughed. "Progress."

"Yeah. So. I just wanna apologize again. For yesterday. I know this is going to be a shock to you, but I'm not one hundred percent great at emotions. I tend to lash out when I feel, whatever. And yeah, you not calling during a really hard week—I know it wasn't really your fault—but it really hurt me."

"I'm sorry," I said. "I wanted to call you the minute I got home, but I no longer have a phone and they've been basically babysitting me."

"Imagine that. Parents with boundaries," he said.

I knew what that meant, but also I didn't really get it. I mean, who asks for more boundaries from their parents?

"I guess," I said.

"So, a story. This week, this kid started at the Gaiety. Says he's eighteen, but there's not a chance in the world. Sixteen tops, and a young sixteen. I'm watching him and it's like, I'm completely horrified, because he's so young and he thinks he's so in charge, and he just isn't. Twice I gave him condoms and he gave me this blank look, like he didn't know why. It hurt my heart. Because he clearly doesn't know what's going on, or if he does, he doesn't care. And he told me the story of his first time, and he tells it like it's sexy, but . . ."

CJ swallowed and looked away.

"It wasn't sexy. He was thirteen, and the guy was thirty, and anyway. The point is that I asked him if he'd ever been tested for HIV, and he said no. It broke my heart, because he's so young, and no one cares. It made me almost want to stop dancing, because he's getting used. I'm eighteen and I can take care of myself. This kid may think he can, but he can't."

He paused.

"Wow," I said, a little relieved. I had been scared he was gonna tell me something bad had happened to him.

"Yeah. And, well. This is the hard part, because you have been so nice and I'm not sure I deserve nice, and there's one more lie, Micah."

My stomach flipped.

"I've never been tested, either."

"What?"

He lowered his head and chewed on his lip. "Well, I did technically get tested, last year. But I never went in for the results. I mean, if there was some kind of medicine or a cure, but there isn't. So finding out is kind of fatal."

My head went fuzzy. I thought about all the things he'd told me. I tried to catalog all the things, and then my mind was flooded with memories of us at the train tracks. And we'd used a condom, but still. We'd kissed. And this was a death sentence. And he hadn't been tested.

"Please tell me you're careful," I said.

"I am. Truly. I've been careful every time, but." He stood up and adjusted his pants and sat down again.

"But?"

He sighed. A jogger ran by and CJ ran his hand through his hair.

"I haven't told you this because I haven't told anyone, okay? And it was the kid's story that made me realize that I'm a fucking idiot, okay?"

"Okay," I said, my face hurting because my jaw felt so tense. "What happened, CJ? Just tell me."

He took a deep breath.

"Back when she was alive, my mom and Jack used to take me to East Hampton in the summers. This was a bunch of years ago. It was the summer before ninth grade, 1984, and I was a live wire. I was fourteen; I had just hit puberty and I was incredibly curious. Think me with a double portion of hormones."

"Oh boy."

"We used to go to this beach called Two Mile Hollow. It's a private beach and really nice, and we had a permit to go there. One time, as we're driving home, Jack says something like, 'Les boys were out in force. All the way to the left, if you walk.'

"My mother chuckled.

"Something about that stirred my interest. I didn't really know what it meant, so I asked.

"'The boys who like other boys. *Playin' for the other team.* Those boys.'

"I knew that was Jack's way of saying gay, and I knew I was gay, even if I had never told a soul. Once he said that, I couldn't get the idea out of my head! And I was so scared the next morning, when I told them I was going for a bike ride, that they knew I was going to check it out. But they didn't seem to care, or say anything, so probably they didn't know?

"I'd never met a gay person. I didn't know how. I was fourteen. I had seen porn because my friend Casey had lent me a dirty magazine, and I had found myself always looking at the guys instead of the girls. I just needed to know for sure.

"So I biked six miles to the beach by myself. I used to do a lot of stuff by myself. Parental supervision, anyone? And when I got there, I walked left along the ocean, kicking at the waves, glancing toward the beach whenever I could without being too obvious. I got to the part where the crowd shallowed out, and suddenly it was just men, mostly couples, and then, as I walked farther, the men on towels didn't seem to have bathing suits on! I think my eyes could have popped out of their sockets. I noticed a man running toward the water as I passed. He was totally naked. I turned around and he waved at me. I waved back but kept walking. I knew that it probably wasn't a good idea, because he was a full adult and I was fourteen, but I was really curious, you know? So after I went a bit farther, I turned and I walked back to his towel.

"'Do you know what time it is?' I asked the guy. He was naked and, let's say, aroused.

"I won't bore you with the details, but basically I was like, 'I've never talked to a gay person before. Are you gay?' But he was pretty single-minded in his interest. Not much for small talk. Any talk, really. He told me his address and invited me to stop by later.

"I left the beach and biked home thinking no, obviously I can't do that. He was older than my stepdad. But I had braces on my teeth, and I was ugly and skinny and I couldn't imagine the next time I'd have that opportunity again, so I . . . well, I made this thing up about going to the movies with my friends in town, even though I didn't have friends in town. My mom by this time had checked out. Jack hadn't, but he was in vacation mode and I think he was just happy to get rid of me. He drove me to town, and I walked to this guy's house on the edge of town.

"I think it's kind of funny now. I was thinking we'd talk, but we definitely didn't. He took me inside and he laid me down on his bed and he did whatever he wanted to me. When it got to the last part, I have to admit, I was like, I don't see how that adult-size thing will, you know, fit. I said as much and he told me not to worry and he put me on my belly and, um. Yeah, didn't fit. But that didn't exactly stop him and I screamed and I cried and he kind of held me down and did what he did and then he pulled out and said, 'You're bleeding,' and I went to the bathroom and sat there and was like, *Well, I guess that's sex.*

"So it wasn't the greatest first time ever. And I think it colored everything, you know?"

His face looked tight. His neck. I could see inside him, almost, and I couldn't look away.

"I mean, to the extent that I am self-reflective, which is not a ton, I see it has definitely impacted me. Like, you're not dancing at the Gaiety, I am. It definitely introduced me to a different side of the gay world than I would have known otherwise, and while I took a year off after that, when I started up again, it was always with adults, like my sophomore English teacher, which is a story for another time. Also, I don't do that getting penetrated thing almost ever, because, yeah, no thanks.

"So when I say that I didn't have adult supervision, I kinda mean it. Like, who lets their fourteen-year-old son go bike riding alone all day? Who leaves their kid alone at home all weekend? They did that, too.

"But also. Um. He didn't use a condom, because. I don't know. It was 1984. I knew about condoms and that you should use them, but I didn't know as much as I know now, obviously. I asked him if he had AIDS, and he laughed. 'Would I be hanging out at the beach if I had AIDS?' he said. I didn't know if that made sense, but he was an adult, you know? So we did it, even though I didn't know if a person could have the virus and not look sick.

"And the point is, when I told you that I'd been tested a bunch of times, I lied. I did get tested that one time last year, but obviously the lack of follow-through means it doesn't really count. So I lied to you about that, but I've been thinking, and honest to God, I don't think there's any other lie left, anything I haven't told you. You said you loved me, and I don't know if you really love me, but I figure I can't keep saying I'm damaged goods without telling you what that means. And if you want to walk away and cut your losses I will totally understand. But. I will tell you anything and everything if you'll still be my friend. Because you are a good friend, Micah, and I want to tell you everything."

I was frozen. No part of me could move. I wanted to hug him. I wanted to walk away. I wanted to never, ever leave.

So I said what was true. "I've never used condoms with Napoleon or Lucas."

His mouth shot open. "Are you serious?"

I nodded.

"Why would you do that?"

"We're in high school. I am pretty sure they've never been with anyone else. I haven't. Other than you."

"You're not at risk from me. We used a condom, and you can't get it from kissing. I told you that."

That may have all been true, but honestly? I was now more worried about what I did with CJ than what I had done with the other two guys. And that was something I was gonna have to keep to myself.

"Well, thanks for telling me," I said.

"Ouch. Cold."

"I'm sorry I don't know how to process life and death in like two seconds."

"I get it."

"We have to get tested. Both of us. You know that, right?"

He closed his eyes and sat down. He put his head in his hands and he sighed loudly and dramatically.

"Yeah," he said. "And thanks, by the way."

"Whatever for?"

"For the 'we.' "

CHAPTER TWENTY-TWO

WHAT HAVE I DONE TO DESERVE THIS?

December 1987

We had to wait until my period of being grounded ended, so it wasn't until the Monday before Christmas that CJ and I went to the Gay Men's Health Crisis offices in Chelsea to get our HIV tests. I told my mom I had to buy presents for Deena and other friends, and she was too tired to insist on coming along.

The nurse, a brassy redhead with a cougar tattoo on her right forearm, drew my blood, counseled me on safer sex, and then delivered the fantastic punch line.

"You'll call in two weeks for your results. Merry Christmas and Happy New Year."

"What?" I almost yelled. No way. They couldn't make me wait for two whole weeks. That was inhumane.

"Two weeks," she repeated as she deposited the needle in the red medical waste bin. "I know it sucks. But look at the bright side."

I waited for her to continue. "Which is?" I asked after she didn't.

"I just meant it like the saying. You know. 'Look at the bright side.'"

CJ and I met up in the waiting room, both with our elbows wrapped in gauze.

"Two weeks," I said.

"I figured you knew." He opened the door and we walked out onto Twenty-Fourth Street.

"I did not."

"Chelsea Square Diner?"

It sounded as good as any other place to begin the interminable waiting period.

We ordered cheeseburgers with steak fries and sat in a booth in the back, and we proceeded to have the world's most awkward conversation.

"What if I have it? We, I mean," I asked, covering my fries with ketchup.

His eyes went wide, and that communicated fairly well the macabre truth of what that would mean.

"You're not gonna have it. Neither of us will. I had risky sex with one stranger, basically. You had it with two non-strangers. It's gonna be fine," he said, but his tone was uncharacteristically checked out, un-CJ-like. "I haven't had any symptoms and it's been three and a half years. I think it's probably fine."

It sounded to me like he was trying to convince himself.

He shook his head, and I sat there, wishing I knew what to say to make the butterflies in my gut stop fluttering so wildly.

"What in the world would I even tell my mother? She'd

kill me before AIDS did. I just. I can't believe this. Any of this. How did this happen?"

CJ threw his hands up. "Don't look at me! You put yourself here before you even met me. No condom? What were you thinking?"

I wanted to scream at him. I wanted to rewind to a place where I didn't know CJ and I never had to worry about AIDS, and that thought was so unfair that it made me hate myself. My choices had brought me here. Not CJ.

"You look pissed," he observed before he took a bite of cheeseburger.

"I'm fine," I said. "Don't worry about it."

We ate in somber silence for a bit. I was thinking about that night on Greenwich Avenue, when I told him I loved him, and he responded by going home with Sammy. And maybe he was "damaged goods," but that didn't make it hurt any less. The tension grew, and I silently said goodbye for the zillionth time to CJ. Who didn't love me. Who had introduced me to a world that was undeniably scary. Who had, in the time I'd known him, brought me from where I was to this place. Even if it wasn't his fault, here we were.

He took a pickle spear off the silver tray, the communal one that had been on the table when we'd sat down. He started to massage the pickle lasciviously. I cracked up a tiny bit despite myself. Then he licked it slowly while looking in my eyes. Finally, with the sexiest of looks on his face, he started to slowly insert it into his eye.

That got me.

"Ow!" he said. "Pickle juice in my eye. Major ow!"

"Why are you like this? Who hurt you?" I asked.

He gave me that toothy smile and raised his eyes twice in quick succession.

"For once in my life, I'm sitting with someone who actually knows the answer to that question."

My heart melted, and reality smashed me in the face, in a good way. Here I was with CJ, whom I still happened to love, on a Monday afternoon, at a diner in Chelsea, watching him eye fuck himself with a pickle.

"Is there some way we can just start at zero and have a mass apology and be okay? I'm tired of being weird with you. I want to go back to before the weirdness," I said.

He fluttered his fingers in a majestic manner, then rotated his palms above his head as if it were some sort of religious cleansing ceremony.

"We are hereby back at zero," he said, and we shared our first real smile in a while.

We talked about positive things, pun intended. What we'd do when we both found out that we were negative. Unspoken was my out-there love for him. We put it away; we didn't discuss. Instead, I told him about my future as a movie director. He told me about becoming a *Solid Gold* dancer, only back in the early 80s, when their dances were more innocent.

"Back before everything was so sexualized," said the guy who had just publicly made love to a pickle.

"I totally get it," I responded, and I grabbed a pickle, put it between my lips, and sucked it in.

That night, when I started to go a little stir crazy with no one knowing about the test, I waited until my parents were fully distracted by Barbara Walters and finally used the business card Rick had given me. It took him a few moments for him to figure out who I was, even when I said my first and last name. Then he was like, *Oh!*

"Remember when I asked if you'd keep a secret and you said no?" I asked him.

He laughed. "I do."

"Well, what if I told you I have something going on that I really need to talk about, but I can't talk to my parents about it because they'd totally freak, but a gay man would probably not freak out as much if I told them?"

"How about lunch tomorrow?" he asked. "Can you come by my office?"

"I can and I will," I said.

Rick's office was located on East Fifty-Fourth Street, a part of town I never went to because I never had a need to be among the yuppies dashing for lunch in between meetings in impossibly tall skyscrapers. I looked around at all the businesspeople rushing who knows where, and I prayed to God I would never be one of them, that I'd be talented enough to make a living as a producer or a director or something like that.

Or marry someone who could make enough money so I'd never have to yuppify.

Rick looked relatively sharp in a gray suit and blue tie, his hair shiny and perfectly parted. He gave me a slightly uncomfortable hello, told his secretary to hold his calls, and took me to Jackson Hole on East Sixty-Fourth for ginormous burgers.

"So," he said once we were settled and ordered. "Spill."

I took a sip of my Dr. Brown's cream soda. "Yesterday, I went and got an HIV test."

He exhaled and closed his eyes. "Okay," he said once he could look at me again. "Is there reason to be concerned?"

I felt frustration rise into my temples like heat. "Well, yeah. I mean, if it's positive, I die."

"No," he said. "I mean, is it likely you've been infected? Have you been unsafe?"

I bit my lip. "With two kids from school."

He sucked in his teeth. "How unsafe?"

I told him the details, which was super weird. We barely knew each other, and at the same time, it felt good getting rid of the secret.

"You into them is less risky, but not without risk," he said. "And what do you know about them?"

"I think they're both virgins, but then again, how would I know that? I was a virgin until Lucas, and then I wasn't when I was with Napoleon, but we never talked about it. Who's to say they aren't doing the same?"

He nodded. "True. Have you had other contacts?"

I told him about CJ, and to my relief, he echoed CJ on the risks.

"If you got HIV from kissing a boy or having oral sex with a condom, you'd be the first, I'm sure. That's just not how it's transmitted."

I ate a fry, relieved to hear someone say it, and also grateful to CJ, for rolling that condom on me.

"So what happens next? I ask. "I'm supposed to call, like, the day after New Year's for my results. What if I'm positive?"

"First off, I don't think you will be. But if you are, we'll talk to your parents about it. It's not easy to talk about, believe me."

He sipped his milkshake.

My heart slipped into my throat.

"Wait." I said.

"Yes, Micah."

"You have it?"

"I'm HIV-positive. Which is different from having AIDS. That's where I am, for now."

"Oh," I said, and my hands and feet went numb.

He shoveled fries around his plate with his fork. "I'm fine, so far. Found out last year. I got tested and I was positive. My lover, Gabriel, took the news worse than I did, even though he tested negative. He left me."

"Oh."

"Oh well," he said, but his tone told me it was anything but "oh well."

"Does my dad know?"

Rick shook his head.

"Oh," I repeated.

"Yeah. Not sure how that would go. People get pretty irrational about HIV and AIDS. You can't get it from casual contact, but as soon as I tell people, they stop wanting to play racquetball with me."

I tried to imagine what that would be like. If I turned out to be positive. Would Deena stop wanting to hang out with me?

Would my parents?

I was pretty sure CJ would be okay with it.

For all the people in my life calling him a troublemaker or dicey, that fact had to be worth something.

Sitting and talking to Rick was better than I thought, once I got used to it. He was kinda funny for an old guy, and he really listened to me. That was nice in one way, and terrible in another.

Because this guy I'd just figured out was nice was probably going to die of AIDS.

A Christmas Eve call with CJ:

"I thought you were dancing tonight?" I asked.

"Yeah, I took the night off. The idea of spending Christmas Eve dancing for strangers struck me as a little too depressing. Thought instead I'd sit in the apartment alone, since Jack is off skiing."

"Yes, that sounds way less depressing."

He laughed. "Well, at least I'm not also waiting for a test result that will tell me if I'm going to die before I turn twenty-five."

I couldn't laugh back.

"Nothing?" he asked. "C'mon. Give me something. If I don't laugh, I'll cry."

"Yeah, not my favorite Christmas Eve, either."

"I thought you're Jewish?"

"Yeah, but usually I go over to Deena's. Her family does stuff. But I can't be with her right now. She'd know in half a second that something was wrong, and I'd spill the beans, and I just can't handle that."

He sighed. "Let's play a game."

"What's the game?"

"Future Christmas wishes."

"Ooh, I like that."

"You have thirty seconds to describe the perfect Christmas in ten years. The best one wins."

Immediately, despite everything, despite the fact that our lives had just become somehow existential, my thought was, *With you. You and me. Someplace safe. Somewhere where death cannot get us.*

"You go first," I said.

"Okay, okay. Well, I guess I live in Los Angeles, because my memoir, ghostwritten by Jackie Collins, has been turned into a movie, with Tom Cruise playing me, of course. I'm sitting in my swimming pool, looking out at the Hollywood Hills. My house is huuuuge, and there's a big Christmas tree, with zillions of presents under it. The phone is ringing off the hook because *Entertainment Tonight* and *People* want to interview me, but I'm like, *No, not again.* And my houseman, Thomas, brings me hot chocolate by the pool and asks if there's anything else he can do for me before he heads up to bed, and then the gay porn music starts, and, you know . . . duh dah duh dah."

I laugh. "Sounds perfect."

"Okay, yours."

"Okay," I say, finishing up the fry I was chewing. "I have a lover and we're happy. We live in the mountains somewhere, maybe Vermont. We have a nice house and maybe a dog, and because it's Christmas Eve, we invite our neighbors over to sing carols by the tree. I'm still Jewish but celebrate Christmas as a national holiday, of course. There's a lot of laughter and warmth, I guess. Yeah."

He was quiet for a while, and we shared a nice silence, all things considered.

"I like yours better," he said.

CHAPTER TWENTY-THREE

DESTINATION UNKNOWN

January 1988

Worst Christmas and New Year's ever.

Until it was the best.

I rang in the New Year with Dick Clark and the Times Square ball dropping, while CJ kicked off 1988 dancing on a dingy stage, trying to move his feet quicker than a disease that either was or wasn't inside him, barely missing him thus far, or already silently scheming to take him out.

On New Year's Day, I went to Deena's for the world's most awkward brunch.

"So what's actually going on with you?" she asked over mushroom frittatas and mimosas. "You've been ultra-weird all break. Is this some sort of CJ drama? How come I think it absolutely is? You weren't like this before CJ."

I shrugged. "It's nothing."

"But it isn't, is it? Some shit is going down, and you used to tell me everything, and now you tell me nothing, and it sucks. Are we even still friends?"

My heart pulsed. I didn't want to lose Deena—any more than I already had, anyway. Ever since that night at the Gaiety, something had come between us, and it wasn't actually CJ.

But the idea that I could lose her if I told her what was actually going on was too much.

"My dad's best friend has HIV," I said.

She stopped chewing. "What?"

"Yeah," I said. "I've sort of been leaning on him because I need some adult advice about some things, and he told me. It's not exactly the best Christmas gift, knowing that. My dad doesn't even know, and that's kind of hard to keep from him."

"Jesus, Micah," she said. "That sucks."

"Yeah. It all fucking sucks. Did you know Ronald Reagan didn't even say the word *AIDS* for *years* while tens of thousands of people died from it? All because those people are mostly gay or drug users."

She wiped her mouth on a napkin and seemed to consider this. "I feel so bad for people who got AIDS way back before we knew how it was transmitted. That's so horrible. At the same time, can you believe people are still getting it? It's like, if there's a disease that could kill you, maybe keep it in your pants, right?"

Sometimes my hair caught fire. Like I could feel my scalp heating to a scald, and my choices were to say something or to say nothing.

And I always said nothing, because in a way she was right? And in a way totally wrong. But it wasn't something I could explain in simple, logical words. The level of wrong was blistering my forehead, and if I even said a single word to convey that, our friendship could end.

"Yeah," I said. "Sure."

That afternoon Napoleon called. Unlike with CJ, I'd been able to tell him in school that I'd been grounded.

I just hadn't bothered to tell him when I was ungrounded.

"What'cha up to?" he asked now.

"Nothing," I said, wishing I hadn't picked up. This was a call I didn't need today, given that tomorrow I was going to find out if I had the virus that caused AIDS.

"You wanna come over? My parents are out."

And I suddenly felt so guilty, as if the weight of the world were on my chest. Like poor Napoleon, who I may have given AIDS. Except that, in reality, he could have given it to me and I didn't even have the guts to say anything about it. "I can't today," I said. "Still grounded."

"Oh well. No big deal."

Yeah, I thought. *No big deal at all.*

I went down to the Lortel an hour before showtime that night to see Felicia for the first time since everything had gone down.

"Oh, honey," she said when I told her what had happened, and she came over and sat next to me and put her arm around me.

"Yeah."

"You're almost certainly gonna be okay. I mean, have you been doing things you haven't told me?"

I shook my head. I hadn't told her specifically about Napoleon and Lucas, and I wasn't going to tell her now because if she freaked out right now, honestly? I wasn't sure I could take it.

"Call me as soon as you find out either way, okay?" she asked.

I nodded. Then I asked, "How's Walter?"

She sighed deeply and looked at the floor. "Hospice care," she said.

"Shit," I said.

"Yeah." She closed her eyes, and then her face contorted, and suddenly Felicia, my rock, was crying. "He looked so scared when we left last night. Like, he was pleading with us not to leave him there with the hospice worker, and we kept delaying leaving, but at some point, you know, we had to go. I can't get that look in his eyes out of my head. It's absolutely haunting me."

For the first time since I'd known her, I put my arm around Felicia.

"You're a really good friend to him," I said.

"Yeah. But I can't fix it. I want to be able to fix it, and I can't."

I squeezed her into me and said nothing, and for a full minute I let her cry, which made my eyes tear up, and I wondered if all the death and despair would ever come to an end.

Finally, I spoke up. "Is there anything I can do?"

She put her head on my shoulder. "You're growing up, kiddo. We got this. Me and Raina and several other friends have put together a schedule, and we have it covered. His folks are around, too. That's really sweet of you to offer, though. Thank you."

"That's what friends are for," I said.

I took the subway up to the Gaiety. The lady buzzed me in as if I were now a regular.

"Did I ever tell you the Italian tourist story?" CJ asked

after we'd hugged. I was backstage with him before he went on. Sarge, this steroided-looking guy about ten years older than us with pronounced bags under his eyes, was busy putting tight jeans on his stocky legs, over his G-string.

"Oh good, a story," I said.

"Yeah, this is a good one. I'm sixteen. I meet an older guy on the street after school. We're talking on the corner down from our building—I know, not a great idea—about meeting up later in Columbus Park. I look to my left and see my mom walking toward us, coming home from work. This was about three months before she got sick. I panic. I tell the guy and he says, 'Don't worry, I'm a good actor.'

"So my mom, who definitely has seen us, walks toward us with a blank face, and the guy, in this ridiculous accent, says, 'Thank-a you for the directions, signor.' It's so fake, so cheesy! He walks off and I walk with my mom toward our building and she says nothing. Not a thing. We take the elevator up. Not a thing. And nothing later, when I made some stupid excuse for going out."

"Wow."

"Yeah. It's interesting. She just gave up on me, which wasn't ideal, because I actually loved my mom a lot. And then she got sick, and she went fast, and she left me with Jack. And Jack was okay, but the gay thing was not his favorite when he found out. You met him. Marlboro Man. The first time I told him, he said right away he had no problems with it. I made a joke. I said, 'I guess now you'll know I'm fantasizing about Terry Bozzio and not Dale.' He laughed and we went and threw the football. Then we didn't talk again for six months.

Seriously. I was sixteen, and for six months he gave me the silent treatment. This was back when Mom was already checked out, but before she got sick. It was like living in an emotional vacuum. So I dropped out of school and started just living. Met Carl, who was my boyfriend for a couple months after I turned seventeen. He was thirty. Nice guy. Still talk on the phone sometimes."

The story made me want to cry out. Want to scream. I could do neither, because here we were, backstage at a strip club. In the real world, where things like that happened to people all the time, apparently.

"Wow," I said.

CJ limbered up his upper body with stretches. "Well, I'd better make a lot of money tonight," he said.

"Why? You need some new records?"

He shook his head. He stretched his leg on the makeup counter and bent into it. He touched his chin to his knee. "I need a new place to live."

"Oh! Moving out?"

He turned and lowered his voice. His head was still down near his leg, and I leaned in closer, painfully aware of his beautiful body and its proximity to my mouth.

"I told Jack about the test. He told me if I'm positive, I'd better find a place to live. I decided that means if I'm negative, I'd better as well. That's not a home. Not anymore."

I felt like crying. I felt like screaming. And I felt if I did either, no one would hear me.

What would become of CJ? What would happen to me if I were positive? In what world was this fair?

And unlike every other time I'd thought something like this, something about the unfairness of it and the closeness of finding out made me do something I'd never done before.

A tear fell from my left eye. Then another one. Then my right eye. I didn't even rub my eyes. It was like too much. I let them fall.

CJ's face turned and he tightened his mouth, and I was sure he was gonna call me a pansy or something. But instead, a tear fell from his right eye, and our eyes caught and we stared into each other and cried for ourselves, and for our world.

I wished there were an adult we could go to who would make it all better. But our president wasn't doing anything, and my mother and my father didn't know I was being tested, and Jack didn't care, and Rick had the disease, and Felicia was there, but she couldn't fix it all.

"I love you," he said. "I love you, Micah."

My world sighed and stopped spinning so chaotically. I looked at CJ. Really looked at him. Here was a guy who had seen some things, and I couldn't make it all better, but I could at least try. And mostly, all I could do was think: *Me! He loves me!*

"I love you, too," I said.

I leaned in and kissed his lips, and slowly he stood, and I rose with him, and we put our arms around each other and it was sensory overload and I felt I could explode into a million stars and cry out in gratitude, even if God had brought this horrible disease here, because he had brought me CJ. My CJ. Finally, mine.

The kiss went long, and I took the part of my brain that

could imagine virus particles in everything and sent it away. Because maybe I had the virus, maybe he did, but a kiss wouldn't transmit it, and this was bigger than a virus.

This was love.

"Why me?" I whispered into his mouth.

I could feel his mouth curl into a smile, and mine curled, too.

"Because you're so . . . you. You're kind. You're earnest. You're incapable of artifice. I used to have fantasies of the kind of guy I'd marry. You're him. You're the only one who's ever known me. And stayed. You're my best friend. And also, you have no idea how cute you are, which is so freakin' sexy."

"Don't go on tonight," I said. "Just stay here with me, okay?"

"I have to go on. But tonight I'll be dancing just for you. 'Kay?"

Please tell me this is forever, I thought. *Please tell me there are no takebacks.* Because there could never be any takebacks from me. I was fully hooked on CJ. I had been for what felt like a long, long time.

"Promise me," he said. "No matter what happens tomorrow, we will stay for each other. I can't handle the idea of you going. Like, I truly can't."

"I promise," I said. "With my whole heart."

CHAPTER TWENTY-FOUR

BOY BLUE

January 1988

After my parents went to work and I did a good amount of pacing, I called GMHC to get my test results.

"Code number?"

"Um. What? My name is Micah and—"

"Don't give me your name. Never give your name. There are lists. If you're positive, you don't want to be on that list. Look at the slip of paper you were given. There's a five-digit code number."

"Oh, um. Sorry." My heart was pounding in my ears. I told him the number.

"Okay, hold, please."

I held. For an eternity. Or for three minutes. It was hard to tell. My entire body was shaking. The only thought I had was what it would be like if he said those words: *You're positive. HIV-positive. You have HIV.* What would happen to my life.

"Thanks for holding. Please state your five-digit code again."

I did.

Silence. Finally: "Negative."

"Oh. Okay. Thank you. Thanks. Thank you."

"Stay that way. Use a condom. Every time. Hear?"

"Yes. Thanks. Thank you. Thanks."

I got off the phone and I jumped in the air, feeling lighter than I'd felt in a while. And then I cried. I cried because it could have been positive. I cried because CJ's still might be positive. I cried for every person who had ever dialed those numbers and heard the word *positive*. I cried for Rick. I cried for my mom, and my dad, and the tears they would have shed had my test gone the other way.

I called CJ.

No one answered. I tried not to read too much into that. It was six minutes after the hour, and my call had taken a minute less, but that didn't mean anything, right? That was insane thinking, right? He might not have called yet. Last time he didn't even call for his results.

So I hung up and called Rick.

"Oh, thank God," Rick said after I told him. "And CJ?"

"I don't know yet."

"Okay. Fingers crossed. He's gonna be fine. I know it."

God, did I hope so. "How are you doing?" I asked.

He cleared his throat. "I'm okay. I've had nothing. Nothing at all. Not even swollen glands, which is a good sign. This disease is weird. It's been around six years since it was discovered, and lots of people have died, but some people haven't. You get it and it's a death sentence because there's no cure, but maybe it isn't, because not everyone gets sick."

I wondered if this were true. If it was that some people didn't get sick ever, or that some people hadn't gotten sick *yet*.

My call waiting beeped. Thank God. "Gotta go. It's CJ, I think."

"Fingers crossed," Rick said. "Talk later."

I pressed the hang-up button to switch calls. "Hello?"

Silence.

"Hello?"

Sniffles on the other end of the line.

Oh no. No. No.

"Hello?"

More sniffles.

"Will you come look for apartments with me?" the small voice on the other line asked.

"Oh," I said. "Um, okay."

Sobs from the other end of the line.

No . . . No.

I closed my eyes. I shook my head.

Terminal. Funny word, that. Sounds like a bus station, smells of death.

More sobs. I couldn't. I don't know why. It was like I was watching a movie of my life. CJ. Cee Jay. CJ Gorman. HIV-positive. This was the scene when CJ called to tell me, and I was utterly unable to do the scene. Be the mature boyfriend who says, *Don't worry. Everything's going to be okay. I'm here with you. I'll always be here.*

"No one's gonna want to . . . touch me. Ever again."

"No," I said, but I wasn't sure. CJ had the virus. The one Walter had that had aged him forty years in the half year I'd known him. I'd kissed CJ yesterday, and they said that was okay, but who kisses someone with a fatal disease that is spread by bodily fluids? That didn't make sense.

"You're negative," he said, not a question.

"Yeah."

"Well . . . good. At least there's that."

"Yeah." I couldn't say more. If I said more, I'd say the wrong thing. If I opened just a little, everything smothered up in my heart would bleed out.

"Say something," he said. "Please."

I opened my mouth. Nothing. Words were not there.

"You can't do this to me," he said, and I could hear the panic in his voice.

"I'm not. I just don't know what to say."

"Just say something, Micah. Tell me I didn't just become a walking pariah. Tell me that you're still my boyfriend. That you love me, because. Right now, I need it. Please."

"I do, but—" I burst into tears. Ugly, snotty tears. High-pitched, babyish, unrefined. *I can't do this. I can't. I can't. This is too much.* I couldn't stop crying. It was like my body had taken over and I couldn't stop its convulsions. I had to put the receiver down on my parents' bed. I didn't want CJ to hear this. *I don't know what to do.*

When I finally calmed down enough to breathe, I picked the receiver up again.

"Hello?" I said.

But there wasn't any response.

He'd hung up.

I grabbed the phone and called him back, tears still falling, my voice still choked.

No answer.

Shit.

I called again. Left a message. "CJ, this is me. I'm sorry. I didn't know what to say. I was overwhelmed. But I'm here, CJ. I'm always here. Please call me."

I hung up feeling utterly wasted, panic wafting through my veins.

I had to go to him. Right this minute. And also I couldn't. What would I say? What would I do? I wasn't strong enough to handle this. This was adult stuff and I wasn't an adult. Two months ago, I'd never gone anywhere without telling my mother, and now I had a boyfriend with HIV.

Or did I?

I'd failed him. In his worst hour.

I called again. No answer.

I put on my sneakers and my jacket, but then I thought, *What if I go down there and he calls and I'm not here? I can't just go. But I have to. How can you be in two places at once when you absolutely have to be in both?*

I called Deena, because at least that way, if he called, I'd hear the beep.

"Hey," she said, and I realized I was utterly unprepared for this conversation. But that's what friends were for, right? So I just dove right in.

"CJ has HIV. I don't. I got tested and I don't, but he's positive. I don't know what to do. Help me know what to do. I just. It's too much."

"Oh my God," she finally said.

"Yeah."

"Were you . . . with him?"

"No, yeah. I mean, we fooled around but with a condom, and we kissed yesterday because we both said 'I love you.'"

"Oh my God," she repeated.

"Yeah."

"You have to tell Napoleon if you were with him after you were with CJ."

"Yeah," I said, because I was used to agreeing with everything Deena said. And then I said, "Wait, what?"

"You have to tell them. You could have infected them."

I stared in the mirror on my closet door. "No. I told you. I'm negative. I couldn't give it to someone because I don't have it."

"But you were with someone who is positive. That's like, you have to tell Napoleon if you've been with him recently. There are innocent people involved."

I was silent. I felt splayed open, attacked.

"Micah," she said. "I didn't mean—"

"I totally get it. Napoleon is innocent. Not like me. Not like actual gay people, who deserve it."

"Micah," she repeated.

"Guilty as charged," I said, and I hung up.

I lay on the floor, wishing for an earthquake. Stupid New York doesn't get earthquakes, and I needed one then, something to swallow me up and drag me to the pit of the earth, never to re-emerge.

I wasn't sure what I would say to CJ, but I knew I had to say it in person, and that the sooner I did it, the better. On the 1 train downtown, I felt particularly useless in my big blue down jacket, like a puffy infant. *Look at me,* I imagined telling CJ as I stared at my reflection in the dirty glass. *Does this look like someone who can take care of you when you get AIDS? I can barely remember to comb my hair some days. I'm not like you, with your elaborate outfits, and your zest for life, and your fighting spirit. You prick me, I bleed. You, on the other hand, protected us when we were in trouble. By pricking yourself.*

The farther south the train went, the more certain I was. I could pledge to be a better friend, no problem. I would and could be around for phone calls and visits, even if it was scary to think about death. If I needed to cry or something, I could do that on my time and not bother him with it. But no, being in a relationship with a person with HIV was too much for Micah Strauss to deal with. This was real life, and I had to know my limits. And yes, maybe Rick's boyfriend was terrible for leaving him, but he was an adult and that was different. I was seventeen. I deserved more time without having to think every day about the person I loved most in the world dying. So I would make it not so in a calm and friendly and real way, and I would touch him when I told him, so he'd know I wasn't leaving, because no one should be left. But people were always telling me who I had to be in relation to them, and I kept letting them step all over me, and it was time to put up the stop sign.

I got off at Franklin Street and when I ascended to the street, a frigid gust of air hit me and woke me up to the reality of what it felt like to be vulnerable. And that was okay. It was necessary, in fact, and the icy feeling across my face felt like just punishment for what I was about to say to CJ. But I had to say it. I prayed he was home and would let me see him.

I buzzed and stood out far enough into the street so he could see me if he looked out. I didn't see anyone approach the fourth-floor window, and my heart sank. I needed to find CJ now. I needed to tell him that I would be there for him always. As a friend. I needed him to know that not everything was about me, and I could handle the tough stuff, if he'd just let me try one more time.

When it became clear he wasn't answering the buzzer and was probably not home, I ran down the icy street toward a pay phone. I fumbled my freezing hands into my pockets, looking for a quarter, and I found one just as the freeze began to seep into my bones. I dialed his number and waited. When the machine picked up, I tried to unchatter my teeth in order to leave him a message.

"Hey, CJ, I'm on your corner. I need to see you. Please let me see you. I'm gonna go back to your building now. Okay?"

I hurried back down the street, and my feet caught a patch of black ice and I went sailing backward. My butt and back hit the pavement with a smack, and then my elbows, and my hands got scraped, and the pain in my bones was like injury to insult, and I sat there in my humiliation as New Yorkers raced past me like I didn't exist.

Maybe that was the lesson here. Being an adult means closing your heart. I wasn't sure I loved that idea, yet I wasn't sure how to change it.

I dusted myself off and walked my sore body down the block.

And there was CJ, standing with one leg on the street, one leg still in the elevator. I felt my body lighten at the sight of him.

"You're bleeding," he said, and as I approached, we both laughed because of course the day I went to see my HIV-positive boyfriend, I'd be bleeding, an open wound.

The heat of the elevator brought me slightly out of my stupor.

"So many questions," he said, and I could tell he wasn't okay, not by a long shot, by the softness of his voice. He'd been punctured and I'd done some of the puncturing, and it took me everything I had to not embrace him right then and there.

"A few answers," I said.

The elevator stopped, he opened the chain-link gate, and we were in the warmth of his apartment. Wordlessly, he took me into the bathroom and handed me gauze and a clean wash-cloth, and I doused it with warm water and tended to my scraped hands. The sight of my own blood made me wince, and the fact that I was hanging out in the bathroom of a person with a transmissible disease with an open pathway to my bloodstream was loud in my head. I realized that being afraid of a virus didn't make me a bad person; it just made me a human one, and that wasn't all good or all bad.

I bandaged my palms and soon I was gash free and standing with CJ in his small bathroom, and I looked in his eyes, and it was all my heart could take.

I still loved him. There was no virus in the world that could make me love CJ less, because that was some brain-over-heart bullshit that didn't have to be part of being an adult. And in an instant, it became clear to me: There was no *Let's just be friends* speech in me. I didn't want that.

I wanted CJ. In sickness and in health.

I grabbed him and embraced him tightly, and he let me, he let me take him in my arms and he made a sound that was a mix of grief and pleasure as I held his face in the crick of my neck, and I rubbed his neck, and I enveloped his thin body in my thick one.

"I'm always gonna have this. Even if I don't get sick."

"Shh," I said.

"You can't come and go from my life every time you get scared."

"I know."

"I'm so scared."

"Me too. We can be scared together."

"This won't end well."

"Shh."

I pulled my head back so I could gaze deeply into his eyes, and I saw the fullness of his lips, and, petrified but aware that I needn't be, I planted a kiss on his lips, one as tender as everything I felt for CJ poured into one impulse.

He took me by the hand and led me to the bed, and, still clothed and shoed, we lay down facing each other.

There was nothing that needed to be said, because our eyes said it to each other. I didn't need to tell him that I was sorry for not being able to contain my own emotions in order to let his in. He didn't need to tell me how much that had hurt, because I saw it in his eyes, which I kissed gently. His eyelids were soft, innocent.

There are so many songs that say *I want to hold you forever.* It's an impossibility. And yet that afternoon, we did just that.

CHAPTER TWENTY-FIVE

COLOR IN YOUR LIFE

February 1988

CJ ascribed to me life-saving words that I was pretty sure I'd never said.

"That thing you said on the phone about taking one affirmative action," he told me when we met in front of the Lesbian and Gay Community Services Center after school on a Monday. "Just do one thing. That's what I'm gonna do."

I had said that part, but the affirmative action thing wasn't me, because that meant something totally different. Nonetheless it was good news. CJ had been in an understandable funk for the past month, sometimes holing up in his apartment for days at a time. Our phone calls had become mostly diatribes about Reagan and the *New York Times*, and how neither had almost anything to say about dying faggots. A few times he'd gone apartment hunting, as Jack was giving him a wide berth and the silent treatment at home. (He'd refused to tell Jack his results, so Jack didn't know what to think.) I'd gone with him to see one particularly cool studio on Perry Street, a second-floor walk-up that stunned me by how small it was. He'd applied, but the landlord turned him down because of his place of employment. The Gaiety, apparently, set off some red flags for potential landlords.

These were not problems I had anticipated when the school year had started back in September.

Anyway, it was a frigid February afternoon, the sun was going down, and I was being hugged tight under a rainbow flag by the guy I loved, who was finally ready to take some "affirmative action," in front of a redbrick building on Thirteenth Street, around the corner from St. Vincent's Hospital, where hundreds of gay men were currently dying of the very virus that lived in CJ's bloodstream.

He wanted me to go with him to a meeting that night, this group called ACT UP that had been formed by a guy CJ called Larry. CJ always talked about people I'd never heard of and that he barely knew on a first-name basis. It was cute and kind of annoying.

We took shelter from the cold inside, in a big and colorful front room with high ceilings. The walls were covered in rainbow graffiti. CJ took my hand and led me to a small room behind it that served as a library. Wordlessly he grabbed a New York *Native* that had on the cover in big letters, *Good News! Fusidic Acid: Another Promising Antibiotic.*

"This was a few months ago," he said, pointing at the headline. "Another dud. Rest in peace, fusidic acid. Now the big thing is AZT, which could extend my life but is super expensive. The company that makes it charges eight thousand a year for it just because they can, and no one gives a shit because it's mostly gay people who are getting screwed over."

A couple weeks back, CJ had gone to the Gay Men's Health Crisis for an intake interview. His counselor got him connected to a doctor who treated people with HIV, and talked to him about getting counseling, which he refused. "If I start being sad all the time, I'll do it," he'd told me after. When I'd pushed him on it, he'd shut the conversation down.

Now he flipped the page on a newer edition of the *Native* and showed me a chart of AIDS cases by state.

"Forty-four thousand cases and counting," he said. I glanced at it. Apparently North and South Dakota each had five cases. I wondered what that would possibly feel like, to be one of five cases of AIDS in an entire state. The idea made me shiver.

At the bottom of the chart it read, *Of these, 25,363 (approximately 57 percent) are dead.*

"Larry says the real numbers are much higher."

"Ah, your best friend Larry."

He smirked. "At the last meeting, he told me I was cute and to go find a boyfriend."

"I hope you told him that job was taken."

He shrugged, and I slapped him lightly on the shoulder.

The whole boyfriend thing felt really tenuous. Like we used the term and we held hands and we made out at his apartment when Jack wasn't there, but we hadn't done more than that, physically. The idea of having sex was the furthest thing from my mind. I just wanted to hold him. Forever. As for CJ, he said he wanted to wait until he had his own place and he could "relax." But truthfully, I think he was still freaked out about his diagnosis. Which was why I wished he'd talk to someone.

I knew I would like to. I was still way jittery, but it didn't matter. What mattered was being there with him, for him.

The fact that I was a junior in high school was immaterial.

For me, having no one to talk to about it was a big part of the problem. Deena and I now avoided the topics of CJ and HIV, ever since our phone call. We seemed to be drifting apart, and there seemed to be no way of closing the growing divide. I talked to Rick once in a while by phone, but he was going through his own thing, and talking to him about sex things seemed super weird. And I hadn't seen Felicia in person since the day she'd cried about Walter.

CJ then got started on his affirmative action for the day, paging through the classifieds, hoping against hope he'd find an affordable apartment in Manhattan, with a landlord who was cool enough to rent to an exotic dancer.

"It's kind of hard. As a newly recovering flirt, I can no longer use my masculine wiles to get men to do things for me."

I narrowed my eyes at him.

"Hey," he said. "You know who I am. I'm trying, okay?"

While he went through classifieds, I looked at the schedule on the information desk. The Center was the place for all sorts of groups, from ACT UP to Gay Men of African Descent to Queer Scrabble to Lesbian, Gay, Bisexual, and Transgender Teens. I made a mental note to come for one of their Saturday meetings sometime.

Soon people started arriving for ACT UP and my heart fluttered. I'd never been in a group of all gay and lesbian and trans people before. What if I stood out as the least fashionable? The chubbiest? The youngest?

We moved into a big auditorium, maybe a hundred of us, and we started listening to speakers.

"We need to disrupt," said this muscular lesbian wearing a bandana and a cool cartoon shirt that read IGNORANCE = FEAR, SILENCE = DEATH, with an image of three people covering their eyes, ears, and mouth. People cheered loudly. "Last time we did Wall Street, we didn't disrupt the market nearly enough. A bunch of pictures of angry homos isn't enough. This time? We stop trading! Assholes cannot get rich while people with AIDS who can't afford Burroughs Wellcome's prices die!"

Cheers from all around. I couldn't stop peering around at all the people, representing so many races and identities. Men and women and everything in between and beyond, in suits, dresses, jeans, leather. All coexisting. I didn't really stand out, except maybe for my age. I could see some of the men looking at me, and that felt weird and made me want to shrink into myself.

They were all looking at CJ, that's for sure. It was his height, his nonchalant grandiosity.

One of the most obvious things was that this meeting was run as a true democracy. Everyone had a voice, and we'd be sitting there for hours if it came to it, because everyone would be heard. Points of order were called out, and men were told to let women speak, and white people were told to cede to people of color, and it felt like I'd finally found a family that I'd actually choose. One where fairness at all costs mattered.

People got up randomly to speak, and the topics ranged from a slight a man felt when an action group didn't call him like they said they would, to someone who wanted a moment of prayer for a man named Bobby who was at St. Vincent's. The affirmative grunts made it sound like people knew him, and that made me wonder how it could be that in a city as big as

New York, some semblance of community existed, as if this were a small village.

Like *The* Village, maybe. I wasn't sure, but I wanted to be part of it.

CJ raised his hand and a man onstage, possibly Larry, pointed at him.

"Let's hear from the youth," he said.

I grimaced. What version of CJ was going to show up this time? I wasn't sure I had patience for another con. Not now. Not here.

"I'm CJ Gorman," he said. "I'm eighteen and I have HIV." Murmurs of support drifted through the room.

"My stepfather is kicking me out of my home. I'm scared." A tear fell from his right eye, and as much as I wanted to comfort him, put a hand on his shoulder, I didn't. This was his moment, not mine.

"I actually have put away some money. I dance at the Gaeity, so . . ."

"Oh, Mary!" a tittering voice in the back whispered, and immediately that person was shouted down.

"Seems like no one wants to rent to an eighteen-year-old gay stripper without a credit card, so, I'm looking for a place to live. Preferably with a true friend attached. I have a special one"—he pointed at me—"but I could really use others. And yeah, I really do want to help. With ACT UP. I'm ready to fight back because it's fuckin' not fair!"

"Amen!" someone shouted. Another person yelled, "Yeah!"

"I got you," the first woman who'd spoken said. "See me after."

"Thanks," CJ said, and I could hear the tears in his throat.

Larry spoke. "You boys want to get involved?"

CJ looked at me. Sometimes an idea just comes to fruition, and suddenly, without speaking, I knew that affirmative action meant something new right now. Silence equals death. So does inaction.

"Sure," CJ said, while simultaneously I said, "Yes."

Hoots from the crowd. "All right," Larry said. "That's the spirit."

After the meeting, the muscular woman came over to us and gave CJ a bro-handshake-slash-hug and introduced herself as Becky.

"You okay with a roommate?" she asked.

"Um, I guess. Who?"

She ignored the question. "Drugs? Drinking?"

"Not my thing."

"Promiscuous? Lots of men in and out of the place?"

He pointed at me. "Just one," he said.

She smiled for the first time. She had a pronounced under-bite and dimples that made me immediately like her.

"Awright," she said. "Roomie."

"Oh," CJ said. "Um. How much? Where?"

"A block from here. Can you do three hundred a month?"

He nodded, apparently dumbstruck.

"I have a small second bedroom I use as an office. I don't need it. Just don't be a dick, okay?"

He laughed. "Promise. Thank you. Thank you so much."

"We're family here," she said. "Welcome to the family."

A warm feeling passed through my chest and gut. I wanted to stay forever in this feeling.

Then a rail-thin mustached Black man about my dad's age came up to us. "Did they put you on AZT?" he asked.

CJ shook his head.

"Good. It's poison. It's killing people. No AZT. If you want to know what's what, take me out for coffee." He handed CJ a card.

"Thanks," CJ said.

"No sweat," the guy said.

We'd walked in feeling overwhelmed by this thing so much bigger than us. But now, we felt *plugged in* to something fierce and strong. And that gave me just a tiny bit of hope that we could fight this.

CHAPTER TWENTY-SIX

GIDDI UP BABY—BE MINE

March 1988

When I got to CJ's new place a few weeks later, Becky answered the door in sweats and a tie-dye tank top.

"Glad you're here," she said. "He's having a bad day. Maybe you can get him up."

It was a Wednesday after school. Becky was completely awesome, and CJ, for once, had space of his own. I'd been coming over after school on days when he wasn't dancing or delivering meals for God's Love We Deliver.

We were making great strides as a couple, now that we had a place to hang out. I hadn't ever spent the night, but one time after school and before his work, we fell asleep in each other's arms. It was glorious.

Sex was still out of the question. For all we knew about safer sex, neither CJ nor I could seem to get our heads around having sex with this virus a permanent presence in our lives. For my part, I had fantasies all the time, but the reality still scared the hell out of me. I had no idea what it was like from CJ's point of view—whenever I asked, he'd deflect.

"Bursulous, the God of Sex, has decreed it not to be," he'd say. Or something equally maddening.

The walls of his tiny room were covered in posters: One of Dale Bozzio from the *Spring Session M* era, one of the entire band Missing Persons in concert, and one of Terri Nunn of Berlin, which was fast becoming his new favorite band.

I went into his room to find a lump on his bed, under a big blue comforter. A song I'd never heard before was playing.

"You in there?" I asked.

"No."

"No?"

"No."

I sat down on the bed next to him. "And why aren't you in there?"

"Just listen to this song."

I listened, and to my surprise, the vocalist was unmistakably Dale Bozzio. The song didn't sound like Missing Persons, though. She was singing about the feelings she had being so strong.

"What is this?"

"It's Dale. That's what she's going by now, which means Missing Persons is done. Done. The album is called *Riot in English* and it's on Prince's label, Paisley Park. It just came out, found it at Tower. I love Prince and I love Dale, but this is a union that was not meant to be. There is a song called 'Giddi Up Baby—Be Mine.' It made me unsure I can still live."

I massaged the lump under the comforter. "Poor baby. And this hibernation is all because of Dale's new album?"

His sigh was loud enough to be heard through the layers of down. "This is the kind of time where if I didn't have you, and I didn't have HIV, I'd be out on the prowl."

"Okay . . ."

"Yeah. Because sometimes it's the end of an era, and everything is a little bit shit, and you just need to take the edge off,
but then you find out you have this disease, and you get a
boyfriend and you have to be on your best behavior because
without him you'd have nothing, but what you really, really
want is to be in a dark room with a stranger, swapping spit and
pawing at each other like animals in heat, and obviously that's
a no go, so you don't even say it or think it, even though it's
very, very true, and one of the reasons you shouldn't be in a
relationship anyway, because you're not worthy of love from
a real live actual person, obviously."

I got under the blanket with him. Inside, it smelled like a
combination of cinnamon and bitter that I'd come to know
and love.

"Mind if I join?" I said.

"Whatever," he said. "Fine."

"What happened?"

"Nothing happened. Nothing ever happens. I talked to
Jack today. He did this whole thing where he told me how
proud of me he was. That I've been able to make it on my own
and that makes him feel good about the job he did with me.
And I'm like, *Yeah, good job throwing me out, Jack! Nicely
done!* Except I didn't say that. I basically just said thanks,
and then he talked about us getting together and healing this
rift—his words—and I said I'd be up for that, and then,
when I got off the phone, that's when all the words I should
have said came to me. I should have been like, *Sure, Jack. I don't
mind that you threw me out of my mother's house because I have*

HIV. No problem at all, Jack, you fuck. Fuck you so hard, Jack."

"Wow."

"Yeah, not a great day. Also, I asked Mira for a Saturday night shift, because there's good money to be made, and she said I've been slacking off lately, missing too much time, but really I think it's because I'm not muscle-y enough or hot enough."

"You're crazy. You're too hot, if anything. You're always the life of everything. No one can look away from you."

He snorted. I couldn't quite see his eyes, but my own eyes were beginning to adjust to the darkness, and I could see the shape of him.

"I'm lust boy in love with himself."

"What?"

"It's a song I wrote last year. Don't ask me to sing it. It's more like poetry and I don't sing. It goes like this: 'Lust boy in love with himself/Don't know rejection is something I've felt/ They call me sleazy and crazy and all/They leave me lonely/ I've been through it all.'"

I touched his hand and massaged it.

"That may be who you were, but you're not that now."

"The hell I'm not."

"Well, it can't be you."

"Why not?"

"Because I'm not leaving you lonely, for one thing."

He took my hand in his and squeezed. And then he sang, his voice warbly and not entirely on any recognizable key. "'Lust boy in love with himself/They take advantage of his uncommmonwealth . . .'"

"Eek," I said.

He laughed. "Not great?"

"It's perfect . . . but maybe some quiet time?"

"Mmm," he agreed, and he laid his head on mine.

I stopped by the theater to see Felicia on a Saturday afternoon.

"A sight for sore eyes," Felicia said, hugging me.

"I missed you, too. How are you? How's Walter?"

She let me go and I could see it in her face before she even said it.

"Walter's passed, Micah."

I had to sit down. My head spun. Here we were in the room where Walter used to pop in and say nice things to me. And now he didn't exist anymore.

"It's been hard," Felicia said. "He was such a fighter and he gave it his all, but in the end his body gave out."

"Yeah," I said, still shocked.

Felicia came and stood behind me, putting her chin on my head. "This is your first, isn't it?"

I nodded. "Yeah."

"The first is really hard. They're all really hard. I wish I could tell you otherwise."

"CJ and I are in ACT UP," I said, after a bit of silence.

"Oh, really? Wonderful! I'm so proud of you. And are you and CJ . . . together?"

It felt a little wrong to be smiling, so I suppressed my smile. "Yep."

"That's great," she said. "Just great."

"He has it."

"Shit."

"I don't."

"Well, that's good. Keep it that way."

"We're not having sex. Too scared."

"You don't have to avoid sex completely."

"I know, I just. I can't right now. We can't."

"Totally understand. If you need me, I'm here, okay?"

"Okay. And thanks."

A Sunday call from Napoleon:

N: Hey, what's up, wanna come over?

M: Nah, sorry. I'm seeing someone.

N: Oh. Cool. Okay. Whatever.

M: It was fun, though. Thanks.

N: Sure, yeah.

M: Hey, Napoleon?

N: Yeah?

M: Make sure you use condoms, okay? There's a disease out there and it's not something you want. I don't have it, but you never know, you know?

N: Okay. Thanks, dude.

M: Later, dude.

CHAPTER TWENTY-SEVEN

BEDS ARE BURNING

March 1988

Skipping school to spend time with CJ had become something of a bad habit, but on this particular Thursday, I knew it was the right thing to do.

We gathered in front of Trinity Church with a ragtag crew of misfits old and older, mostly. CJ and I stood out, as we had at the initial meeting. Some of the people looked very ill, others totally healthy, like us. The way we fit in, though, was our signs, which had been created by CJ.

The one I carried read ONE AIDS DEATH EVERY HALF HOUR.

CJ's said CORPORATE GREED IS KILLING ME.

This was a side of CJ I was just getting to know, and it both scared me and made me love him even more.

"I've seen you at the meetings," a Latino guy with maybe six piercings in each ear said to CJ.

CJ nodded, and the guy smiled and winked.

"Good thing," he said. "We need some younger blood."

I flinched at the use of the word *blood*.

A bald man with a bullhorn got our attention, and the milling around ceased.

"First, we stop traffic. We chant 'ACT UP! FIGHT BACK! FIGHT AIDS!' Then, once our front liners are set and the police show up, we do our die-in. Jacko will hand out our gravestones. You hold it upright above your head, you lie down, and you wait for the cops."

"My arms don't reach that high," a voice yelled.

Another voice yelled back, "Put your legs over your head, Mary!" and there was a mixture of laughter and insults shouted back and forth before the bald man took control again.

"You DO NOT fight the officers. You go limp, then let them carry you. You can scream, you can shout, but you do not harm, okay?"

"Fuck that. They harm us. They kill us!" someone yelled.

"And that's why we're out here," the bald guy said, and there were murmurs of assent and dissent.

Before I could even catch my breath, there we were, an army of protesters, marching toward traffic on Broadway.

I looked at CJ. He looked at me, shrugged, and lifted his placard over his head. It was like a question: *You in?*

I was all in.

It took me a bit to find my shouting voice. At first I matched the pitch with the people nearest me, but it was too low for my voice to be heard. So I took a deep breath, as if standing at the edge of a cold pool, and I jumped in, my dissonant pitch melding with the rest as I shouted our slogan as loud as I could.

"ACT UP, FIGHT BACK, FIGHT AIDS! ACT UP, FIGHT BACK, FIGHT AIDS!"

A shivery feeling flooded my veins as I felt a new power

emerge from my body. I glanced over at CJ, and he was crying freely. I reached over and took his hand and squeezed, and he responded by gripping my hand harder and allowing his voice to warble our war cry.

Cars stopped. They had to. Horns honked, then honked some more, a battle cry of those who didn't give a shit, who were mad that their commute was being ruined without caring that our entire lives were at stake. I felt hatred and pride merge in the muscles of my arms. I raised my sign higher and raised my voice even higher than that. I knew tomorrow I'd have no voice left—and that was okay.

The police arrived, and there were whistles blown and shouts through megaphones ordering us to disperse immediately. I held CJ's hand even tighter. The part of me that was pre-CJ felt the urge to run, felt petrified that I was maybe about to find out what true loss of freedom felt like. What if a police officer hit me with a billy club, or dropped me because he hated me so much for my message, for who I was?

But I stayed with it, and when I was handed my gravestone, which read I DIED FOR THE SINS OF THE FDA, I lay down on the cold pavement and let my body shiver and the pain of the truth of the message merge with the thrill of taking action.

CJ's gravestone read KILLED BY THE SYSTEM.

Being part of a die-in was weird, because it got unnaturally quiet. And lying there, I had a lot of time to think about death. How one day, AIDS or not, I was going to die. All of us were. I thought about how many years of good life had been stolen by this disease, from people just like me, just like CJ, and that was so deeply unjust.

Soon I could hear the defiant screaming of our people, and without even looking I realized they were being carried into police wagons, one by one. As they were, we cheered from our reclined positions, sending truth and power to our family in arms, and tears were now falling from my eyes. I wanted to reach out for CJ and make sure he wasn't carried away from me, but my hands were needed to hold the gravestone above my head, so I held on, and as the screams of those carried away closed in, I again felt that urge to run, to avoid the figurative blood on my hands, to stay clean, to stay safe.

But I held on.

It wasn't CJ who was grabbed first, which I had just assumed would happen, because wild things always happened to CJ.

It was me.

With a rough grip, the officers grabbed both of my arms and pulled, tweaking my shoulder, and I screamed, I screamed so that CJ would hear me, so that the world would hear me and feel the injustice, that this was so wrong, to be hated so very much just for being who I was, for being part of a group that was being slaughtered by inaction, and the voice coming from the middle of my chest was a roar I hadn't known I was capable of, and it sustained me as I was dragged backward, my arms in an unwieldy position that I knew with one change of direction might take my shoulder out of its socket. I was totally goddamn free, and exhilaration swept through my chest and into my stomach and groin and I kicked my legs until another officer grabbed them, and roughly I was thrown into a dark vehicle, where my hands were cuffed to each other above my head. I could smell the slightly sour breath of the person lying next to me, and I turned my head and my eyes met the eyes of a man with lesions covering his face, and he had tears in his red eyes, and so did I, and we smiled at each other and I realized we were truly all one, all connected, and if he had AIDS, we all had AIDS, because one death unnoticed was a million deaths.

"Attaboy," the man said, his voice rusty like the color of his hair. "I'm proud of you, kid."

My voice spent, I whispered back, "I wouldn't be anywhere else."

As it turned out, CJ was not arrested that day. They arrested about a thousand of us, mostly in front of the stock exchange but many in front of the church, too. And thank God for CJ not being one of them, because he could be the one who posted my bail.

After a few hours of sitting in a dank cell with no water to quench my dry throat, I walked toward the 1 train with him, in shocked silence.

CJ didn't have to ask. He handed me a Popsicle and I wolfed it down, craving the moisture against my hoarse vocal cords. When my vocal cords were quenched, I sighed, completely dazed by the day's events.

"You are my hero," CJ said. "You were fuckin' badass."

I couldn't believe the words CJ was saying to me. And in response, instead of just denying it or making a joke, I turned and kissed him on the mouth.

It was a deep kiss. Our tongues united and my heart sped

and my hair even stood on end. All my hair, from my legs to my arms to my head.

Kissing my boyfriend, who had HIV. And not caring, because I knew better now. That wasn't how it was passed. And I loved him more than I feared him finally, truly.

"Fags," a voice barked.

CJ and my voices merged, barely backing away from our kiss.

"Screw you" was my response. "Fuck off" was his.

I no longer cared.

CHAPTER TWENTY-EIGHT

ONE MORE TRY

April 1988

The fifty-third (or so) time I saw CJ, he was wearing a clone outfit.

Not like a gay clone with a mustache and a leather jacket. More like a clone of Micah Strauss. Ill-fitting jeans, a green Lacoste shirt, and the kicker: a brown Members Only jacket. The kind you find in a secondhand store, maybe?

He was standing at the door to our apartment. I broke out laughing.

"Oh my God," I said. "What is—what is this?"

He smiled his goofiest smile and shrugged. "I figured your parents like you, so maybe they'll like me better this way?"

CJ. Always in costume.

My mother greeted him with a cross between a handshake and a hug. She'd been working on it, I knew. Getting past her feelings that he was a bad influence and focusing on accepting him as my first boyfriend.

"I've heard so much about you," she said.

"I'm so deeply sorry," he responded.

That made her laugh.

My dad gave him a curt handshake. "I love your jacket," he said.

"Yeah," CJ replied. "This does not surprise me."

We'd decided that for a first visit, no mention of HIV was necessary. It was enough that my parents were willing to meet CJ, I felt, and CJ seemed fine with that.

Rick joined us for dinner, as support. We five sat awkwardly while my mom served us chicken kreplach soup, making intermittent conversation.

"This soup is perfect. Never had kreplach before, but it's scrumpdillyicious," CJ said, using the word from the Dairy Queen commercials.

"I'm so glad," my mom said, giving him a sweet smile.

"Mom could be a chicken soup magnate," I said, trying to fill the awkward space in the conversation. "Every kind is always really good."

Dad said, "She needs a good brand name. The Kreplach Lady. Chicken Soup Kitchen. Chicken Soup for the Hole."

CJ snorted involuntarily, and that made me laugh. Finally, so did Rick, and even my mother laughed, though she looked fairly horrified.

"Oh, come on, grow up. I mean the hole in your face," my dad said.

CJ patted his mouth with his napkin. "No, I like it. It's very biological, very descriptive. I think all restaurants should be that way. My mom took me to California when I was younger, and they have a burger place called In-N-Out Burger. Almost too descriptive, really."

"CJ!" I said, shocked, because I thought he was going to try to make a good impression.

My mom, though, seemed willing to save the conversation. "Do they really? That's very California, very zen, very . . . body accepting."

CJ cracked up. "I was joking. In-N-Out refers to the fact that it's a drive-through place and they get you in and out quickly."

My mom turned white, then a little pink. "Oh," she said, staring down at her plate.

The silence was awful. Finally, Rick saved the day.

"The pizza place near me should be called 'Stopped-Up Pizza.' "

This cracked up my dad. Everyone laughed, thankfully.

My mother knew CJ was political because of his impact on me, so she found safe ground in her liberalism after she offered everyone lamb chops.

"Reagan's reign is nearly over, thank heavens," she said.

"Sing it, sister," CJ said.

"He's done such a number on education. It's going to be a huge problem for our public schools if the Democrat doesn't win in November. Thankfully it's looking good for them. No one likes Bush," she said.

"The way he's ignored AIDS is nothing short of criminal," CJ said.

My mother nodded her head. "Yes. I've been reading in the *Times* about that, about how he really didn't say a word about it for so long, just like Reagan. The disease killed my hairdresser a few years ago."

CJ laughed. "The disease killed my hairdresser: a history of the eighties."

"CJ," I admonished, but no one seemed particularly burdened by his joke.

"I think it's wonderful that the disease is getting more press. Although, I must say, I find some of the activism a touch distasteful."

CJ and I looked at each other and then I stared beams into my mom, hoping she'd stop.

"I mean, why disrupt trading on the stock exchange? All that does is get the common man against your cause. I think most people would agree they're for helping people with AIDS. Sometimes the radicals go a little too far."

I felt that sinking in my gut that told me we were probably in for a storm. I turned to CJ, who seemed to be asking for my permission, and in a flash he had it. I gave him a subtle nod.

"Burroughs Wellcome, the drug company that makes AZT, the only proven drug to treat AIDS, has priced the medicine at eight thousand dollars a year, well beyond most people's ability to pay for it. They do that strictly out of greed. They don't need to. The ACT UP protest at the stock exchange got them to talk to us, and is going to result in a price decrease," CJ said.

My mother replied, "Oh, of course, I didn't mean . . ."

"Us?" my father said.

Another look between CJ and me. "Yes, us," CJ said. "I was there."

"And so was I," I added, meeting my father's eyes.

"Oh!" my mother said. "Well. That's—" She didn't finish the sentence.

"Sometimes you need to shout to be heard. And then you're still not heard. Where did you read about the demonstration?" CJ asked.

"The *Times*, I'm sure."

"Ah, but you didn't read about it, actually, because there was no article. Just a photo with a four-line caption on page B-three the next day, a caption that didn't even include why we were demonstrating, I might add."

The table was quiet for a bit. My head was dizzy from warring impulses: to say how I really felt, which CJ had just done. And to protect my mom from a truth that was getting very close to being said.

"Please be careful. The men who go to those things aren't like you boys, they aren't like Rick. Many of them are promiscuous, and that community is just saturated with disease. It's so sad, but that's the reality."

This sickly feeling was weighing down my gut, and I realized we were at the precipice of another coming out.

"I have it," Rick said, diverting the attention away from me and CJ.

"What?" my father said.

"I have HIV. I found out last year. So it isn't really a matter of *those* people. It's *these people*. It's me."

My father stood up from the table.

"Me too," CJ said.

My father froze. Then he put his hand on his forehead and sat back down.

CJ helped himself to more mashed potatoes, and I watched my mother as he did so. Her expression was inscrutable, and I wanted to scream to both my parents, *Say something!* But I also understood. Because I had been there just a few months ago with both Rick and CJ.

Rick put down his silverware and looked at my father. "I'm sorry I didn't tell you. I was afraid. Afraid you'd drop me as a friend. That's why Gabriel really left—he couldn't handle it when I tested positive."

"Oh, Rick," my dad said, and he stood up again, knelt behind Rick's chair, and hugged his best friend tight.

Rick seemed to tense a little for a moment and then he let his body relax. He put his hands over where my dad's were on Rick's forearms.

"I don't have it," I said. "But I know CJ does and we're together."

My mother nodded a couple times, and then she swallowed, stood up, and walked into the kitchen.

Mom stayed in the kitchen for a while, my dad and Rick retired to the living room to talk, and, as it turned out, shed a few tears together. CJ and I sat alone at the abandoned dining room table, and I took his hand in mine and traced the back of his hand with my index finger.

"Well, that went very well," CJ said.

"It's gonna be okay. She's just shocked."

He nodded. "I think I'm gonna go."

"Only if you promise that you know that we're okay. Because we are. Totally okay."

He smiled a shy smile, a rarity for CJ, but something that was happening more and more since his positive diagnosis. "Somehow I do know that," he said.

After CJ left, I went into the kitchen. My mom was sitting on the stool at the kitchen nook, crying.

"Hey," I said softly.

She shook her head. "Why? Why are you doing this?"

"I'm in love, Ma."

"But you don't have to be. Sometimes we have to let our head win over our heart, just for self-preservation. He's nice and he's very handsome, but honey, he has AIDS."

"HIV," I corrected her.

"I really don't know the difference."

"HIV causes AIDS."

"So no real difference. Why would you hook your wagon to a train that's terminal?"

"Should I do what Gabriel did? Leave him because he has a disease? Is that the person you want me to be? If Dad had cancer, would you pack your bags? Believe me, at first I thought about it. Nobody wants this. But I love him, and I'm not going anywhere, okay? That's not the person you raised."

She shook her head back and forth repeatedly. "Oh, bubby," she said, her voice filled with regret. "I just don't know. I'm so sorry you're going through this."

"It's fine."

"It most certainly is *not* fine. You're too young to be dealing with this."

"I can't choose who I love. I love CJ."

"I'm not saying that you don't. I'm saying that you're young, and this is hard, and don't give up on your friend. This will leave scars, Micah. The rest of your life, your story will be that you fell in love with a terminally ill—"

"Stop saying that! We don't know—"

"We do know. This disease has no cure. And no, I'm not *that* afraid you'll get it from him, because I have faith you know how to protect yourself. I'm worried about your heart."

She began to cry again, and I felt like I was six inches tall for putting her through this. But there was also something else brewing in my gut. This fury, this hot ball of fire that wanted to erupt and tell her to stop, stop, stop putting this pressure on me and stop telling me to do something I couldn't do.

I simply wasn't going to stop being in love because it made logical sense.

That wasn't an option.

So instead I went to the refrigerator and I got myself a Dr Pepper, and I poured her a seltzer water with ice. When I brought her the drink, she said, "You're a special person, Micah."

"You gonna be okay with this?" I asked.

"I'll try my best," she said.

My dad came into my room that night. I was on my computer, playing *Transylvania* for the fifty millionth time. I was stuck on how to open the sarcophagus and had been for the past month.

I looked up and saw that his eyes were red, and I almost told him no, that I couldn't take one more conversation where I disappointed someone for how I felt.

He flopped down on my bed and rubbed his eyes.

"Quite the night," he said.

"You okay?"

"What? Yeah, I'm fine. I'm stressed about it. Too much disease, happening to people I care about. Please let CJ know I'm here for him, okay? It was just very hard, hearing about Rick."

I nodded.

"He wasn't like that. He wasn't promiscuous, not at all. Or not that I knew of? No. Not at all. We even talked about it. One time after racquetball a couple years back, he told me about friends of his who were dying, and I didn't really know what to say. And maybe he saw that, maybe he saw how afraid I was, because he immediately put me at ease. 'They went to the baths,' he said. 'I don't do that. I never did. I'm more of a serial monogamist.' I guess I let it go then. I figured that, yes, gay men were dying of an incurable disease, but it was men of a certain ilk."

I tensed my jaw.

"I'm sorry, Micah, by the way. I'm sorry for what you're going through, and if I ever said the wrong thing, I'm sorry for that, too."

The tears were now falling.

"All these years, playing racquetball and shooting the shit. He's my best friend. My only friend, really. And there's a virus in his body that will probably kill him, and I don't have a clue, actually, of how to react. I want to fix it. I want to eradicate this disease, and I want to make you know how much I love you, and how I get that you must feel . . . I don't even know how you must feel."

So I showed him by going in for a hug. And he opened his arms and let me in and we sobbed together over this disease that was likely to kill my boyfriend and his best friend.

"You cannot get this, Micah. Do you understand me? You have my blessing and my support in this relationship. But you cannot get AIDS. I forbid you from doing that."

Maybe it wasn't the most rational thing for him to say, but I have to admit: I liked it anyway.

"Okay," I said.

CHAPTER TWENTY-NINE

LOVE DON'T NEED A REASON

May 1988

The second time my parents met CJ, he was decked out in jean shorts and a pink tank top, or what he called "full twink mode."

It was the fourth annual AIDS Walk, and a couple hundred people, some being pushed in wheelchairs, had gathered at Amsterdam and Sixty-Eighth in front of a makeshift stage. As much as I was glad my parents had come, and Deena had come, and Rick, it was a weird merging, and I couldn't help but see it from their eyes. My mom was craning her neck, checking out the crowd. A couple in leather holding hands. An emaciated skeleton of a man who may have been twenty-five or eighty, sitting in a wheelchair, being pushed by another skinny man. Two lesbians in SILENCE = DEATH T-shirts with the pink triangle, their arms around each other.

"Good to see you, CJ," my father said, sticking out a hand for CJ to shake. "How've you been?"

"I just won third place in a beauty contest. I collected ten dollars," CJ replied.

"Oh good," my father said, smirking.

By his side was Rick, who still looked like a straight guy with his chinos and button-down shirt.

Of course, I looked like one, too.

I got hugged from behind. It was Felicia, beaming at me, her eyes jetting back and forth between me and CJ. Raina was with her, and there was a joyful reunion as we got caught up.

She handed me a box of Dots and a package of Twizzlers.

"I raided the concessions stand. Today we're handing out Dots and Twizzlers as a way to honor Walter. You in?"

I smiled. I was definitely in.

A man got up on the stage and introduced the first speaker, the actor Tony Randall. I sneaked a look at my mom. Her eyes were wide. He was famous, from *The Odd Couple* on TV. I hadn't known he was gay, and maybe he wasn't? From the looks of it, she had the same thoughts going through her brain.

"Hello, great people of the AIDS Walk," he said. "You might wonder what I'm doing here. You see, I was told it was *Goy* Men's Health Crisis."

Cackles and shrieks of laughter rang through the crowd. His speech was warmhearted and full of empathy, and as I listened, I realized it didn't really matter if he was gay or straight. What mattered was his heart, and his heart was open and kind.

Then the emcee asked everyone in the audience to bow their heads and observe a moment of silence to think positive thoughts for someone named Nathan Fain, who apparently wasn't doing well. There were murmurs of recognition throughout the crowd, and again I was amazed at how at once small and large New York City could be.

Then Michael Callen was introduced, and an emaciated

guy climbed up onto the makeshift stage, sat behind a piano, and began to play and sing.

If your heart always did
What a normal heart should do
If you always play a part
Instead of being who you really are
Then you might just miss
The one who's standing there
So instead of passing by
Show him that you care
Instead of asking why
Why me, and why you?
Why not we two?

I grabbed hold of CJ's hand. It was like this guy was singing my life, and I could tell CJ understood, and I didn't care that this was the first time my mom and dad saw me holding hands with a guy, and for a brief moment, seeing the world through my mom's eyes ceased, and I saw it through my own tired but hopeful eyes.

'Cause love don't need a reason
Love don't always rhyme
And love is all we have, for now
What we don't have is time

All around us, grown men and women wept openly. The words were so earnest, so honest, so true, for so many. For the piano-playing singer, possibly. For CJ and all the people with the disease in their bloodstreams, probably.

I looked over at my boyfriend. My boyfriend. His face was wet with tears and he did nothing to hide it. I kissed his neck, not caring who saw.

During the walk, Deena did her best to ingratiate herself to CJ and me. Things had been awkward since our fight, but the last couple of months had seen us achieve something of a detente. We weren't back to calling each other every night, and now she was nicer, and in that way more polite, than before.

"Great crowd," she said as the crowd approached Riverside Park at Seventy-Second Street.

"I can't believe I'm here with my parents," I said back softly.

"Go Ira and Dalia," she responded, and I cracked up and smiled at her and took her hand in mine, and the three of us walked together in silence for a while.

Rick, for his part, walked with my dad. Until he saw someone that he knew, and then he ran over and hugged the guy, who was about his age, Black and tall and handsome. And then, suddenly, he was gone, and my parents walked alone in front of us, holding hands. And I think we were all thinking it: *Please, God. Let that be someone for Rick to love.*

I thought about the future. About how little I knew of what was going to happen, and whether this would be the last year of the AIDS Walk, because they'd find a cure, or whether, twenty years from now, it would be like this but massively larger. I hoped to God it wouldn't be.

I looked over at CJ, who was the picture of great health,

and again, I hoped God would hear me. *Please let him live. Please let this amazing man live a long and happy life, because the world needs CJ. He is not done with the world yet, and the world, most definitely, is not done with him.*

I just hoped I'd be there for the entire journey. And that it would be very, very long.

EPILOGUE

Present Day

You will always be the love of my life, CJ Gorman.

From those very first days, then learning about your "death sentence." To those dicey early 90s, when we almost lost you to toxoplasmosis in '92, and then again to cryptosporidium in '94. I will never forget the sleepless night holding vigil by your bed at St. Vincent's as you lay in your own filth, your breathing labored, and I tried to make some semblance of peace with a life after you.

It wasn't a real peace. I lied to God that night. I said I'd be okay without you. But of course not. How could I be?

You are me, CJ, and I am you. You are my skin and my conscience and my spirit. We are intertwined. No one has ever known me like you. I have never known anyone the way I know you.

You made it through toxo and crypto and pneumocystis, and you went on disability and we hunkered down in our Chelsea studio. Sometimes we played the victims and wondered why this would happen to us, and sometimes we fought terribly, because you loved your stories and sometimes fiction and fact blurred with you and that was just your nature. And sometimes I forgot that I could do this, and wished that I wasn't chained to a person who had to take medicines so many times every day, who had to run to the bathroom so frequently.

We marched and protested and got arrested and vowed this was our last time, but then we did it again and again and again, because it was something we could do. We needed to take action, just to keep our hopes alive.

You saw me through Rick's painful death in '95. You weathered every storm I had with my parents when I decided to produce off-off-Broadway. You buoyed me when that didn't work, and you saw me through the raw early years of me trying to write, first nonfiction, then fiction.

And you somehow persevered. You made it through the mid-90s without too many issues, and then the protease inhibitors in '96. We couldn't believe . . . couldn't allow ourselves to be optimistic because so many times before, our hopes had been dashed. But this was different. And suddenly your T cells, jumping, catapulting, from eight to two hundred to a thousand. And the virus in your blood suddenly undetectable, and all the weight gained back, and your face (mostly) full once again, full and vital and not the face of a young, naive CJ but a weathered soldier, somehow wiser, more real. Once you've weighed a hundred pounds at twenty-five, it's hard to embrace vanity and artifice again, isn't it?

And yes, in that haze of realizing you would live again, you needed to explore, and you needed to breathe, and you fell in love with Mark, and those were dark, dark days for me, CJ. The darkest. I didn't know I could be so angry and still survive. I didn't know if you would come back. I lost you all over again, and you will never be able to remove that hurt from my heart. Never.

But you did come back, and you nestled into me, and I welcomed you back into our life as a unit, and we grew in our careers, and we moved to Phoenix, and we aged, and we got min-pins, and we bought a Volvo, and we moved to the suburbs.

And now here you lie, next to me, snoring gently. Your once-wavy brown hair much shorter, thinner. And my love for you is so strong it hurts a little, still, to see you next to me and not be able to climb inside you and breathe as one, every minute, every day.

The Mormons believe marriage is eternal. We will never be Mormons. But eternal we shall be. We already are.

Thank you, CJ. Thank you for protecting me that first night at the Tunnel. And thank you for becoming my life.

If you'd have asked me back in 1987 where I'd be in 2022, I would have laughed.

Everywhere around me was death, and I was just coming of age as a gay person. I was lonely, precocious, and rebellious. I was three parts CJ to one part Micah, and it wasn't completely clear how HIV was transmitted yet. I assumed from quite an early age that I would contract AIDS and die like so many other young gay men around me in New York City.

In fact, one of my earliest thoughts as a gay person was the misguided idea that I was going to be the youngest person ever to die of AIDS. There was no Internet to help me understand the facts; there was precious little information at all in the mainstream media.

That's what it was like to come of age in the early days of AIDS, in the epicenter of the disease. I equated sex with death. I felt that who I was wasn't worthy of living, and that no one really cared at all if people like me died.

Thirty-five years later, I'm still here. The guilt I feel about being spared HIV is too painful, so I try to avoid that line of thinking. What I can say is that my friends who passed away were the same as me, made of the same stuff. I think of them often and marvel at what they would have accomplished if given more time on earth. The loss of talent is beyond catastrophic.

I wrote this book so that people could experience what I experienced in that time and place. While this is a work of fiction, all references to 1980s people and places are historically correct, with two exceptions: I attended the AIDS Walk and saw the scene described, with the late Michael Callen singing "Love Don't Need a Reason," but it was the third annual AIDS Walk in May of 1987, not the fourth in 1988. And Brian McNaught's book of essays *On Being Gay* was actually released in 1988, not 1987. The cameos of Larry Kramer and Marsha P. Johnson were taken from actual conversations each legend had with me when I was a teenager. I delivered meals every week for God's Love We Deliver in 1988 and 1989. I attended several ACT UP meetings at the Lesbian and Gay Community Services Center on West 13th Street between the years of 1988 and 1990, though I was not an active member of ACT UP in that I never attended any of the major protests. This is something I still regret, that I could have done more and failed to do so.

I think this happened because I was sadder than I was angry.

When I think back to the eighties, I realize now that my anger was turned inward. The impact of having literally no representation of people like me in books and television and movies was that I got depressed, that I hated myself instead of hating the enemy: rampant homophobia. I bought into the idea that I was lesser than straight people, and I felt great shame about my burgeoning identity. After all, revealing my identity to my family had created huge tidal waves of angst and fury. I felt that I was the problem.

Oddly enough, for all the work I've done on myself over the course of three and a half decades, one of the best resources I've ever come across for truly exorcising the shame that came from coming of age during the early years of the AIDS pandemic is The AIDS Memorial on Instagram (@theaidsmemorial). This amazing project is made up of thousands of photographs and stories about those who we have lost to AIDS, and it has helped me see my own beating heart, along with those of all the incredible people we have lost to the disease. I find myself coming back again and again to these visual stories for the healing impact they have on my soul.

Destination Unknown is for everyone who has ever been made to feel ashamed of their identity, anyone who has ever been told that their lives are less meaningful because of who they are.

I hope you will see aspects of Micah and CJ in yourself, and I hope you will come to celebrate them.

ACKNOWLEDGMENTS

Writing a book about a pandemic DURING a pandemic was a special kind of challenge.

While COVID-19 and AIDS were and are extremely different, much of the fear that the former brought out in me during the early days of the COVID pandemic reminded me of the fear I felt during the period of time in which *Destination Unknown* is set. There were days I just couldn't face that fear, and many times I thought I might not finish writing this book.

I'm glad I got past that.

First and foremost I wish to thank Chuck Cahoy, my partner in life, who never doubts me even when I do. I love you with my whole heart. Thanks to my mother Shelley, my father Bob, stepmother Roz, sister Pam, and brother Dan. Your loving care means everything to me. To Greg and Terry and Brian and Ray and Joc and Joe and Jim and Lisa and Matt and Kriste and Steve and all my other dear friends: You put up with a lot when I'm struggling, and you stick around. Thank you. A huge thanks to my agent, Linda Epstein, for sticking by my side during a hellish year-plus. To my editor, David Levithan, I could not do this without you. You help make sense of the messy parts. To my Scholastic family, I love you. Thanks for all you do.

Thank you so much to Ed Wolf, who walked me through the medical aspects of what it would mean for someone to test positive in 1987. Thanks to Richard Dworkin for chatting with me about Michael Callen, who I idolized. And to my fans: I don't know how to express to you just how much your support means to me. And finally, to all my friends who died in the 1980s and 1990s: I miss you so damn much.

Bill Konigsberg is the author of many acclaimed novels, including *The Bridge, The Music of What Happens, Honestly Ben*, the Stonewall Book Award– and PEN Center USA Literary Award–winning *The Porcupine of Truth*, and the Sid Fleischman Award for Humor–winning *Openly Straight*. In 2018, the National Council of Teachers of English's Assembly on Literature for Adolescents (ALAN) established the Bill Konigsberg Award for Acts and Activism for Equity and Inclusion through Young Adult Literature. Bill lives in Phoenix with his husband, and can be found online at billkonigsberg.com.